Hann

bu...

amateur dramatic reviewer for a Devon newspaper. The urge to travel was too strong, however, and she became an air stewardess, first with British Caledonian and then on private planes. Many adventures later she ended up in Los Angeles, where she met her future husband – and still lives there with him and their cat.

www.hannahdennison.com

www.hannahdennison.blogspot.com

@HannahLDennison

DEADLY DESIRES
AT HONEYCHURCH HALL

HANNAH DENNISON

CONSTABLE • LONDON

CONSTABLE

First published in the United States by Minotaur Books,
an imprint of St Martin's Publishing Group, 2015

This edition published in Great Britain in 2015 by Constable

Copyright © Hannah Dennison, 2015

1 3 5 7 9 10 8 6 4 2

The moral right of the author has been asserted.

A CIP catalogue record for this book
is available from the British Library.

ISBN: 978-1-47211-470-9 (paperback)
ISBN: 978-1-47211-471-6 (ebook)

Printed and bound in Great Britain by
CPI Group (UK) Ltd, Croydon CR0 4YY

Papers used by Constable are from well-managed forests
and other responsible sources

MIX
Paper from
responsible sources
FSC® C104740

Constable
is an imprint of
Little, Brown Book Group
Carmelite House
50 Victoria Embankment
London EC4Y 0DZ

An Hachette UK Company
www.hachette.co.uk

www.littlebrown.com

For Jason

Acknowledgments

When I first started writing this series about an ancient crumbling country house and its inhabitants, little did I realize that I would quickly share my heroine Kat Stanford's passion for preserving and protecting the magnificent country houses of Great Britain. It's a sad fact that since the Second World War, nearly two thousand distinguished country houses have been demolished, destroyed, or today stand in ruins. The reasons range from crippling inheritance tax laws to the demands and expectations of twenty-first-century living, not to mention the financial reality of keeping these vast estates going.

With this stark fact in mind, I invite Anglophiles and lovers of English cozy mysteries everywhere to join me in applauding the National Trust, English Heritage, the Battlefields Trust, and the Society for the Protection of Ancient Buildings in their tireless endeavors to safeguard the England we know and love.

Perhaps that is why the inspiration for the plot in *Deadly Desires at Honeychurch Hall* was sparked by the Action Alliance, a protest group who continue to fight against the construction of HS2, a high-speed railway line that will destroy a further three hundred cottages, Georgian manor houses, medieval rectories,

viii ACKNOWLEDGMENTS

and ancient churchyards, to say nothing of decimating woodlands, hedgerows, and, inevitably, threatening all wildlife in its path. You definitely have my support!

And speaking of support, this book wouldn't have been possible without the help and encouragement of my amazing posse. I would like to extend my heartfelt gratitude to my wonderful agent, Dominick Abel; my editor, Marcia Markland—who always knows exactly how to make my stories better; the super-efficient Quressa Robinson; Shailyn Tavella—who embraced my quirky publicity ideas with grace and good humor; and the fabulous Talia Sherer— whose enthusiasm always made me smile. Special thanks must go to Mary Ann Lasher—your book covers are exquisite and it's no surprise that they have spawned a Mr. Chips fan club.

As always, I couldn't do any of this without the support of my daughter, Sarah; my family and the Elen clan; my boss, Mark Davis, chairman of Davis Elen Advertising; and my talented comrades in the trenches—Elizabeth Duncan, Clare Langley-Hawthorne, Daryl Wood Gerber, Kate Carlisle, and Mark Durel.

And last but always foremost in my heart, there are no words to express the deep love and gratitude I feel for my husband, who has supported my writing dreams from the very beginning. Jason— this book is for you.

DEADLY DESIRES
AT HONEYCHURCH HALL

Chapter One

"I'd rather die than let the wretched government build a high-speed rail network through here." Mum pointed to a green flyer that was pinned to the post of a five-bar gate.

STOP OPERATION BULLET!
SAVE MINUTES, LOSE CENTURIES!
JOIN OUR PROTEST GROUP TODAY!

"Operation Bullet," Mum went on. "What a silly name. More like operation bunkum."

"Bunkum?" I scoffed. "Who uses the word 'bunkum' these days?"

"Don't you care about all this?" Mum put one Wellington boot–clad foot on the first bar and used her good hand to haul herself up.

"Careful," I teased as Mum began to wobble. "Remember your age."

"I'm not seventy *yet,* thank you very much," Mum declared. "Anyway, it's got nothing to do with age. It's my gimpy hand."

"Which is why I suggest we just lean over the gate and admire the view."

"I'll be glad when you go back to London and stop nagging me," said Mum. "When did you say you're leaving?"

"When I'm sure you can manage on your own," I retorted. "And you promise not to get into any more trouble."

"Me? Trouble?" Mum gave me a withering look. "I'm sure I don't know what you mean."

It had been nearly six months since Dad died and two since I discovered that my mother had secretly sold our small family home in London and moved over two hundred miles away to Little Dipperton in Devon. If that wasn't enough of a shock, thanks to a broken hand, Mum's request for me to help her with "some typing" led to an astonishing discovery. My conventional, respectable mother was actually Krystalle Storm, the internationally bestselling romance writer of racy bodice-rippers. Furthermore, Krystalle Storm's real identity—and the extent of her earnings—was a closely guarded secret. Fortunately my father never discovered her alter ego—nor has HM Revenue and Customs, which is all the more ironic given that my father had worked all his life as a tax inspector.

But that was just the beginning.

Following my retirement from hosting *Fakes & Treasures*, Mum and I had planned to open our own antiques business and now she'd changed her mind. To say I was perplexed was putting it mildly. And now here we were, bickering as usual.

"Well, I'm definitely joining that protest group," said Mum with a hint of defiance.

"You see?" I exclaimed. "You're already asking for trouble. Stay out of it, Mother. Anyway, the government hasn't even built the HS2 from London to Birmingham yet. It will be years before they start this one."

"I don't see why we need a new line down here," my mother went on. "What's wrong with the one we've got?"

"It's archaic," I said. "That's why."

"I didn't expect you to understand."

"Please let's not argue," I said.

Mum breathed in the crisp October air and exhaled with a sigh. "None of that city pollution here. You'll miss this, just you see."

"Cows and manure? I doubt it." The problem was, I knew Mum was right. I would.

It was a day of fitful sunshine and spiteful showers. Around us sprawled a mosaic of undulating farmland enclosed by ancient hedgerows that rolled down to the River Dart. Thick belts of pine forests were interspersed with lush woods sprinkled with rust, gold, red, and myriad shades of green that shimmered in the autumnal breeze.

"Did you know that Honeychurch Hall was a Royalist stronghold in the Civil War?" said Mum wistfully.

"Yes."

"The Roundheads and the Cavaliers fought up here," Mum went on. "It's haunted of course."

"Of course."

"Can't you just hear the sound of cannon fire?"

"Not at the moment. No."

"Sir Ralph commanded his troops from up here."

"So you keep telling me."

We were walking Hopton's Crest named after Sir Ralph Hopton, a Royalist commander in the first Civil War who secured the southwest of England for King Charles I. The rough track that had run along the top of this ridge nearly four hundred years ago would have afforded panoramic views. Today, they were still spectacular but marred by banks of overhanging trees and unruly hedges. At the end of the crest, the track narrowed to a steep path that wound down through sloping woodland and past a marshy swamp aptly named Coffin Mire.

Below, on one side of the ridge, nestled the small village of Little Dipperton, and on the other, tucked between trees and centuries-old dry stone walls, lay the magnificent Honeychurch Hall estate in all its fading glory, along with the peculiar equine cemetery, ornamental grounds, Victorian grotto, and vast walled garden that was lined with near-derelict glasshouses.

Mum's Carriage House stood adjacent to her estranged neighbor Eric Pugsley's hideous scrapyard. At one time a thick belt of trees separated the two but Eric soon cut that down—just to annoy my mother, or so she claimed.

From our vantage point and with autumn in full swing, we were treated to an eyeful of old bangers—or as Eric liked to call them, "End-of-Life Vehicles"—a hearse, pyramids of tires, and discarded pieces of farm machinery. There was also a car crusher machine and Eric's red Massey Ferguson tractor that was parked outside a battered old caravan that served as his office.

"Let's look on the bright side," I said. "If Operation Bullet really happens it will be the end of Eric's kingdom."

"And that's supposed to give me consolation?" Mum said. "Actually, it was Eric's idea to form the protest group for Little Dipperton. The railway line will cut right through the village as well as Honeychurch."

"Good luck to him," I said. "As the saying goes, 'you can't fight city hall.'"

"Oh yes we can," said Mum. "I've decided to join him."

"What?" I gasped. "You're going to be in cahoots with *Eric*?"

"Yes, I am," Mum declared. "In fact, there's a protest meeting on Thursday evening at the pub."

I started to laugh. "I thought you couldn't stand him."

"I can't," said Mum. "But what choice do I have? Apparently Eric asked Lord Honeychurch for his support but was told to leave well alone and mind his own business."

"And it isn't yours, either," I said.

"Of course it is! I live here."

"What does Edith think?" I asked.

"Her ladyship, you mean." Mum still couldn't bring herself to call the dowager countess, Lord Rupert Honeychurch's mother, by her first name despite being invited to do so on numerous occasions. As far as my mother was concerned, being over familiar with the gentry—as she insisted on calling the upper classes—was inconceivable. "We're not supposed to talk to her about it, either," Mum continued. "His lordship doesn't want her upset."

"That's a first," I said. "Just weeks ago Rupert was trying to get her committed to that retirement facility—"

"Sunny Hill Lodge," said Mum. "But I do think she's got *some* form of dementia, Kat."

"Well, I'm sure Edith's seen the flyers all over the countryside. They're hard to miss," I said. "And Muriel from the post office has been running a petition for weeks."

"That's true," Mum admitted. "Perhaps his lordship doesn't see the point in distressing her, knowing that the railway line won't be built in her lifetime."

"Possibly," I said. "How old is Edith now? Eighty?"

"Eighty-five but you'd never think it," said Mum. "She could live on for years."

I had to agree with her on that point. Lady Edith Honeychurch still rode sidesaddle every day, ran the local pony club, and was altogether a formidable character.

"Do you know how old the Queen Mother was when she died?" said Mum.

"I have no idea," I said. "But since the royal family is your area of expertise, I suspect you're about to tell me."

"One hundred and two!" Mum exclaimed. "Yes! One hundred and two! *And* she still had all her teeth."

I waved the wicker basket I'd been carrying. "Come on. Let's go and find those sloes for Mrs. Patmore."

"Mrs. Patmore?" Mum frowned, then grinned. "You're right! Our Mrs. Cropper *does* look like the cook from *Downton Abbey*. It must be the uniform and mobcap."

Mum pointed to a small wood at the bottom of the field below. "She told me that the sloes are along the blackthorn hedge down there."

"Near Coffin Mire." I pulled a face. "The place gives me the creeps. And besides, with all the rain we've been having, it'll be boggy."

"Suit yourself." Mum strode a few yards farther on and paused at the foot of a stile embedded in a dry stone wall. "I'm going."

"Wait." I gave a heavy sigh. "Someone's got to keep an eye on you."

A sign saying TRESPASSERS WILL BE PROSECUTED & POACHERS WILL BE SHOT was accompanied by the added warning BEWARE OF THE BULL roughly painted on a piece of wood and nailed to the top rail.

"That's that then," I said with relief. "There's a bull in the field."

"There's no bull in there," said Mum, making a meal of climbing over in her ungainly Wellington boots. She was wearing a green wool skirt that more than hampered her progress. "It's just to frighten off trespassers." There was the sound of material ripping.

"Blast!" she cried.

"I told you not to wear a skirt," I said. "I may be a Londoner but I know how to dress for the occasion." I had donned jeans, and bought myself a three-quarter-length Barbour jacket and pair of Barbour boots from nearby Dartmouth, a little fishing port with real shops.

After helping Mum disentangle the fabric from the barbed wire, we set off again.

She was right. There were no cows to be seen.

"Told you so," Mum muttered.

"I hope Mrs. Cropper appreciates your efforts," I said.

"When it comes to making sloe gin, I'll go above and beyond," said Mum. "Besides, she's shorthanded in the kitchen. They can't find a new housekeeper. Vera was a hard act to follow."

We both fell silent. Although it had been weeks since I'd discovered Eric's wife Vera's body in the grotto, I would never forget it.

Mum squeezed my arm. "Sorry, dear," she said gently. "I know you still think about her. But as Lady Edith would say, life goes on—wait!" She gasped. "What on earth—?"

We came face-to-face with a large rectangular placard that had been staked into the ground. Garish red lettering on a black background announced HS3 CROSSING FROM HERE.

"Operation Bullet." Mum's expression hardened. "They've already started marking the boundaries!"

A further nine placards, spaced at regular intervals, split the field in half and continued all the way to the bottom of the hill.

It was a clear indication of what destruction lay ahead and I was surprised to find I was as upset as my mother. "What are you going to do?" I asked.

"I'll talk to Eric and we'll call an emergency meeting," said Mum grimly. "If I get my hands on whoever put those boards up their life won't be worth living."

"Shall we pick the sloes tomorrow?"

Mum shook her head. "We're here now and those signs aren't going anywhere."

We followed the footpath that hugged the boundary where mounds of upturned earth bordered a recently cleared ditch. Birds took flight as we walked on by, a reminder that it wasn't just people who would be affected by the proposed new railway line, but wildlife, too.

To the right of the blackthorn hedge another five-bar gate stood open revealing a muddy bridleway that eventually came out at the rear of Eric's scrapyard. From where we stood there were more wretched placards standing in the field that rose up the other side of the valley.

"They're going to destroy this entire valley," said Mum.

"Look at all those sloes!" I said, hoping to distract her. Even at this distance, the blue-black berries were visible in the hedge that stood diagonally opposite us.

"Let's cut across here," said Mum.

A vast expanse of marshland stood before us. "Are you kidding?" I said. "That's a swamp. We should follow the hedge line where the ground will be firm."

"Rubbish. Follow me and do what I do."

Tufts of marsh grass sat in black, inky puddles. The air smelled stagnant and we were soon ankle deep in scummy water. As the sun disappeared behind the clouds again, the wind picked up.

"You know it's haunted down here, don't you?" shouted Mum over her shoulder.

"According to you, everywhere is haunted," I shouted back.

"Remember I told you about Sir Maurice?" said Mum. "This is where he lured a platoon of Roundheads to their doom by pretending to be their commanding officer. They drowned in Coffin Mire."

"Harry's version is much more interesting," I said and recounted the earl's seven-year-old son's graphic embellishment of the tragedy where the men were eaten alive by alien worms with piranha-sharp teeth.

"There is something wrong with that child," said Mum. "Now watch how I pick my way through this bit." She suddenly picked up speed, shouting, "Only tread on the tussocks and don't stop moving."

I gingerly put one foot on top of a clump of grass but the ground literally quivered under my weight. "It's like walking on jelly!" I cried as my boot sank up to the shin with a horrible hissing, suction sound. It emitted the most awful smell.

"Mum! Wait!" I wrenched my foot out and hopped from tussock to tussock after her.

"Keep going!" Mum yelled. "This is very, very boggy. Follow me—Oh!"

She pitched forward but her feet were stuck fast. Instinctively, I grabbed the edge of Mum's raincoat and managed to haul her sideways. Her feet shot out, causing enough momentum for us both to do a wild tango before landing on muddy but firm ground.

"Great. That's just great," I said, extricating myself from under her. Mum was beside herself with mirth. "You should see yourself," she gasped. "Covered in mud and oh, you stink!"

"Thanks," I said. "If I wasn't here you could have drowned just like an escaped convict on Dartmoor."

"We'd better go your way." Mum clutched her nose, sniggering. "But I'll go ahead. I don't want to be downwind."

Five minutes later we had set the wicker basket on the ground between us and were picking sloes.

"Speaking of escaped convicts," said Mum casually. "Did I tell you that my brother is on parole?"

"Your stepbrother, you mean?" Up until two months ago I hadn't even known Mum had a brother. In fact, I'd discovered she had had two stepbrothers. Both had been boxers with Bushman's Traveling Boxing Emporium back in the 1950s and '60s. It was yet another of the many skeletons that seemed to continuously tumble out of my mother's closet.

"I had wrongly assumed that Alfred must be out of prison given that he helped you move to Devon," I said. "Why? Are you planning on seeing him again?"

"Oh, yes. I thought he could have your room."

"What?" I squeaked. "He's coming to *Honeychurch*?"

"That's right," said Mum. "On Thursday, in fact."

"You can't be serious!" I said. "You hardly know him! He's a criminal!"

"Rubbish. It was just a few forged passports and whatnot. Such a fuss over nothing," said Mum. "Alfred is going to join our protest group. He's very good at organizing that sort of thing. Do you remember hearing about a riot at Wormwood Scrubs prison a few years ago?"

"Don't tell me—"

"That's right. Alfred was the ringleader."

"Then how did he get out on parole?"

"He has his ways," said Mum. "Alfred tells me he can get hold of T-shirts. We can put the Stop-the-Bullet logos on them—SAVE MINUTES, LOSE CENTURIES."

"And I suppose Alfred will stay with you rent-free?"

"Aha! That's where you're wrong," said Mum triumphantly. "As a matter of fact, her ladyship is thrilled. It's all arranged. He's going to help with the horses and do a few odd jobs around the place."

"What?" I said again. "He's going to work at the Hall?"

"Yes. I just told you that. Don't you ever listen?"

"Since when did you decide all this?"

Mum paused for thought. "A couple of weeks ago, or perhaps it was longer."

"Why didn't you tell me?"

"I'm telling you now."

"Why do you do this?" I exclaimed. "Is it to deliberately torment me?"

"It's hardly any of your business," Mum said. "Besides, they need a new stable manager with William away—"

"Not *away*," I reminded her hotly. "William is in prison for manslaughter, or have you forgotten?" *Prison again*, I thought. *There seems to be a recurring theme here.*

"It was an accident."

For a moment I was speechless. "William strangled the housekeeper, Mum."

"I don't want to talk about Vera," said Mum quickly.

"What's more, he impersonated your stepbrother. I suppose you've forgotten about that, to say nothing of how he attacked me!"

A glazed expression crossed my mother's features. She started to hum. I could see I was wasting my time.

"Does Alfred even *know* anything about horses?"

Mum inspected the contents of the basket. It was already a quarter full. "Lady Edith and Lady Lavinia needed help—"

"*I've* been helping with the horses—"

"*You're* going back to London. This weekend if I remember correctly."

"Mum, please," I begged. "You hardly know Alfred."

"He's family," said Mum. "Alfred needs a job and he was very good with the horses we had on the road."

"That was over half a century ago," I reminded her.

"We used to call him Dr. Doolittle because he could talk to the animals."

"Whatever." I groaned and tried to focus on pulling the berries off the hedge and not getting stabbed by the vicious thorns. Mum was right. It was none of my business.

"That's why it's better that you *are* going back to London, dear," said Mum. "Although promise me one thing—"

"What now?"

"Don't get talked into taking Dylan back."

"His name is David!" I said. "And that's none of *your* business." With a mother's uncanny intuition, she had hit a nerve. It was true. I *had* been toying with the idea of at least meeting my ex-boyfriend for coffee.

"Well, Dylan's clearly trying," said Mum. "I've never seen so many flowers. Your bedroom looks like a funeral parlor. I do wish you'd meet someone else, darling. Someone available. Someone who wants to have children."

"Don't start that—"

"Hello?" came a male voice. "I thought I heard voices."

There was a rustle of leaves and a tall, clean-shaven man in his late forties wearing a smart tweed jacket and flat cap emerged from the bridleway. He had a slight limp and was using a beautiful antique walking cane.

"Well, well, well," said Mum in a low voice. "Here comes a romantic contender!"

Chapter Two

"Ladies, good afternoon," the stranger said. "I hope I haven't disturbed your walk."

"We're picking sloes," said Mum, openly giving him the once-over. "I'm Iris Stanford and this is my lovely daughter, Katherine."

I gave a nod of greeting. My mother couldn't be more obvious about her intentions for me. It was embarrassing. But even more embarrassing was the fact that we both stank of bog.

The man stared at me intensely. I took in his gray eyes with their long, dark lashes, sexy cleft chin, and full sensual lips and felt my face redden. Clearly my mother's descriptive accounts of her male heroes in her latest tome had infected my powers of observation.

"There are more sloes on the other side of this hedge. Valentine Prince-Avery." He smiled and offered his hand—then promptly withdrew it, wrinkling his nose.

"Sorry, I know we smell," I said.

"Valentine!" Mum's eyes widened. "Goodness. What a wonderful name. Very Regency."

"*Kat* Stanford?" Valentine snapped his fingers. "Of course!

I thought I recognized you! *Fakes & Treasures*! They call you Rapunzel! It *is* you, isn't it? Your hair gave you away."

As a former TV celebrity-of-sorts, my waist-length chestnut hair was my trademark feature. "I'm thinking of cutting it all off."

"Kat inherited her lion's mane from my side of the family," said Mum proudly. "Her father went bald at an early age but as you see, that is unlikely to happen to her—or her children. When she has children, that is."

"I'm glad to hear it," said Valentine, suppressing a grin. "It's a pity you retired, Kat. I never missed an episode. I'm a bit of a collector myself." He gestured to the walking cane.

"I was admiring that." The ox bone cane had a distinctive ivory handle fashioned in the head of a French bulldog. "It's unusual."

"It belonged to my great-grandfather," said Valentine. "He was a collector of curios. As a matter of fact, I've come to Devon for the Chillingford Court auction. Such a shame."

It was an all-too-common theme. The Jacobean house had been in the family for centuries and had passed to the son who no longer wanted—or could afford—the upkeep of a twenty-thousand-square-foot mansion. Every single thing, including the walls, fixtures, floors, and doors was to go under the hammer on Wednesday.

"We're going to the auction, too!" Mum exclaimed. "Perhaps Kat can give you some tips?"

"That would be very nice," said Valentine.

Our eyes met and I was glad to see his sparkled with amusement.

"Will your wife be joining you?" Mum asked bluntly.

"Mother!" I hissed and mouthed "sorry" to Valentine. "Lovely to meet you. Come on, Mother, we have sloes to pick."

"To answer your question," said Valentine. "I'm a widower."

"Oh, I am so sorry," said Mum who had the grace to look embarrassed at last. "But I'm sure your children must be a great comfort."

Right at that moment I would happily have thrown my mother back into Coffin Mire but Valentine seemed unfazed.

"They would be if I had children," he said.

Mum brightened. "I keep telling Kat, don't wait too long."

Valentine laughed. At least he seemed to have a sense of humor. "I'll let you ladies continue with your fruit picking. Oh, by the way, I'm staying at the Hare & Hounds." He withdrew a business card and pushed it into my hands. "In case you feel like a drink this evening, I'd really like to hear your opinion on a couple of lots I've got my eye on. That is, if you aren't too busy."

"She's not," said Mum firmly.

I gave Valentine's business card a quick glimpse and gave a start of surprise.

The irony of the situation was not lost on me but I doubted that Mum would see it that way—VALENTINE PRINCE-AVERY. COMPENSATION CONSULTANT: HS3. There was a mobile phone number and a website address.

Mum looked over my shoulder and gasped. "Why! The nerve of it! Those placards littering the countryside must be your doing!"

"Mum," I protested, "Mr. Prince-Avery is only doing his job."

"You deliberately misled us!" she fumed. "Why did you say you were here for the auction?"

"I *am* here for the auction," said Valentine calmly. "But I'm also here to talk to property owners who will be affected by the new railway line."

"You are trespassing!" Mum went on. "I've a good mind to report you to the police!"

Valentine listened placidly to Mum's outburst that went on to include a conspiracy theory, the prime minister, and inexplicably,

9/11. Finally she ran out of steam and ended with, "So there. Put that in your pipe and smoke it."

I was mortified. "I apologize, Mr. Prince-Avery—"

"Valentine, please. And I'm used to it," he said wryly. "But I do want to explain your options, Mrs. Stanford."

"I don't want options—"

"Especially regarding the location of the rolling stock depot—"

"Rolling stock depot... rolling *stock*..." Mum sputtered with indignation.

"We'll be in touch," I said. "I think you'd better go."

A Klaxon horn startled us all. "Get off this land!" came an angry shout. "You're trespassing!"

We turned to see a four-wheel mobility scooter trundle into view. Plastic shopping bags overflowed from the front wicker basket and others dangled from the handlebars. Perched in the captain's seat was a florid-faced woman in her seventies. She was dressed in a purple-knitted wool coat and matching wool cap embroidered with red flowers. A younger version—wearing an identical outfit in orange—was trailing behind. Over the crook of her arm was a broken twelve-bore shotgun.

"Oh God," muttered Mum. "It's the Gullys."

Valentine looked startled. "Who?"

"Joyce and Patty. Mother and daughter." Mum pointed to a small patch of woodland where a cottage was just visible through the trees. "They live at the end of the bridleway in Bridge Cottage."

"Bridge Cottage? The place by the river?" Valentine said. "I knocked there earlier today but no one answered."

"They are a bit odd," said Mum.

"Good heavens!" he exclaimed. "Is that a real shotgun?"

Joyce sounded the horn again and stopped her mobility scooter just yards away from where the three of us were standing. She turned to her daughter and gave her a curt nod. Patty fumbled in her pocket and withdrew two cartridges.

"What is she doing?" Valentine said with growing alarm. "Is that thing loaded?"

"It is now," said Mum as Patty expertly popped the cartridges into the barrels and handed the gun to her mother.

We looked at each other in horror.

"Surely she's not going to fire?" said Valentine.

A deafening shot rang out that echoed around the valley, sending startled birds soaring into the sky. Mum grabbed me and screamed.

"The next bullet is for you!" Joyce shouted and pointed the twelve-bore at Valentine.

He didn't hesitate. He turned swiftly on his heel, clambered over the stile, and took off across the field as fast as his limp could take him.

Joyce trained her gun on his retreating figure and fired again. Luckily, it missed him by miles.

"You shot at him!" I exclaimed, unable to believe what had happened.

"He was trespassing," Joyce exclaimed.

"You shouldn't have done that." I was appalled. "Yes, he was trespassing, but he wasn't poaching."

"Mother is very upset," said Patty. "Muriel from the post office told us that Bridge Cottage isn't eligible for compensation. The cutting will pass just yards from our front door and there is nothing that we can do about it. He'd better not show his face around here again or next time, Mother won't miss."

My mother finally found her voice. "Goodness. Well done. That certainly scared him off, didn't it?" She gave a nervous laugh.

Joyce looked at Mum and muttered something unintelligible under her breath. It didn't sound complimentary.

We all eyed each other warily. There was something unnerving about the four of us standing in the bridleway—mothers and daughters, all about the same age.

"There is a protest group meeting on Thursday," said Mum. "You should come."

Neither Joyce nor Patty answered. Instead, Joyce broke the barrel and handed the shotgun back to her daughter. Joyce started the mobility scooter and the pair returned the way they had come without another word.

"You're so lucky to have me," said Mum.

"I know. I am." And I meant it. "Especially since you don't have a deadly weapon. Poor Patty. Fancy having a mother like that."

"Patty's just as bad as Joyce," said Mum. "They're like two peas in a pod."

"Wait a minute—is that *the* Patty who worked up at the Hall recently?"

"Lasted all of three weeks," said Mum. "Apparently she can't hold down a job—at least, that's what Mrs. Cropper says."

"Why?"

"Her mother needs her more, apparently," Mum said. "Joyce has got a weak heart, high blood pressure, some kind of neurological disorder—you name it, she's got it. Patty is working part-time at the pub to make ends meet but I doubt if that will last long."

A car engine sputtered into life. Across the other side of the valley, I saw the roof of a metallic-blue SUV move along the hedge line and disappear from view.

"I bet that's Valentine's car," said Mum. "I've never seen anyone walk so fast with a limp."

"Well, so much for *that* budding romance," I said dryly. "Shall we see if he was right about the sloes on the other side of the hedge?"

Mum and I cut through a gap and into the bridleway. On one side stood a bank of old oak trees. Lying on the ground at the base was a Merrythought Jerry mouse dressed in a hand-knitted red cardigan.

"Mum!" I said with dismay. "Look." I bent down to pick up the toy. "It's Ella Fitzgerald."

"Where is that naughty boy?" Mum scanned the area.

"Harry!" I called out. "We know you're hiding. Where are you?" Frankly, I was concerned. Harry and Ella Fitzgerald were inseparable.

Mum and I fell silent, listening for any giveaway sounds. This was the third time he'd run away from boarding school in the past four weeks.

"Harry!" I said. "We're not cross with you, we want to make sure you're alright, that's all. We're not angry. Please come out."

There was a rustle from above. We looked up to see Harry, standing on a wooden platform high in the oak tree. He was dressed in his Biggles helmet, goggles, and white scarf. A pair of binoculars swung around his neck.

"Squadron Leader Bigglesworth, I presume," I exclaimed, addressing Harry's alter ego.

"I wonder if Lady Lavinia even knows he's missing?" said Mum in a low voice.

"What on earth are you doing up there, sir?" I said.

"I'm on surveillance, Flying Officer Stanford," said Harry. "I'm afraid the enemy is afoot. The Germans are trying to build a runway but we soon saw 'em off, made 'em run."

"He must have seen Joyce shoot that gun," Mum said anxiously.

"Have you got Flying Officer Fitzgerald down there?" Harry demanded.

"Yes, sir," I said and lifted up the velveteen mouse. "Fortunately, she's fine—just a little shocked from falling out of that tree."

"She didn't fall! She was shot down," said Harry grimly. "We need better defenses."

"Why don't you come down and give us a full report, sir."

Mum rolled her eyes at me and whispered, "Stop encouraging him."

"It's just a game, Mum," I said.

"Our first casualty," Harry went on. "And there'll be more. We've got the Honeychurch dormice to protect. Are you with me, Stanford?"

"Yes, sir," I said giving a snappy salute.

"Good. Because we're now officially at war."

Chapter Three

"Do you think the bag ladies are double agents?" said Harry as he joined Mum and me at the bottom of the tree.

"Bag ladies?" Mum exclaimed.

"Mummy calls them the bag ladies," Harry went on. "Because they always have tons of bags everywhere. She says they live in a rubbish dump."

"Oh—you mean Joyce and Patty Gully," said Mum, stifling a grin.

"I didn't think much of their tank," Harry declared. "And the purple bag lady was a terrible shot. She missed that German by miles."

"The gun went off by accident," I said quickly. "Joyce didn't know it was loaded."

"That was silly," said Harry. "Father's told me everything about guns. Ours are kept in a locked gun cabinet in the gun room."

"Here is the wounded warrior." I handed him the Jerry mouse, anxious to steer the subject away from guns. "Flying Officer Fitzgerald will survive."

"But what will happen to the other mice—the real ones?" Harry bit his bottom lip and suddenly, Biggles was forgotten. Standing before us now was a very worried little boy.

"I remember those mice as a child," said Mum.

"William told me it was important I protected them but I can't if I'm at that horrible school."

"I'm sure they'll be safe," I said.

"Not if these woods are cut down," Mum said.

"Shh," I hissed.

"When is William back from the Himalayas?" Harry demanded.

"The Himalayas?" Mum and I were both taken off guard at the mention of the stable manager's name. We exchanged looks of confusion. I knew that the family had kept William's true reason for his absence—namely a charge of manslaughter and prison sentence—a secret from Harry, but I hadn't thought to ask what it might be.

"Mummy says that William and Vera have gone on a mountaineering expedition to the Himalayas and that they'll be gone for a very, *very* long time," said Harry solemnly.

Yet again, when it came to Harry, I was at a loss as to what to say. Often he would come out with brilliant comments that showed him to be extremely bright. Other times—such as now—he seemed so gullible. Boarding school must be sheer torment for someone so sensitive and with such a vivid imagination. I was fond of Harry and it troubled me.

"Well, enough of that now," said Mum briskly. "Let's take you home. Your parents must be worried sick."

Harry dug in his toes. "I'm not going back to the front and you can't make me!"

"Don't be silly," Mum scolded. "You're a grown boy now."

"I'm sure we can work out whatever's worrying you," I said, glaring at Mum.

"You promise?"

"Yes," I said. "Let's go"

"You're asking for trouble, Kat," Mum muttered.

"Now...where's your school uniform?"

"Oh. *That*." Harry slipped behind the tree. More rustling followed and a few minutes later, he reappeared dressed in his school uniform of blazer, gray trousers, striped tie, and cap.

"I'm afraid that Squadron Leader James Bigglesworth has left the building," Harry said gloomily.

I laughed. "Of course he hasn't," I said. "He's disguised as Harry Honeychurch."

Harry brightened. "Yes! He is! I mean, yes! I am!"

The three of us set off for the Hall.

"How did you get back here from school, Harry?" said Mum. I had been thinking the same thing. It had to be at least fifty miles away.

"I took the bus," he said. "I'm not stupid."

Mum leaned in and whispered, "Just think! He could have been abducted, for heaven's sakes. The country is full of perverts these days."

"Be quiet, Mother!" I whispered.

"But it was a jolly good thing I *did* escape," Harry went on. "Because someone had to keep an eye on the enemy."

"That's true," I said.

"That man with the limp was waiting for you for ages," said Harry.

"What do you mean, *waiting*?" I said sharply.

"He waited until you were picking the sloes." Harry laughed. "I saw you fall into the bog. You were really lucky you weren't eaten by alien worms with piranha-sharp teeth!"

"I wonder why he was waiting for us," Mum mused.

"To see *you*, Mum," I said. "Remember? He wanted to tell you about the rolling stock depot and discuss your options?"

"What's rolling stock?" Harry asked.

"Let's talk about this later, Mum," I whispered.

Harry's eyes widened. "Like somewhere to store ammunition and bombs? Like a factory?"

"No, nothing like that," I said. "Harry, why don't you tell me about the dormice? Where do they live?"

"Oh! They live in Cavalier Copse. They're arb...harb...arb... they live in trees and hedges."

"Arboreal?" I suggested.

"Yes!" Harry beamed. "William says they travel from tree to tree and never touch the ground. They're going to hibernate now until April." His face fell. "William says they build their nests in hollow trees and roots but...what if all the trees are cut down?"

"They won't be," said Mum grimly. "Not if I have anything to do with it."

"Tell me what the dormice like to eat," I said, hoping to distract him.

"Insects," said Harry. "But hazelnuts are their favorite."

As we walked up to the stile at the top of the field, Harry chattered happily about the Honeychurch dormice, and for a while "the enemy" and boarding school were forgotten.

Suddenly, the five-bar gate in the corner was thrown open and a herd of Devonshire Red Ruby cows and their calves drifted in.

"Cows." I looked over at Mum and said pointedly, "I told you there were cows in this field."

"Oh! Quick. Hurry!" Harry clambered over the stile. "William told me that the cows who have babies don't like us in their field. He said that a holidaymaker was trampled to death last summer whilst walking his dog."

"That's horrible," I exclaimed.

"I heard about that," said Mum. "Apparently, he panicked and started to run. You should never run away from cows, especially if they have calves."

"So says the country girl," I joked as I helped Mum over the stile and we both jumped down on the other side.

"You forget that when I was a girl I spent *every* summer in the country," Mum declared.

"There was a stampede," Harry went on with obvious relish. "He was surrounded by a million cows who stamped on him until all his limbs fell off and his insides exploded." Harry gave a heavy sigh. "I'd rather be trampled on than go back to school."

"Tell me all the good things about your new school," I asked.

"There aren't any."

"Of course there must be," Mum chimed in.

"You'll make friends eventually," I said. "No one likes being the new boy."

"I won't. I hate it. The boys make fun of me." Harry's top lip quivered. "They called me a sissy for taking a toy mouse to school."

"I bet some of them secretly have toys but aren't brave enough to admit it," I said, trying to jolly him along.

Harry slipped his hand into mine. "You promised I would never go back," he said again.

"Told you that was a mistake," Mum whispered into my ear.

"What about changing schools?" I suggested, knowing the moment I said it that it was the wrong thing.

Harry brightened. "I could go to my friend Max's school. I could come home every day!"

"Well . . . that's up to your parents," I said hastily.

"Will you ask Mummy? Please, Kat, *please*!"

We entered the cobbled courtyard at the rear of the Hall and headed for the entrance to the servants' quarters.

"Goodness, someone's been busy with a broom around here," said Mum.

Mum was right. The last time I'd been this way the cobbled courtyard had been cluttered with an assortment of old farm-yard appliances, pieces of wood, and sheets of corrugated iron and mounds of rubbish. Instead, everything had been piled into a large builder's skip that stood in the corner.

Harry started to drag his feet. "Can't I come and stay with you?" he said. "Father is going to be so angry."

"Not angry, just worried," I said. "Come on, shall we go and see Mrs. Cropper first? Maybe she'll make you some hot choco-late. You must be starving."

"Alright," whispered Harry and clung to my hand even tighter.

We stepped through the back door and Mum and I stopped in surprise.

"It looks like the broom has been in here, too!" I said.

The long flagstone corridor that led to the kitchen quarters had always been thick with grime and cobwebs. Not anymore. Even the yellowing painted walls looked as if they had been wiped down.

"What's that pong?" Harry asked.

It was true. There was an eye-watering smell of disinfectant.

"If I had to choose between eau de mire and eau de carbolic I'm afraid I'd rather have the latter," said Mum.

"Look!" Harry exclaimed. "All the doors to the dungeons are open! The prisoners must have escaped!"

The corridor was lined with doorways, each serving a purpose-specific larder for meat, dairy, fish, et al. There was also a flower room, stillroom, and a lamp room. What had been a dull passage-way now shone with cheery brightness.

We peeped in the first doorway—the dry larder. The rectangular room had one window at the far end that was framed by ill-kempt shrubs outside. Although it was still gloomy, everywhere—floor, walls, even the ceiling—looked as if it had been thoroughly scrubbed down. The stoneware storage jars and vats were lined neatly on a central trestle table. The massive dresser that hugged one wall stood equally spotless.

"Mrs. Cropper must have found a new housekeeper after all," Mum remarked. "I wonder if she's from the village?"

Generations of the same families had always worked at Honeychurch Hall "below stairs"—if that term could still be applied in this modern age. Following Vera's so-called unfortunate "accident," Mrs. Cropper had grumbled that finding someone with the right "training" had been impossible.

There had been a series of daily help from Little Dipperton—Patty Gully having been just one—but none had lasted more than two or three weeks.

Harry ran in and out of the open doorways and shouted, "This is *wicked*!"

"I recognize that voice!" Mrs. Cropper stood at the end of the corridor. "Is that Master Harry?"

She was dressed in her usual uniform of a pink-striped pinafore over a plain white linen short-sleeved dress and wore her gray hair tucked under a white mobcap.

"The school called this morning and told us you ran away again," said Mrs. Cropper sternly. "His lordship and Lady Lavinia are waiting for you in the drawing room with Shawn."

I still couldn't get used to calling the local police inspector by his first name despite his being Mr. and Mrs. Cropper's grandson.

Harry scowled. "I'm not going back to the front. Ever."

"That's not for you to decide," said Mrs. Cropper briskly.

"Kat says I can go to the same school as Max," Harry said.

Mrs. Cropper glared at me. "Did she now."

"Did you know that the bag ladies nearly shot someone to death with their gun today?" said Harry gleefully.

Mrs. Cropper's eyes widened in shock. "What is Master Harry talking about?"

"It wasn't quite like that," I said quickly.

"Oh yes it was," said Mum. "This despicable man was trespassing and Joyce encouraged him to leave with her twelve-bore."

Harry nodded eagerly. "The sign says TRESPASSERS WILL BE PROSECUTED & POACHERS WILL BE SHOT."

"But he wasn't poaching, Harry," I said. "My mother's exaggerating. The gun went off by accident."

"What was this trespasser doing?" Mrs. Cropper demanded.

"Laying a runway for the airplanes," said Harry. "There were big black boards with HS3 CROSSING FROM HERE."

"Operation Bullet, I presume," said Mrs. Cropper grimly. "Well, enough of all that. Come along, Master Harry—"

"We almost forgot to give you these." Mum passed her the wicker basket of sloes.

Mrs. Cropper took the basket in one hand and Harry in the other. "Come along, Harry," she said again. "Your father will be wanting to talk to you."

Harry's face fell. He looked as if the weight of the world was on his little shoulders. "Don't forget to write to me, Kat."

"And don't forget to write to *me*," I said. "I love getting your letters."

Mrs. Cropper whisked Harry away.

"I hope he'll be okay," I said.

"I wouldn't mind poking around in these old larders," Mum

mused. "I've got a scene in *Forbidden* that takes place in the meat larder."

"I hope it's not a love scene," I said. "Anyway . . . I thought we'd turned in your manuscript?"

"We?" said Mum. "*We* turned in the manuscript?"

"You couldn't have finished it without my typing expertise," I pointed out.

"*Finished?* It's not finished," she snapped. "Turning in the manuscript is only the beginning of the process. I'll get notes back from my editor any day now. In fact, I should have gotten them yesterday."

"I thought you just sent it off and that was that."

"Of course not! It's a very lengthy process. It's not a sausage factory."

I knew I'd hit a nerve but I was spared further explanation by the appearance of a woman in her early thirties stepping through the doorway of the meat larder carrying a bucket of dirty water. She was dressed in a drab, gray dress under a waterproof butcher's apron. A lock of dark hair flopped over one eye, having escaped from under a neat cap. She was very pretty with a heart-shaped face and large brown eyes.

"Oh!" she exclaimed, bobbing a curtsey. "Beg pardon. You startled me." I noted a broad Devonshire accent.

"Hello. You must be the new housekeeper," I said. "You've done a fantastic job of cleaning up the courtyard."

"Thank you, ma'am."

"You've certainly got your work cut out for you here," Mum chimed in. "What's your name?"

"I'm Parks."

"We can't call you Parks," I said. "What's your first name?"

"Angela."

"I'm Iris and this is Kat," said Mum. "I live at the Carriage

House. Kat is visiting. She lives in London." I caught the dig but ignored it.

Angela regarded me keenly. "Forgive me for saying so, ma'am, but aren't you the lady on *Fakes & Treasures?*"

"Yes, I used to be," I said and swiftly changed the subject. "Do you live locally?"

"No. I'm from North Devon," said Angela.

"That's quite far away," Mum said. "What made you want to move? A broken heart?"

"Don't listen to her." Honestly, my mother could be so tact-less.

"No. Nothing like that." Angela's warm smile was marred by a nasty snaggletooth. "I was in service at Lindridge but the house burned down. You've got to go where the work is. His lordship very kindly gave me one of the cottages by the walled garden—although I'd much prefer to live in."

We exchanged pleasantries and learned that Angela only started working at the Hall a week ago.

"Of course, there's no scullery maid," Angela went on. "And it's just me having to do all the work apart from Mrs. Cropper, but things are different these days, aren't they? A servant's life is not what it used to be."

It was such an odd thing to say. She couldn't have been that much younger than I. Maybe life in rural Devon was even further behind the times than I realized.

"There used to be twelve live-in servants here," said Mum. "And five gardeners."

"That's what Mr. Cropper told me. This house must have been quite something back in the day."

"It was nice to meet you, Angela," I said. "I hope Mrs. Cropper doesn't work you too hard."

Angela seemed to hesitate. "Can I ask your advice?"

Here we go, I thought. *She's going to ask me to value her grandmother's teapot.*

"At Lindridge we used to have a book club. It was fun," Angela went on. "I was thinking of asking Lady Lavinia if we could start one here. What do you think? Would you both come?"

"Kat can't. She's doesn't live here," said Mum with another dig.

"What about you, Iris?" said Angela. "I mean, you're retired. What do you do all day? You must have lots of time on your hands."

Mum looked taken aback. "I'm quite busy, thank you very much."

"Oh, no, no, sorry." Angela reddened. "I didn't mean it like that. I just thought you might be bored."

Angela seemed so upset about her faux pas that I felt sorry for her.

"That's a great idea," I said. "Although, as you noticed, there aren't that many people on the estate anymore."

"I thought we could ask the folks in Little Dipperton as well," Angela ventured. "We could meet once a month in the tearoom in the village or something."

"Angela!" shouted Mrs. Cropper. "Can you come here a moment?"

"I'd best be going," said Angela hastily. She gave us another snaggletooth smile, bobbed another curtsey, and with her bucket and mop, hurried back to the kitchen humming a familiar melody.

Mum frowned. "Isn't that the theme tune from *Downton Abbey?*"

"Yes! Gosh. That's taking job loyalty to another level." We both laughed. Maybe the show's phenomenal success had spawned a whole generation of wannabe parlor maids, t'ween maids, and scullery maids!

"Well, I'm not joining her silly book club," said Mum. "What nerve! Implying I did nothing all day."

"To anyone who doesn't know about your secret life," I said, "it would look that way."

The evening was drawing in. Checking my watch I saw it was almost five and time to feed and bed down the horses for the night. I'd always had a passion for these noble creatures and I'd grown to enjoy this time of day. I knew I'd miss them all. With William incarcerated at HM Prison Exeter, I'd been helping at the yard along with Dawn, the eighteen-year-old daughter of Tom Jones who farmed Home Farm. Maybe Mum's stepbrother Alfred would be a welcome addition, after all.

"I'm going to the yard," I said. "Do you want to come?"

"No. I'm going back to lie on the sofa and do absolutely nothing. Just like Miss Snaggletooth implied."

"Car coming," I said, stepping back onto the grass verge as a panda car came into view.

"It's that nice Shawn," said Mum. "I do wish you'd give him a chance. He's already broken in as a husband and you'd have a ready-made family."

"No thanks," I said. "And stop trying to play matchmaker. Your last effort backfired—no pun intended."

"Very funny," said Mum dryly.

The panda car drew up alongside us and stopped.

Shawn opened his window with a smile. "Evening, ladies."

With his mop of brown curly hair and freckles I always thought he seemed far too young to hold the rank of detective inspector.

Tonight, the lapel on Shawn's trench coat sported a new stain—possibly tomato ketchup—one of the hazards of being a single parent of five-year-old twins.

Redheaded policewoman Roxy Cairns waved from the passenger seat.

"I do wish she'd do something about her mustache," whispered Mum. "Hasn't she heard of waxing?"

"Quiet," I said then leaned in to say, "I hope Harry wasn't in too much trouble again."

"He's very naughty," Mum chipped in. "I'd give him a good hiding if he were my son."

"Mum, for heaven's sakes," I hissed. "You can't say that these days."

"Rupert is taking him back to school tonight," said Shawn.

"Rupert and Lavinia have had a huge fight," Roxy said with relish.

"Roxy!" Shawn said sharply.

I'd noticed that Roxy only addressed Lord and Lady Honeychurch correctly when she was in their presence. She didn't try to hide her dislike of the upper classes much, either.

"Where did you find Harry?" said Shawn.

"Last time the poor kid was hiding in Eric's caravan," Roxy said. "Eric really got it in the neck."

"Harry was up in a tree in Cavalier Copse," I said.

"The treehouse? Oh yes," said Shawn. "William built that. Have you seen it? There's even a little hut."

William and his good deeds again!

"Harry caught a bus," Mum said. "The school is fifty miles away. What if he runs away again and there isn't a bus and he decides to hitchhike?"

I elbowed Mum and said, "We're just happy to know he's safe."

"It won't happen again," said Roxy. "Rupert has threatened to sell Thunder."

"Harry loves that pony," I exclaimed.

"That's as good a deterrent as any," said Mum. "Speaking of deterrents. Did Harry tell you about the little shooting incident this afternoon?"

"Yes he did," said Shawn. "As a matter of fact, we're heading down to Bridge Cottage right now to talk to Joyce and Patty. They can't go frightening off government officials."

"Don't they have to have a gun license?" Mum asked.

"They do. Both have shotgun certificates," said Shawn mildly.

"Should I get one?" Mum mused.

"Why?" I said "Are you planning on using one?"

"Possibly," said Mum. "Did you know that the Department for Transport have started marking out the boundaries for the railway line?"

Shawn nodded. "So I heard."

Roxy leaned over to shout, "This whole business is disgusting. My aunt lives in the path of HS2, the other line that's supposed to take thirty minutes off the travel time from London to Birmingham. Thirty minutes!"

"Actually, Roxy," said Shawn, "it's thirty-two—"

"Disgusting," Mum echoed.

"I must remind you, Roxy," said Shawn sternly. "As members of the Devon and Cornwall Constabulary we are supposed to keep our opinions to ourselves."

"My aunt's place falls under a compulsory purchase order," Roxy fumed. "They've lived there for forty years! What are they supposed to do now? They can't get another mortgage at their age. I've heard that most of the properties around here aren't even eligible for compensation."

"There's a protest meeting on Thursday," said Mum. "You should come."

"Count me in!" Roxy exclaimed.

"If you are planning on doing anything at all, it's got to go by the book," said Shawn.

"We're hardly going to throw paint or set fire to cars," said Mum.

"I don't know. I might," said Roxy. It was hard to tell if she was joking or not.

"I'll tell you exactly what I told Eric," said Shawn. "You need to petition the government. Build a strong case and take it through the Court of Appeal just like the Action Alliance is doing for HS2. Frankly, I think it's too early—"

"But it's not, is it?" said Mum. "Those placards are up right now. It's already begun!"

"Shawn doesn't care," said Roxy. "He loves trains, don't you Shawn—"

"That's enough . . ." Shawn must have hit a button because the window shot up. Their words were muffled but judging by Roxy's contorted face and Shawn's angry expression, their arguing continued.

The car sped away in a flurry of gravel.

"Well," said Mum finally. "Roxy will certainly be an asset to our cause."

"Or a liability."

We stopped where the drive forked in front of a huge horse chestnut tree. On our left was the lane that led to the stable block.

"I'll see you in an hour or so," I said.

"And remember, not a word about the protest group or those placards to Lady Edith."

"I think you'll have a hard job of keeping that a secret," I said. "But it won't come from me. I promise."

The moment Mum was out of earshot, I pulled my iPhone out of my pocket and retrieved Valentine Prince-Avery's business card. He answered on the first ring and seemed pleased to get my call.

"I'm alive," he joked. "But that was the first time I've been shot at by a mad woman with a twelve-bore."

"You have a difficult job. But—" I hesitated. "I'd like to hear about what my mother's options might be. Any chance we can talk tonight?"

We agreed to meet at the Hare & Hounds at seven.

"And can we just keep this between the two of us," I said. "At least—just for now."

Chapter Four

"**Young boys need to toughen up, Lavinia,**" I heard Edith say. They were in the midst of a heated conversation in the tack room and the door was ajar. "You were all for it a few weeks ago."

I knew I shouldn't eavesdrop, but I couldn't help it.

"Harry has run away three times now," Lavinia protested. "He's being bullied and he's frightfully unhappy. I can't bear it. I just can't."

"I've never heard such nonsense!" Edith exclaimed. "As his mother, you must be strong."

"He's seven! And he's frightfully sensitive," said Lavinia. "Didn't you miss Rupert when he first went away to school? I thought I wouldn't mind so much. But I do."

"You can't allow yourself to give in to sentiment, Lavinia," said Edith. "Half the reason we don't have a British Empire anymore is because of the way children are educated these days."

"For heaven's sake," Lavinia exclaimed. "The British Empire died at least half a century ago. If you tell me to keep a stiff upper lip, I'll scream."

"All this touchy-feely American nonsense," Edith went on. "Look at Rupert. Boarding school did him a world of good. You don't see him sniffling like a girl."

"Exactly my point," said Lavinia dryly. "I don't want Harry to be incapable of showing his feelings."

I had to agree with Lavinia. I often wondered if that was my ex-boyfriend David's problem. He'd been sent off to boarding school at age seven, too. David loathed any form of emotion—especially public displays of affection that made him squirm with embarrassment. To begin with, I'd found his old-fashioned gallantry attractive. But I soon discovered he was unable to talk honestly about his feelings, preferring to retreat behind a wall of silence or simply walk out of the room.

"Rupert cried to start with, of course he did," Edith went on. "But he soon pulled himself together like a true Honeychurch must."

"What about trying the local school?"

"Absolutely not," said Edith. "Harry should be mixing with his peers, not the hoi polloi and all the frightful nouveau riche."

"It's different now," said Lavinia. "The hoi polloi *do* go to public schools and yes, I know what you mean about the nouveau riche, but no one cares if one's not listed in *Burke's Peerage* anymore."

"Where on earth did Harry get the village school idea from in the first place?" Edith demanded.

"Apparently, Katherine Stanford told him he could go," said Lavinia. "Rupert was *ab-so-lute-ly* livid. We had the most frightful row."

My stomach gave a lurch. I knew I should have kept my mouth shut. I hurried on by but promptly tripped over a pitchfork that fell down with a clatter. The talking ceased abruptly.

Quickly, I spied an empty water bucket, grabbed it, and headed over to an outside tap. I turned the water on full blast.

Lavinia poked her head out of the tack room door. "Oh, it's you."

I gave a feeble wave of greeting and pretended to find something fascinating in the water bucket. Edith must have made a comment because Lavinia stepped back and closed the tack room door.

Their conversation had unsettled me. I knew I shouldn't have interfered but it was hard not to. The Honeychurch family had really gotten under my skin—and it wasn't just the humans.

Well before I'd discovered the magic of the antiques world, I had desperately wanted to work with horses but my ever-practical father insisted that I would never earn a decent living as a groom. Of course, Dad envisioned me on the lower end of the equestrian world, not the upper. It never occurred to me to disagree with him and follow my dream. I admired Mum for following hers—and against all odds. Much as we both adored my father, I hated to admit he had been rather overbearing or as Mum would say, "protective" and "only wanting the best for both of us."

As I filled up the water buckets and refilled hay nets I realized I'd miss my new equine friends most of all. I had become familiar with all their different personalities. Tinkerbell, the dowager countess's favorite chestnut mare, was notoriously impatient and known to wriggle out of her bridle if no one was watching; Jupiter, a bay mare who Edith claimed was depressed following William's departure; Harry's adorable little black pony, Thunder, who loved Heinz tomato soup and drank it from a thermos flask; and Duchess, a dapple-gray mare that I'd begun to think of as my own. In addition, there were two young horses, Falcon and Kestrel that Lavinia and William had been training for two-in-hand carriage driving competitions. Finally, there were the "old ladies"—Pixie Dust, Rose, and Willow, aged twenty-eight, thirty, and an impressive thirty-five. Every morning I dreaded hearing the news that one of them had died during the night. I wondered what would happen to Edith's beloved equine cemetery should Operation Bullet really happen and with a jolt, I knew I would do my best to stop it happening, too.

I was inside Duchess's stable when I saw Rupert's black Range Rover pull into the yard. Harry got out of the front passenger seat and hurried over to Thunder's loose box opposite. He darted inside.

Lavinia emerged from the tack room and walked over to the car. Rupert opened the window. I couldn't catch their conversation but judging from Lavinia's expression as she went to find Harry, guessed it had not gone well.

A few minutes later, mother and son emerged from Thunder's loose box. Lavinia had her arm around Harry's shoulders. She kissed the top of his head. Harry spotted me in the doorway and broke away to join me.

"Are you off?" I said with false cheerfulness.

"Flying Officer Stanford," said Harry, adopting his Biggles persona, "I'm afraid I've been recalled for duty."

"So I heard, sir."

"I want your word that you won't let anything happen to the dormice."

"I promise," I said. "What about Flying Officer Fitzgerald, sir? Is she going with you?"

"No," said Harry. "She's needed at home."

"Harry!" Lavinia materialized at the stable door. "Come along. Father wants to leave now."

"Good luck, sir," I said and gave a snappy salute. Lavinia rewarded me with a tight smile, then steered Harry over to the Range Rover. As he clambered into the front passenger seat I heard him say, "But I haven't said good-bye to Mr. Chips!"

"He's off chasing rabbits, darling." Lavinia buckled up Harry's seat belt and closed the car door.

Rupert drove away with Harry's face pressed against the

glass—a picture of pure misery. It was awful. I couldn't see Lavinia's expression since she was already hurrying back to the tack room.

I waited until the coast was clear before stepping back into the yard where I was greeted by a burst of frenetic barking. Mr. Chips, the Jack Russell terrier, tore around the corner and bounded up to me. His tan and white body was coated with mud and he smelled terrible.

He dropped a stone that was coated in drool at my feet and looked up expectantly, his stump tail wagging furiously.

I leaned down to fondle his ears and he licked my hand then nosed the stone toward me.

"You want me to throw this, boy?" I said and gingerly picked it up between my fingers.

Mr. Chips danced about on his hind legs, barking with excitement as I threw the stone as far as I could. He bounded after it and was back within minutes to drop the stone at my feet again.

"You've started something now." Edith emerged from the tack room wearing her usual sidesaddle habit. Like Lavinia, even when hatless, she wore her hair clamped under a hairnet. "He won't let you alone."

I threw the stone again and yet again, he was tearing back for another go.

"You bad dog!" Edith scolded. "Where have you been?"

Despite her age and small frame, the dowager countess was a formidable woman.

Mr. Chips sank to the ground, his ears drooped, and he gave her such a look of sorrow that we both laughed.

"He's been down a badger sett again," said Edith, the relief in her voice evident. "One of these days he'll get trapped."

"Can't you block the holes?" I suggested.

"Block up the *setts*! Good heavens, no!" Edith sounded appalled. "Protection of Badgers Act, 1992. Can't touch them."

"I didn't know that," I said. "I've lived in London all my life. They say, 'You can take the girl out of the city but not the city out of the girl.'"

"Do they?" Edith regarded me with curiosity. "Pity you're going back to London. You've been such a help with William away."

There it was again. As far as Edith was concerned, William was "away." I really hoped she wasn't going to elaborate on William's sabbatical. It was all so horribly awkward. I wasn't sure if Edith had convinced herself that William was in the Himalayas or if perhaps the Himalayas was upper-class slang for "prison." The more time I spent with the gentry—as Mum called them—the more I realized that Mum was right. Even in today's modern world there is still a "them and an us."

"How is Jupiter?" *Someone else who is missing William,* I thought.

"Still not eating. Completely off her food." Edith gave a heavy sigh. "She's lost without William. We all are." She fell quiet for a moment. "Tell me about this uncle of yours."

"Uncle?" My mind went blank before I realized whom she was talking about. "You mean Alfred?"

"I remember him," said Edith. "Awful boy. Nothing like his brother, Billy. They camped here every summer, you know."

Of course I knew. It was the main reason why my mother had been drawn back to a place she loved during her unconventional childhood.

I scrambled for something positive to say about Alfred, a man I'd never met. "Mum tells me Alfred has changed."

"I should jolly well hope so," Edith said. "We all knew he was stealing but what does one expect from a gypsy?"

"Oh!" I wracked my brains again. "I thought they were all part of a traveling boxing emporium."

"Those people are all much the same," said Edith with a sniff.

"Did my mother tell you what Alfred has been doing for the past few decades?"

"Of course. Working for a home for retired circus horses on The Continent," said Edith. "Very noble of him. Very noble, indeed."

The Continent. I hadn't heard that quaint British phrase for years. I guessed it was yet another story that my mother had invented.

"Where in Europe was it?" I said. "I've forgotten."

"Spain. The Spanish can be so cruel to their animals." Edith went on, "I think we could offer homes for a few of those horses here. Especially now your mother is restoring the stalls in the Carriage House."

"What a good idea." Outwardly I pretended to be enthusiastic but inwardly I predicted troubles ahead. There were so many lies being told at Honeychurch Hall, I was having trouble keeping them straight.

"I did make it very clear to your mother that Alfred's position is only until William returns," said Edith.

"William is coming *back*?" I tried to hide my astonishment. "When?"

"I know the justice of the peace. We ride to hounds," said Edith. "It won't be for a while but—" She tapped the side of her nose and gave a mischievous smile. "I've got a plan."

Two criminals on the property! Lovely!

I wondered what Rupert thought about his mother's plan. I knew that he was convinced Edith was suffering from a form of dementia. Perhaps he was right, after all.

"Alfred can use William's flat whilst he is working here," Edith declared.

"That's very kind. My mother will be pleased," I said as the stable yard clock chimed six. "Was there anything else you needed me to do tonight?"

"Yes. There is." Edith fixed me with one of her unnerving stares. "Harry mentioned he saw a man putting placards in the two fields by Cavalier Copse below Hopton's Crest."

"Oh, you know Harry, Edith." Lavinia was suddenly beside us. I noticed her face was even paler than usual and her eyes looked red. I guessed that she had been crying. "He loves telling stories, doesn't he, Katherine?"

"Harry has definitely got a vivid imagination," I said carefully.

Edith's eyes narrowed. "Is there something you aren't telling me?"

"No!" we chorused.

"Oh, thank heavens you found Mr. Chips," Lavinia said, quickly changing the subject. "I didn't see him sitting over there. It looks like he's been burrowing underground. And goodness, he does smell."

"We're going to have a bath, aren't we, boy?" Edith snapped her fingers and Mr. Chips leapt to attention. He took up his position close behind her feet. "And Kat," Edith said. "Tomorrow, we will ride to Cavalier Copse and see what Harry was talking about. Come at eleven."

Edith strode off with Mr. Chips trotting behind her.

"I'm frightfully sorry to put you in such a ghastly position," said Lavinia. "Rupert feels there is no reason for Edith to know about this awful train business. It'll only distress her. Ever since Vera's frightful . . . *accident* . . . Edith has not been herself. I mean—" Lavinia lowered her voice, "She's even been visiting William. In *prison!*"

"I can't see how she won't find out," I said. "There are flyers all over the village."

Lavinia bit her lip. "I know."

"And placards in the fields, too."

"What do they say?" said Lavinia. "Will she know what they mean?"

"They're pretty obvious." I said. "HS3 CROSSES FROM HERE."

"I'll talk to Eric. He can get rid of them tonight."

"Did you hear about the shooting incident?" I asked.

"I heard Harry's version of it," said Lavinia. "Joyce and Patty are barking mad. Frightful people. Frightful."

I quickly filled her in.

"Good heavens!" Lavinia actually cracked a smile. "Valentine Prince-Avery! What a name! It sounds like something from one of your mother's novels!"

"Mum and I got a laugh out of that one," I said. "Valentine gave me his business card. Seems he's a consultant who assesses properties for compensation. I think we should talk to him about our options."

"We could," said Lavinia slowly. "But really, he's the enemy, isn't he?"

"But wouldn't it be helpful to know what we're up against?"

"No. I have a better idea. I wanted to talk to Iris about it, too. An old chum of mine—Benedict Scroope—is an environmentalist. Comes highly recommended and is frightfully well connected with all the right people. He even saved an entire village in Kent from being demolished when the Channel Tunnel was built in the early nineties. Managed to get the line diverted."

"That's encouraging news!"

"I think Benedict can be persuaded to take our case," Lavinia went on. "In fact, I told Eric to get in touch with him. I believe he is organizing a meeting in the village but of course, I can't possibly go. One needs to keep a certain air of mystery and distance from one's people. It would be frightfully good if you could go on my behalf."

"I will if I'm still here," I said. "My mother will definitely want to get involved."

"Excellent." Lavinia hesitated for a moment. "I was hoping I could introduce Benedict to your mother tomorrow. We could meet at the Carriage House. Do you think she'd mind frightfully? Such a bore, I know."

"Why don't you call and ask her?"

"Obviously I can't bring Benedict to the Hall because of Edith, and Mrs. Cropper can be a frightful gossip. And then there's the new housekeeper, Parks. One must be circumspect." Lavinia hesitated again. "And I'd rather you didn't mention this to Rupert."

"Won't he find out if you're organizing a campaign?"

"No." Lavinia's pale face turned pink. "Rupert is spending some time—" She made a peculiar gulping sound. "Rupert has had to go to London. On business." She blinked back tears. "Goodness, a fly flew straight into my eye."

"It must have been hard saying good-bye to Harry," I said. "I'm so sorry."

Lavinia looked startled. "Harry? Why? He's fine. *Ab-so-lute-ly* fine. Has never been better, actually."

"I wanted to apologize," I said firmly. "I should never have mentioned the local school option. I hope it didn't cause any trouble between you and Rupert."

Lavinia's face turned even pinker. She seemed horrified at being asked such a personal question. "Trouble? Why would it? Everything is perfectly fine. *Ab-so-lute-ly* fine."

"I'm sure you must miss Harry," I persisted. "I know I do!"

"Miss him?" Lavinia forced a laugh. "Well, one would but one's so busy, isn't one? To miss anything." She gave a bright smile. "Must get on. Good night."

It was dark as I headed for home along the former service road and through the pine forest. When I first took the shortcut, the muffled silence used to spook me. It wasn't just the Hall that had ghosts-in-residence, but the grounds and surrounding fields, too.

My thoughts turned to my life in London that seemed so simple compared to those at Honeychurch Hall. I thought of Mum and her secret identity and now, here she was introducing Alfred, her stepbrother, under false pretenses. Working with retired circus horses in Spain! She may as well claim that Alfred was a champion matador! Or better yet, said that Alfred had returned from the Himalayas! Then, there was the charade between Edith, Rupert, and Lavinia, each hiding something from the other. And mixed up in this was poor Harry, bundled off to boarding school.

And what of Valentine Prince-Avery? My mother wouldn't be pleased if she found out I was planning on meeting him tonight even though I had her best interests at heart. She'd be furious—unless I lied.

But before I could give my social plans any more thought I left the pine forest behind me, slipped through the latch gate, and entered the courtyard to find Mum sitting on the top step of the stone mounting block.

"Where on earth have you been?" she demanded.

"I told you I was at the yard with the horses," I said. "Why? What on earth's the matter?"

"Something terrible has happened."

Chapter Five

"Take a deep breath and calm down," I said.

We were sitting at the pine kitchen table and Mum refused to say anything until she had poured us large gin and tonics. This "sun over the yardarm" lark was becoming a bit of a habit but I told myself that once I was back in London, I wouldn't be reaching for the gin bottle every time the bird clock struck six or there was a problem that only alcohol could solve.

"It can't be that bad," I said. "You haven't run out of gin. Oh!" I spotted the mailing box labeled Goldfinch Press on one of the countertops. "Did they hate the manuscript?"

"Of course they didn't hate the manuscript!" Mum snapped. "Graham, my editor loved it."

"I just thought—"

"I've got to make a few changes and spice up the tiffin—"

"The *what?*"

"The tiffin, darling. Nooky. *Sex.*"

I sniggered. "I've never heard that term before."

"But that's not the real problem." Mum took a large sip and gave a heavy sigh. She pushed a sheet of heavily embossed paper with the logo of a goldfinch toward me. "Look at this."

"Let me see." I read aloud. "*Win a romantic weekend for two on the spectacular Amalfi Coast with Krystalle Storm, the international best-selling author of the Star-Crossed Lovers Series. Stroll through the gardens of her beautiful Italian villa, meet the delightful Pekinese, Truly Scrumptious—*"

"I know what it says!" Mum exclaimed.

"So?"

"Given that Vera had won the contest and now—well, she's dead, isn't she—why wouldn't my publisher have canceled the prize out of respect?"

I skimmed the rest of the letter. "Gosh. There were over five thousand entries," I said. "I know! You'll just have to rent a villa in Italy and borrow a dog."

"Not funny," said Mum. "You obviously haven't read to the bottom of the page."

"It says here that Goldfinch Press is awarding the prize to— good grief!"

"Exactly."

"Eric," I said. "Well. I suppose Eric was her husband. Mum, this is actually a good thing. He knows your secret. Why don't you just pay him off? If your publisher wants publicity photos, we can get them Photoshopped here. Didn't you say that Alfred was good at forgeries?"

Mum's expression hardened. "I talked to Eric in Cromwell Meadows twenty minutes ago. I even took him a cup of tea!"

"And?"

"I said that instead of him going on a mini-break we could come to a cash arrangement," said Mum. "I would simply tell my publisher that Eric preferred to make a donation to charity or something."

"So, you'd pay him off?"

"He flatly refused! And when I asked him why, Eric had the nerve to say it was none of my business!"

"Oh." This was a surprise. Eric was notoriously hard up for money. "He really wants to go to Italy that much? Even when you told him that you didn't own a villa there—or a Pekinese?"

Mum suddenly seemed fascinated by her fingernails.

"You didn't tell him about the villa, did you?" I said. "Of course you didn't."

"He's a horrible man! Why does he have to make my life so difficult?"

"He knows you don't like him."

"I suppose we did get off on the wrong foot this evening," Mum admitted. "You've heard that wretched tractor! Every morning he's outside my window digging out that ditch. It makes a terrible noise and I just can't concentrate. I asked him nicely but he got in a huff and said to take it up with her ladyship if I had a problem. Something about rain, drainage, and flooding."

"If Edith told him to dig—"

"Why can't he dig somewhere else when I'm trying to write?"

"So you had another falling out?" I said wearily.

"What? Why are you looking at me like that?"

"Now that Dad is gone, why can't you come clean? With *everyone,*" I said. "Tell Eric there is no villa or Pekinese dog. And whilst you're at it, tell your publisher—"

"Graham. His name is Graham Goldfinch—"

"That your husband was not an international diplomat, nor did he die in a tragic plane crash, among other things."

"It's too late for that now."

"Graham won't care about your background," I said. "It happens all the time in publishing. Look at J. K. Rowling? She wrote under a pseudonym."

"I'm not J. K. Rowling." Mum gave another sigh. "Alfred would have done such a good job transforming that wall into the Amalfi Coast."

"Now that he's no longer taking care of retired circus horses in Spain?"

"Oh, her ladyship told you. I couldn't say that Alfred has spent the last decade in Wormwood Scrubs prison," Mum said with scorn. "But Alfred will be very useful to our protest group. Just you see."

"That reminds me," I said. "Lavinia is going to call you about an old friend of hers—Benedict Scroope—"

"That's a good name, too. I must write it down—"

"He's an environmentalist. Well connected apparently," I said. "Even managed to save an entire village in Kent from demolition when the Channel Tunnel was built. They want to meet here."

Mum brightened. "Here? Not at the Hall?"

"Lavinia feels—I quote—'*One needs to keep a certain air of mystery and distance from one's people.*' Basically, she wants to get involved but doesn't want to mix with the rabble."

"What an honor." Mum's face flushed with pleasure, then she scowled. "Will Eric be coming?"

"Lavinia said it would be just the three of you."

"Not even his lordship?"

"He's gone to London."

As if on cue, Mum's phone rang.

"I bet that's Lavinia, now," I said.

She snatched up the receiver, said, "Yes, m'lady" several times, "I promise I won't say a word to his lordship," then, "Lovely. Tomorrow at nine-thirty."

Mum put the phone down and turned to me. "Why can't we mention this to his lordship?"

"Rupert told Lavinia not to interfere."

"Of course he'd say that," said Mum with scorn.

My mother did not have a particularly high opinion of Lord Honeychurch ever since we learned he'd tried to sell the estate to an adventure playground development company. Mum still didn't trust Rupert's change of heart and believed it was because he hoped to be reinstated as Edith's heir. I had to admit I thought she could be right.

"Rupert drove Harry back to school and then went on to London," I said. "Lavinia was pretty upset about it. Not that I'm gossiping." But I realized I was!

"Gossip! You must! What happened? They argued over Harry? They separated?" Mum's eyes widened. "Has he met someone else? I wouldn't be surprised. She's such a cold fish. And the way she wears her hair under that hairnet all the time. So unattractive."

"I'll leave all that to your imagination," I said. "I'm going to take a luxurious shower in your wonderful new bathroom."

"I had that shower put in especially for you." Mum looked at the bird clock. "Do you mind getting your own supper tonight? If I'm expecting the gentry tomorrow I need to get cracking on these notes straight away."

"I was thinking about going to the Hare & Hounds."

"Why?" Mum said suspiciously. "Isn't that where that Valentine person is staying?"

I felt myself redden and agonized over whether to lie. "They make a good steak and kidney pie."

"You're a hopeless fibber," said Mum. "You're going to see *him*, aren't you? You're going to talk to *him* behind my back!"

"Why don't we just hear what he has to say about your options?"

Mum grabbed the box containing her manuscript and headed for the kitchen door. "I hope you will both be very happy together. After all, he lives in London. You live in London . . ."

And then it hit me. I don't know how I had missed the obvious. "Would you like me to stay here a little longer?" I said gently. "At least until Alfred has settled in?"

"It's up to you," said Mum but I saw a flash of hope in her eyes and it made me feel like an idiot. As the time for my departure drew closer we'd been bickering more than usual. Why hadn't I realized that my mother was going to miss me, too? For the past forty years I'd practically lived in her back pocket.

"I suppose Alfred could sleep on the sofa in the sitting room," she said.

"It's still more comfortable than a jail cell," I said. "Edith mentioned Alfred could have William's flat in the stable yard."

"I'm not sure if he'll agree to that," she said darkly.

"Come here."

"Why?"

I pulled Mum into my arms and said, "I'm going to miss you, too, but I'm not going to the moon."

"You smell." Mum wriggled free.

I looked down at the clothes I had been wearing all day. I sported manure stains on my jeans and the cuffs of my sweater were brown with mud from our tumble in Coffin Mire.

"Wait! I've had a brilliant idea!" Mum broke into a smile that had devious written all over it. "You can be our spy!"

"What are you talking about?"

"Yes! You must meet Valentine, tonight. I'll bet he's privy—"

"Privy?" I snorted.

"Stop snorting. Yes, *privy*, to all sorts of confidential information that we can pass along to Mr. Scroope. You are going undercover!"

Mum retrieved a Dictaphone from the kitchen drawer. "Here, put this in your handbag."

"I think it's a terrible idea," but I took it all the same.

"But don't put on that awful patterned skirt. It makes you look so frumpy."

It had been exactly what I'd planned to wear.

"I won't wait up," said Mum with a knowing wink.

Chapter Six

One hour later, dressed in the patterned skirt that Mum thought frumpy, I drove the mile and a half from Honeychurch Hall to the village of Little Dipperton. It was a typical chocolate-box Devonshire village consisting of whitewashed, thatched, and slate-roofed cottages with a handful of shops and a seventeenth-century pub. There was also an abandoned forge, a greengrocer, a tearoom, and a general store that doubled up as a post office.

At one time the Honeychurch estate owned the entire village of Little Dipperton but now only a handful of cottages were tenant-occupied with their doors and window frames painted a distinctive dark blue.

Mum and I had walked to the village many times for a lunch-time drink at the Hare & Hounds or stopped in the tea shop for a cup of tea and homemade cake.

My initial six weeks of helping my mother out with her broken hand had turned into eight. Dad had been right to ask me to keep an eye on her and I had to admit I was conflicted about our upcoming separation. It was only now that I was beginning to really get to know my own mother.

Dad and I would groan at her constant "headaches," which kept her in her bedroom for hours. Neither of us had known about her secret writing life and I definitely had had no knowledge of her colorful past on the road with the traveling boxing emporium. For whatever reason, my parents had kept me in the dark about the latter, and far from being intrigued and excited, I felt as if my childhood had all been a lie. Why couldn't they have told me? I had asked my mother many times and her answer was always the same. "We didn't want the neighbors to find out. It was a different time. There was a stigma attached to fairground folk."

As I drove down the hill toward Bridge Cottage, my thoughts turned to HS3. I found it hard to believe that one day this area could be an ugly railway cutting. I still hadn't given up hope that Mum would move back to London and stick to our original plan of working together.

Only this morning I'd heard from my estate agent in London that a shop with a two-bedroom flat above had come up for sale just off Brick Lane in Shoreditch close to Spitalfields Market. I was excited about the location. Spitalfields was named after a hospital and a priory known as St. Mary's Spital that was founded in 1197. The market itself was established in the 1680s and was a huge tourist attraction—the perfect place to start my new antiques business. I decided to drive up on Saturday anyway to take a look, stay in my flat at Putney Bridge overnight, and return to Devon on Sunday.

I was jolted out of my thoughts when my headlights caught the orange glare of Patty's woolen coat. I drew alongside and hit the electric window button.

"Can I give you a lift?" I said.

Without a word, she opened the passenger door and got in. I was practically overwhelmed by the smell of cooked bacon that oozed from her clothes.

"Where are you going?" I asked.

"Work. Where do you think?" said Patty. "Stan was supposed to pick me up at six-thirty but he didn't show up. He's always forgetting and then I have to walk."

"I'm glad I was passing by," I said lightly. "Didn't you call Stan?"

"We don't have a phone," said Patty. "We can't afford it. We can't afford to run a car, either. We can't make ends meet on my mother's pension and disability allowance but people like you wouldn't know about things like that."

She was right. I couldn't know. I also couldn't win.

I scrambled for something to say. "Joyce certainly gave that trespasser something to think about today. I've never seen anyone run so fast."

"Yeah, well, thanks for telling the police," Patty said coldly. "Shawn came round and gave us an official warning."

"I didn't tell the police," I protested. "Shawn had already heard about the incident."

"And you expect me to believe you?" Patty said. "My mother's so upset she had one of her turns. She wanted to come tonight as well but I had to put her to bed. She was in an awful state."

"I'm sorry to hear that." I was already regretting my Good Samaritan gesture and was relieved when we pulled into the pub car park.

"Speak of the devil," Patty exclaimed. "There he is."

Valentine seemed engaged in animated conversation on his mobile phone. He was pacing back and forth alongside a metallic-blue SUV with LUXRY1 on the license plate. The new Suzuki model stuck out like a sore thumb amongst the numerous mud-splattered Land Rovers—the vehicle of choice in the Devonshire countryside.

Even though I couldn't see evidence of a weapon in the string bag Patty clutched to her chest, I thought it wise to park as far away from Valentine's car as possible.

Patty got out, slammed the door, and headed over to the rear of the pub where the kitchens were located.

I checked my reflection in the vanity mirror. For once, I did not have lipstick on my teeth. Even though Valentine was attractive—despite Mum's unkind comment about his limp—I wasn't in the market for romance. My split from David was still raw and the last thing I was interested in was love and all its complications.

I entered the pub. The Hare & Hounds was a typical Devon longhouse with a low, heavy-beamed ceiling and a massive inglenook fireplace. It was so enormous that seats had been cut into the bricks of the enclosed hearth that flanked the grate where a roaring log fire burned in front of a decorative cast-iron fireback bearing the date 1635.

Two threadbare tapestries, depicting battle scenes from the Civil War, jostled with a plethora of pikes, maces, and swords. Dozens of heavy antique keys dangled from wires along the beams overhead and copper of all descriptions filled what little wall space remained.

Tables were grouped in clusters set with oak chairs or embraced by high-backed curved oak benches to provide intimate settings. Through a low arch was a small room known as the Snug from which a back staircase could be accessed through a latch door up to a handful of bedrooms for a B and B. Another door led to the toilets.

In a corner to the left of the fireplace stood a Wainscot chair with a tattered tapestry cushion. I had wondered why it was always left empty until the landlord told me it was reserved for Sir Maurice who, centuries ago, had courted Lady Frances Honeychurch.

Rumor had it that Sir Maurice was the same ghostly Cavalier

who roamed Hopton's Crest on his big black steed. On the fateful night when he'd lured the platoon of Roundheads to Coffin Mire, Sir Maurice had stopped at the pub for refreshments where he sat in that very Wainscot chair. Here, the legend got fuzzy but the bottom line was that misfortune would follow anyone who dared to sit in Sir Maurice's chair. Bottles had been known to explode, dogs refused to lie by the fire, and even I had experienced a distinct "chill" in that particular corner despite the heat from the flames.

The Hare & Hounds was very popular among locals and tourists alike. Landlords Stan and Doreen Mutters had run the pub for forty-odd years and were well known for their unusual pets that roamed around the bar. I never met Deidre, their fourteen-year-old ferret who died just weeks before I arrived, but Mum had. Their newest addition was an Indian Runner duck called Fred who held court at the end of the counter wearing a green bow tie.

Tonight, he was napping next to a large red collection bucket labeled SAVE FRED & FRIENDS! STOP OPERATION BULLET!

I gave Fred's silky white head a scratch and he rewarded me with a quack.

The bar seemed unusually busy for a Monday evening and more than a few familiar faces gave me a surprisingly warm welcome.

"Kat! I knew you'd come!" beamed Stan. With his round, ruddy face, shock of white hair, and corpulent figure, Mum nicknamed him Tweedledee and his equally rotund wife, Doreen, Tweedledum.

Tables were being pushed together and chairs rearranged. There was an air of purpose and when Suzi, one of the waitresses, started laying out notepads and pencils I realized that something was going on.

"We're expecting a good turnout tonight, aren't we, Fred?" Stan said to the duck. "You're early, Kat. The meeting doesn't start for another hour. Where's Iris?"

"What meeting?"

"Didn't Eric tell you?" said Stan. "He changed the meeting from Thursday night to this evening."

Eric had not told either of us and I would bet my last pound that it was because he and my mother had had "words."

"Have you seen this?" Doreen joined her husband behind the counter and set down a stack of green flyers with photographs of local beauty spots BEFORE HS3 and graphically Photoshopped AFTER HS3. They were jarring and, frankly, shocking.

SAVE FRED & HIS FRIENDS! STOP THE BULLET!
SAVE MINUTES! LOSE CENTURIES!
INTRODUCTION BY BENEDICT SCROOPE:
ENVIRONMENTAL SPECIALIST
PROPOSED ROUTE/ALTERNATE ROUTE
COMPENSATION/OPTIONS
FUND-RAISERS FOR APPEAL

"Fred is our mascot," Doreen went on. "We wanted to bring to the public's attention the fact that it's not just our village and the Honeychurch estate that will be destroyed, it's about protecting our wildlife."

"The images are very powerful," I said, surprised at how angry they made me feel.

"Farmers will lose their livelihoods," said Doreen. "Woods and hedgerows will be destroyed. And what about the wildlife? Our bats, badgers, foxes, and deer—to say nothing of the Honeychurch dormice."

Stan put his arm around her shoulders. "We know, my luvver. That's why we're doing something about it. What do you think, Kat? Are you on board?"

"Yes," I said firmly. "I am."

"That's fantastic." Stan beamed. "Having a real celebrity will make a difference."

"Well—I'm not exactly sure I want to use—"

"I don't mind admitting I was wrong—"

"Stan said you wouldn't want to be a part of it but I knew you would." Doreen gave Stan a nod of triumph and held out her hand to her husband. "You owe me ten quid."

"Alright, alright," said Stan. "Now, you'd better make sure Iris is coming."

"I'll give her a quick call." I had a sudden thought. "Do you have someone staying here called Valentine Prince-Avery?"

"You're damn right we do," said Doreen grimly. "I wanted to turn him away but Stan said beggars can't be choosers. We need the business."

"He's only doing his job, luv," said Stan. "I wouldn't want to be in his shoes tonight. Poor bugger's going to get it in the neck. That's the point of the meeting. Put him on the spot."

I thought it strange that Valentine hadn't mentioned this to me on the phone earlier. Now I was in an awkward position. Having a casual drink with "the enemy" was probably not a good idea.

"Excuse me a minute." I brandished my mobile. "I'm just going to give Mum a quick call and see where she has gotten to."

"I'll get you a gin and tonic," said Stan. "On the house."

I slipped through the archway and into the Snug. The two tables and bench seat were empty but a small wood-burning stove made the tiny room feel cozy and I could quite understand why it had earned its name.

Mum was obviously working since she didn't answer even though I knew the phone in her office was just inches away from her typewriter. I dug out Valentine's business card and called him, again.

"It's Kat," I said upon hearing his voice. "I'm downstairs. Did you know there was a protest meeting tonight?"

"No," said Valentine. "The date was suddenly changed for no reason. I feel like I'm about to be thrown to the lions. Is that awful woman in the purple coat downstairs with her shotgun?"

"No. Joyce isn't feeling well," I said. "But Patty her daughter is here. She's working in the kitchen."

"So she'll have access to knives?"

I laughed.

"Look, are you still up for a quick drink?" said Valentine. "I need some Dutch courage."

"Where? Definitely not down here."

"Do you mind coming up to my room?" said Valentine. "I smuggled in some wine." Sensing my hesitation, he added, "I've got the only suite. All very aboveboard."

"Well…"

"You can sneak up the back staircase through the Snug," said Valentine. "No one will see you."

I remembered that Stan had a drink waiting for me on the counter. "Okay. I'll be five minutes."

I reentered the bar just as the front door opened letting in a rush of cold air and Eric Pugsley, who looked relatively smart for a change in a tweed jacket over his jeans. Without his trademark beanie hat, Eric's eyebrows looked more unruly than usual.

To my surprise Angela Parks followed Eric in. She was dressed like an old-fashioned servant on her afternoon off in a mid-calf-length dark gray duster with dainty button boots and a cloche hat.

"Eric's got a new lady friend already," said Doreen with a scowl. "Poor Vera's not long in the grave and he's off cavorting. Although—" She took in Angela's appearance. "She doesn't look his type. Men! They just can't stand to be alone."

"Her name is Angela Parks," I said. "She's the new housekeeper cum parlor maid cum scullery maid, whatever they're called these days."

"Maid-of-all-work, a skivvy, really," said Doreen. "Well. That explains things. Poor Patty." She gestured to Patty who had just emerged through the door from the kitchen carrying a jar of lemons. She put it down with a loud thump and trudged off again.

"Stan and I feel sorry for her so we've given her a job here— not that we can afford it," Doreen went on in a low voice. "Patty has a rough time with her mother, you know. I think she was hoping it would work out at the Hall because she would have gotten one of the cottages on the estate if they'd kept her on. She'd still be close enough to keep an eye on Joyce but have a bit of freedom as well and some money of her own."

"How long has Patty been taking care of her mother?" I asked.

"Let me see—" Doreen thought hard. "Ever since Joyce's Dennis—that's Patty's dad—died of a heart attack. About twenty years—and of course, she's an only child."

Struck by the similarities of our situations, I felt a pang of compassion for Patty. I suspected it couldn't be easy.

"Oh! Mercy, me!" shrieked Angela in her broad Devonshire accent. "Would you look at that duck!"

"This is Fred," I said, rubbing his head once again. "Here, give him a scratch. He loves it."

Angela stepped back. "Oh, no! I couldn't. He might bite me. I'm scared of ducks." She gave Doreen a beaming smile and waved at Patty who was giving her a filthy stare.

"I wondered if you needed any help with the sandwiches," said Angela.

"No, thank you. I'm quite capable of bringing out my own sandwiches," said Doreen with a sniff. "Our contribution to the cause."

"Be nice to her, Doreen," said Eric, joining us. "She's a newcomer—oh! Kat, I didn't know you were coming."

"Yes, I'm here." I said, glad that he looked sheepish. "Why didn't you tell my mother that you'd changed the meeting date?"

Eric puffed out his chest. "I don't know what Iris's problem is. I was just going about my business. Her ladyship orders me to clear out the ditches, so I clear out the ditches and Iris goes mental, screaming at me and the like—"

"I can't imagine anyone screaming at you, Eric," said Angela coyly.

"So that's why you didn't tell her the date of the meeting had changed?" I demanded.

"We don't need her help."

"I think my mother was upset about all the noise under her office window, that's all," I said.

"Office?" said Angela. "She has an *office*? I thought she was retired."

I was about to say "writing her books" but then I remembered that only a handful of people on the Honeychurch estate knew of Mum's secret life and Angela was definitely not one of them.

"I meant to say bedroom window," I finished somewhat lamely. "My mother suffers from headaches."

"She'll have more than a headache if your place gets flooded," said Eric. "With all this rain, you've got to keep the ditches clear of branches and leaves and that's what I told her. She owes me an apology."

Fortunately, my phone vibrated so I didn't have to answer.

"Ah, this will be from Mum," I said, waving it at no one in particular. "Excuse me."

I was glad of the chance to escape. A quick glimpse confirmed my hunch that it was a text from Valentine. "Where are you? I'm dying of thirst."

"Just dashing to the loo," I said to anyone within earshot. I slipped into the Snug and up the staircase feeling oddly guilty.

Chapter Seven

"I thought afterward that my invitation to entice you to my boudoir was highly inappropriate," said Valentine as he ushered me into a tiny bedroom. Dressed in a sports coat, teal cashmere sweater, smart trousers, and Italian leather shoes, he reminded me briefly of David.

"I thought this was a suite?" I said.

"You should see the single room! This is luxurious." Valentine laughed. "But there is a bathroom en suite."

I felt uncomfortable, not because he made me nervous, but seeing his personal things spread around the room smacked of a certain type of intimacy that I wasn't ready for.

"Do you drink red?" said Valentine. "Actually, that's all I've got."

I brandished my gin and tonic. "I'm fine, thank you. Compliments of the house."

"Good. I only have one tooth mug. Take a seat." He gestured to a wingback armchair that stood next to a Victorian fireplace where an arrangement of dried flowers sat in the disused hearth. "You can have the chair."

Valentine disappeared into the bathroom. "I never travel anywhere without my own wine," I heard him say. "The muck they serve in pubs is awful."

I took in my surroundings. The bedroom with its exposed beams could be described as quaint with its rose-patterned curtains and matching hangings that fell around the four-poster bed. Of course, the bed was a reproduction and far too large for the small room but I suspected it was popular with the tourists that passed through Little Dipperton on their way to neighboring Dartmouth, Totnes, and Greenway—Agatha Christie's much beloved summer home.

As well as a large mahogany armoire, there was a chest of drawers and rolltop desk. On a luggage stand behind the door sat a light brown monogrammed holdall of soft calf leather. Valentine's ox bone cane, with its distinctive French bulldog handle, rested on top.

I settled into the wingback chair—never very comfortable and always reminded me of hospital waiting rooms—and put my glass down onto a pretty octagonal side table. A set of keys caught my attention. The fob was a circular piece of thick leather painted in bright red. In the center was a white half crescent moon cradling a five-pointed star under which was stenciled PEMBA ISLAND.

Valentine emerged from the bathroom carrying the open wine bottle and a tooth mug filled to the brim. "That's my lucky key ring," he said. "Got it when I was traveling this summer. It's supposed to bring me luck."

"I have a lucky mascot, too," I said. "A Merrythought Jerry mouse called Jazzbo Jenkins."

A flash of amusement crossed Valentine's features. "A *mouse?*"

"Do you remember the *Tom & Jerry* cartoons?" I said.

"Who could forget the little mouse that always managed to outwit that cat?"

"That's why I think Jazzbo's lucky," I said.

"Can you lend him to me tonight?" He took a deep drink. "I'm going to need all the luck I can get."

"I left him at home." Of course I hadn't. Jazzbo was in his usual place on the dashboard of my car but I was very particular about whom I might loan him to—especially a stranger.

"Do you know why the meeting date was changed?" Valentine pulled out the chair in front of the desk and sat down. "It's very annoying. I haven't had a chance to talk to everyone individually whose properties are going to be affected by the railway line."

"So it puts you at a disadvantage?"

"People panic, you see," said Valentine. "With all due respect, look at this afternoon! At least your mother didn't shoot at me."

"I think it was the phrase 'rolling stock depot' that did it," I said. "Why do we need an extended line down here anyway?"

"Let me show you." Valentine opened the rolltop desk and pulled out his iPad.

"I didn't know the pub had the Internet," I exclaimed.

"It doesn't," said Valentine. "But if I stand by the window on one leg and lean at an angle of ninety degrees, I can get a BT hotspot."

"I tried that at the Carriage House but there isn't a signal anywhere. We're too remote."

Valentine opened a document and handed the iPad to me.

"I'd like you to look at this map of the Great Western Railway that I downloaded earlier today," he said. "It's an old map—dated 1930—but it gives you an idea of how extensive the railway system was back then. There are seventeen disused railway stations between Plymouth in Devon and Penzance in Cornwall."

I was astonished. There were dozens of red lines that covered the southern peninsula of Devon and Cornwall—some straight, some elaborately curved to follow the natural line of hills and rivers; others just dead-ended at stations with quaint names like Copperhouse Halt and Defiance Platform.

"I had no idea there were so many," I said.

"The storms last winter really put the nail in the coffin," Valentine went on. "The flooding that hit the West Country completely wiped out the line south of Dawlish, and even though it's been repaired, it illustrates just how vulnerable the old network is. It needs to be modernized."

I remembered those storms. I'd watched the footage on television and had been shocked by the ferocity of the elements and the misery and suffering of so many people who were cut off for weeks. The floods on the Somerset Levels had been particularly brutal.

"But what's the connection with Operation Bullet?" I asked.

"It's all one and the same." Valentine took a sip of wine. "Devon needs a new rail system. There is no escaping it."

I looked at the map again. "But why does the line have to extend so far south?"

"I couldn't tell you," said Valentine. "My job is to solely assess the properties affected for compensation."

"You should use this map tonight," I suggested. "I always feel that people respond more to visual images."

"Have you tried getting anything printed in Little Dipperton?" Valentine polished off the wine in his tooth mug and poured himself another. "But try telling that to the ministry. They've completely thrown me under the train—no pun intended."

"What a horrible position to be in," I said.

"Not only that, I arranged to have my presentation materials shipped to the pub from London but they never arrived," he said. "To be honest, I think someone stole them."

"Really?" The idea seemed a bit far-fetched. "How?"

Valentine shrugged. "The post office? It's put me in a terrible bind."

"But the placards came in time."

"Oh yes. Yes, they arrived." He gave a heavy sigh. "Anyway—enough of that. You wanted to talk about your mother. She lives on the Honeychurch Hall estate, I believe."

"Mum lives in the Carriage House," I said. "But the Hall is a Grade I listed building. It's stood for six hundred years. There's been a Honeychurch living at Honeychurch Hall since the reign of Henry V. It's harbored fleeing priests during the English Reformation and was one of the last Royalist strongholds against Oliver Cromwell in the English Civil War. There's even an underground tunnel. In fact, the entire area is steeped in history." I realized I was actually getting quite heated up. "Surely that must count for *something*?"

Valentine kept an easy smile on his face but I noticed a flash of what appeared to be alarm begin to register in his eyes. "My job is to solely assess the properties that would be directly affected by the construction and discuss compensation. That's it."

"It sounds so vague."

"A lot depends on whether properties fall into what's known as the safeguard zone."

"Which is—?"

"How far away from the track a property is. If it's in that zone owners will be paid the market price. In some instances, they may even be able to rent back their homes until they have to move out for demolition."

I shook my head with disgust. "Rent their homes *back*?"

"It's better than some who are not entitled to any compensation at all and are stuck overlooking the cutting—which I'm afraid will happen to most of the properties around here."

"Like Bridge Cottage," I said recalling the Gullys' outburst earlier. "So basically, they're stuck."

"I'm sorry," said Valentine. "I'm just telling you the truth. All I can suggest is that they should fight it."

"How?"

"There will be an environmentalist speaking here tonight called Benedict Scroope. He might have some suggestions. There could even be a way of proposing an alternate route. You said yourself that you didn't understand why the train was coming so far south."

"But that would cost a fortune!" I exclaimed. "There would have to be land surveyors and permits and civil engineers involved."

Valentine looked miserable. "I'm just trying to help."

"These folk don't have that kind of money," I said. "This is not an affluent village in the Cotswolds where many people commute to the City and earn huge salaries," I went on. "This is a farming community."

"What about the landowners?" Valentine said. "The Honeychurch family must be pretty well-off."

"The Honeychurches are like most of Britain's old families," I said. "Land rich but cash poor."

"But they must have connections," Valentine persisted. "The old boys' network for one. Can't they rustle up some funds?"

"You're right. They do," I said and thought for a moment. "And so do I."

One of the advantages of spending years with David Wynne was being introduced to people in positions of power. As an international art investigator David's skills were highly sought after. He was a notorious social climber and on first-name terms with a number of cabinet ministers. "Who do you work for at the Department for Transport?"

Valentine looked startled. "Why?"

"I know people there, too."

"I've said far too much, already." Valentine seemed flustered. "This conversation was in confidence and I work for a consultancy firm, not directly for the Department for Transport."

"Don't worry," I said. "Maybe there is a different way to approach this. I can find out on my own. I won't mention your name, I promise." I checked my watch. "It's just gone seven-thirty. I should go back downstairs. It would be really awkward if I was seen leaving your room."

"Wait just one minute," said Valentine. "I hadn't intended to talk business all the time. I really did want to hear your thoughts on the Chillingford sale."

"Of course!" I said. "I'm always happy to talk about *my* line of business. I love it."

Valentine retrieved the sale catalog from his bedside table. He opened it and pointed to a photograph of an automaton dressed as an English country gentleman wearing a red coat and top hat. "This is the one. Lot sixty-two."

The item was described as "*A rare English gentleman smoking automata by Roullet & Decamps, circa 1880*" with a staggering estimate of £20,000 to £30,000. Clearly, whomever Valentine worked for as a consultant was paying him well.

"That's rather specialized," I said. "Did you see the film *Sleuth*?"

"Of course, and like Laurence Olivier's character, I like collecting the weird and wonderful, too."

"If you're talking weird and wonderful," I said, "you should see the Museum Room at Honeychurch Hall. As well as a life-size polar bear, there's a stuffed giraffe head, a Polyphon music box, and an armadillo handbag."

"I think I'll call this chap George," said Valentine suddenly. "Don't you think he looks like a George?"

"Definitely a George."

"Why don't we drive to the auction together?"

"I don't think you'd want that," I said. "I'll be bringing my mother and if you think I gave you a hard time tonight, that's nothing compared to what she would do."

"Fair enough," he said. "Why don't you give me your mobile number and we're arrange a meeting point instead—if I survive tonight's lynching."

"You already have my number in your mobile." I got up and took my empty glass.

I opened the bedroom door and bumped straight into Angela on the landing.

"Blast!" I muttered but forced a smile. "Hello, Angela."

"There you are!" she exclaimed. "What on earth are you doing up here? Eric and I have been looking for you everywhere."

"Well, you've found me," I said.

Valentine materialized by my side. "I rather think the cat is out of the bag," he whispered.

"Oh!" Angela turned pink and regarded Valentine with suspicion.

"I'll be there in a minute," said Valentine and stepped back into his bedroom.

"Um. Sorry for interrupting," said Angela.

"You weren't," I said and wracked my brains for something to say.

Unfortunately, it wasn't just Angela who had seen us leaving Valentine's bedroom. As I swept past her, Patty was standing at the top of the stairs and judging by her expression, she must have seen me with Valentine and I was certain must have gotten the wrong impression.

I was about to say something but she shot me another filthy look and turned away.

"Come on. They're waiting for you," said Angela. "Everyone's so excited."

"Whatever for?"

"Whatever *for*?" Angela beamed. "Because you're the face of Operation Bullet!"

Chapter Eight

The crowd was much bigger than I expected with many familiar faces. Tom Jones—who looked just like his namesake in tight leather trousers and a rockabilly quiff—from Home Farm Muriel, the postmistress and her husband and the two elderly sisters, Violet and Lavender Green, who ran the tearoom.

All the seats were filled forcing many to stand including Roxy Cairns who was out of uniform and dressed in jeans and a sweatshirt. I could not see Shawn and overheard someone say that he was attending a piano recital for his kids at the local school.

Everyone had made short work of the sandwiches. Plates were empty but glasses were continuously being filled from Stan's seemingly bottomless pitcher of homemade scrumpy. The air was fuggy from a combination of heat from the log fire and the number of bodies in the room. The mood was defiant and conversation lively.

Set up at the front of the room was a freestanding easel. Valentine—looking distinctly nervous—stood on one side of Eric. On the other was a lanky man in his late forties with a mop of blond hair. He wore a green Guernsey sweater with suede shoulder and elbow pads and beige corduroy trousers. Heavy framed glasses gave him a Clark Kent look that was marred by an unnatural tan. I assumed this had to be Lavinia's friend Benedict Scroope.

"Here's the face of Operation Bullet!" Eric cried. "Let's have a round of applause for Kat."

The *face* of Operation Bullet! Lending my support was one thing, but being the actual face of the campaign, a completely different thing altogether. I couldn't think of anything worse but before I could protest, the clapping abruptly stopped and the room fell silent. Those standing parted like the Red Sea as Angela appeared carrying the Wainscot chair from the fireplace.

"Coming through," she said happily. "Coming through!"

There was a universal gasp of horror. One woman even screamed.

Angela turned ashen. "What's the matter? What have I done?"

"You've moved Sir Maurice's chair," shouted Patty from somewhere within the crowd. "You're cursed."

Still no one moved.

Angela gave a cry and threw the chair away from her. It fell to the floor with a clatter. Angela, looking stricken, raked the audience for help. I jumped up and hurried over. "Go and sit in the front row." I put my arm around her shoulders and whispered, "They're just superstitious. Take no notice."

Angela nodded miserably.

Sir Maurice's chair was left laying flat on the flagstone floor. Luckily, I was not superstitious. I stepped forward and picked it up. "I'm sorry, Sir Maurice," I said in a loud voice. "Let's put you back by the fire, no harm done."

There was a murmur of appreciation and relief and then conversation picked up once again.

"Three cheers for Kat!" said Stan.

There was another enthusiastic round of applause. I took a silly bow. Angela had scooted along the bench and I just managed to squeeze in between her and a young earnest girl from the local newspaper, the *Dipperton Deal*. She introduced herself as Ginny and promptly took my photograph.

"Are you okay?" I whispered to Angela.

She gave a weak smile but I could tell the "chair incident" had shaken her up.

"First of all, please give Benedict Scroope a warm welcome," said Eric. There was more applause and catcalls. "As you know, Benedict is here to help us Stop-the-Bullet!" Another deafening round of clapping followed.

"And on my right, meet Valentine Prince-Avery who I am sure, by now, needs no formal introduction."

There was an icy silence until someone gave an unsporting "boo!" Valentine straightened his shoulders. He caught my eye and I shot him a sympathetic smile.

Benedict stepped forward and offered his hand for Valentine to shake. He did. The two men gave curt nods of greeting as if they were about to enter a duel.

"Mr. Prince-Avery, why don't you begin by telling us exactly what will happen to our community," said Eric. "Then Mr. Scroope will discuss the impact it will have on our environment. Following that, we'll open the floor to questions."

"You'll have to forgive me for not being as prepared as I would like," Valentine began. "My presentation materials did not arrive."

"That's okay," said Eric. "We got hold of some stock footage showing other high-speed rail networks from around the world. I'm sure they will give everyone here a clear idea of what's in store."

Valentine smiled again but I detected a flash of alarm. A part of me wondered if he had been set up to fail. Maybe the materials *had* been stolen.

"Thank you, Eric," said Valentine graciously. "I had hoped to have talked to everyone prior to this meeting but I do want to stress that I still intend to visit each of your properties and speak to each of you individually and in private about your options."

His statement was met with silence and hostile stares.

Eric gave a nod and looked over toward the bar. The lights dimmed and a PowerPoint presentation appeared on the white screen.

The images were harsh and had the desired effect of creating a desperate situation. "Before" and "after" photographs showed the beautiful countryside, ancient churches, idyllic villages, period homes, and lush woodland intercut with ugly concrete-and-gravel strips hundreds of feet wide. The tracks were sealed off with high security fences and tall metal gantries. Even worse, the boundaries were floodlit at night emitting an almost alien-like glare.

The presentation ended with an ear-splitting sound bite—bursts of noise that afterward, Eric claimed registered ninety decibels. Each lasted several seconds. We were told that these trains would run every two or three minutes from early morning until midnight. The noise would be enough to rattle windowpanes a quarter of a mile away.

The final image was a collage of woodland animals corralled into a pen. Of course, this was heavily Photoshopped but the message was plain. Doreen's comment about the wildlife hit me afresh.

When the lights came up, the audience erupted into cries of outrage and calls for action. Eric gave an ear-piercing wolf whistle to try and restore order. Slowly people calmed down.

Someone shouted out, "Where's Prince-Avery?" Another called out, "He's buggered off!"

It was true. Valentine had vanished—and frankly, I didn't blame him.

"Couldn't take it," said Eric with a nasty laugh. "Coward."

Benedict was grinning, too, as more insults about Valentine's manhood flew around and soon everyone was jeering.

Eric gave another wolf whistle and once again, order was restored. "Now it's time to listen to our expert environmentalist. Over to you, Benedict."

The meeting moved swiftly on as Benedict reeled off facts, statistics, and unheard-of laws dating back to feudal times. He was charismatic and everyone seemed transfixed—even me. It was only when Benedict pinned a large map of the neighborhood onto the easel that the atmosphere changed.

Using a laser pen, Benedict pointed out the affected areas that were shaded in red, pale blue, and orange. It was blatantly obvious that a quarter of the village—including the Norman church of St. Mary's—was marked in red for DEMOLITION. The remainder—Honeychurch Hall, the grounds, a wide swathe of farmland including Cavalier Copse and Bridge Cottage—fell into the pale blue SAFETY ZONE and would overlook the cutting. Two large blocks of orange blotted out the Carriage House, Eric's scrapyard, and the equine cemetery. This was labeled ROLLING STOCK DEPOT.

In short, the entire community would be destroyed if the plan went through.

No one spoke. Everyone seemed to be in shock—including me. I was glad that Mum hadn't known about this meeting.

Benedict cleared his throat and turned to face us. "What Mr. Prince-Avery would have told you was that those properties standing in the pale blue area—the so-called safety zone—although not earmarked for demolition, are also not eligible for compensation, either."

Patty stood up. "So it's true. Bridge Cottage is in the pale blue zone—"

"Most of Little Dipperton is in the pale blue zone!" came a shout from the back. There were more cries of dismay as those whose homes also fell in the safety zone realized that they couldn't sell their properties now and would be condemned to living close to the cutting. They would also be subject to the horrendous noise and rattle of passing trains.

"This is wicked! It's wrong!" Patty shouted. "Prince-Avery shouldn't be allowed to get away with it!" Many got to their feet, shaking their fists—one woman was in tears. It was awful.

I wanted to say it was hardly Valentine's fault, he was just doing his job but I didn't have the courage.

"You should have shot him when you had the chance, Patty," Doreen called out. There were cheers of agreement that were slowly drowned out by another of Eric's wolf whistles.

Benedict stood up on the nearest table and clapped his hands. "Listen!" he called out. "Listen to me! We can fight this! We can fight this if we all work together!"

Slowly people sat down but the mood had turned ugly.

"We could suggest an alternative route," Benedict went on. "As you know, I'm an environmentalist. Much of the woodland and hedgerows in the area are hundreds of years old. Has anyone heard of the South Cubbington Wood proposal?"

No one had.

"You can find it on the Internet," he said. "The South Cubbington Wood community formed an action group and drew up a plan to bore a tunnel *under* the wood."

"How do we go about that?" said Roxy. "None of us are experts here—and nor are you!"

"We hire land surveyors and civil engineers—just like they did," said Benedict. "And then we submit the proposal."

"What about the Civil War angle?" Eric said. "There was a decisive battle fought on Honeychurch land."

"Lots of areas in the West Country can claim that honor. No." Benedict shook his head. "We need to be clever. I feel we can definitely submit a solid plan—if not for a tunnel, for rerouting the line."

"Why can't the track just go around Little Dipperton?" Roxy demanded. There was a chorus of agreement.

"I'm afraid modern technology demands a straight track," Benedict said. "It was true, in Victorian times, tracks could circumvent archaeological sites, ancient monuments, and homes, but not now."

"I presume you aren't offering your services out of the kindness of your heart," said Roxy. "You don't even live around here."

"As a matter of fact, I was born on the Devon-Cornwall border," said Benedict. "So yes, I feel I qualify as a local."

"And how do we go about paying for all this?" Roxy said.

"My fees are very low," said Benedict.

"We'll have fund-raisers," Eric declared. "And for those of you who know how to use a computer—" There was a burst of laughter that clearly indicated that not many people could. "We've already set up an online donation fund with Stop-the-Bullet as a domain name."

"And of course, Kat here has very kindly agreed to be the face of our campaign," said Benedict, gesturing for me to step up to join him.

This comment was met with more applause and whoops of delight.

"Kat—over to you," beamed Benedict. "Thoughts?"

I scrambled for something to say. "How about holding an auction?" I said. "Take a look in your home and see what you can part with. I'll offer a free valuation. It'll be a glorified car boot sale—"

"Joyce and Patty know all about car boot sales," someone yelled out. "They live in one."

There was a ripple of unkind laughter.

"We can host an auction here at the village hall," I went on. "And support it with homemade cakes—"

"We'll contribute the cakes," chorused the sisters from the tea-room.

"Can you get television coverage?" said Ginny the reporter. "You've got all the right connections."

"I'll see what I can do." This was the last thing I wanted but it seemed I was now involved whether I liked it or not.

"Let's get the Dartington Morris Men in," called out Tom Jones.

"How about a Heritage Hike?" Roxy suggested. "You know, a sponsored walk around all the places that are going to be destroyed. We could get that televised, too."

It looked like my plan to go back to London was about to be postponed again.

"We could sell T-shirts with STOP-THE-BULLET: SAVE MINUTES, LOSE CENTURIES on them," Ginny enthused.

"How do we pay for this?" Roxy said again.

"I've already told you, Roxy," said Eric. "We've established a fighting fund."

"A fighting fund for Fred!" Doreen echoed as she made her way to the front holding the duck—wings flapping—amidst the sound of ragged cheers. "And we'll start right now."

Stan appeared with the collection bucket and it was passed around. Pockets were emptied and wallets pulled out. I put in ten pounds. Even Angela put in a fiver. Patty, however, got up and headed in the direction of the ladies' loo.

Patty's exit prompted everyone to head to the bar. The meeting was over. I said my good-byes to Ginny and we exchanged phone numbers.

"I know you must get this all the time," said Ginny shyly. "But I'm one of your biggest fans."

"Thanks," I said. "And I'll see what I can do about a camera crew."

"We'll meet in a month," Eric shouted, trying to make his voice heard above scraping chairs and excited chatter.

Benedict joined me. "Thank you for your support," he said. "I believe Lavinia and I will be meeting your mother tomorrow morning at the Carriage House?"

"Yes."

"Pity about that Prince-Avery fellow," said Benedict. "I must say I was a bit disappointed that he scuttled off like that. I had been looking forward to a bit of a fight."

I noticed Muriel from the post office knock back a schooner of sherry and recalled Valentine's suspicions of theft. "Do you think Mr. Prince-Avery's presentation materials really were stolen?"

"Take a look around," said Benedict. "What do you think?"

"The placards still made it though." I hadn't thought to ask Valentine exactly how so many boards got shipped to Devon and where they had been delivered.

"Placards?" Benedict frowned. "What sort of placards?"

"I saw ten," I told him. "There could be more. They said HS3 CROSSING FROM HERE and are staked out in the two fields near Hopton's Crest leading down to Cavalier Copse."

"That's the perfect photo opportunity," said Benedict. "We could have you standing next to one of them looking angry."

"Alright." I felt so conflicted. On the one hand, of course, I wanted to lend my support, but to be practically spearheading the campaign was definitely not what I had wanted.

Angela bobbed up from nowhere. "Hello!" She beamed. It would seem that she'd gotten over her earlier mishap with Sir Maurice's chair. "Sorry for interrupting but I need to ask Kat something."

"Not at all," said Benedict. "Excuse me, I am being summoned by the hordes."

"Do you mind if I cadge a lift back with you," she said. "Eric's not ready to leave and I'm really tired. I've got to be up at five tomorrow to blacken the grates."

"You do know it's the twenty-first century," I teased.

Angela reddened. "I like doing them. Really."

We fought our way through the throng to the front door but were stopped by Doreen who still had Fred tucked under her arm.

"Patty asked me if you wouldn't mind running her home," she said. "It's not out of your way and Stan's tied up at the bar."

"Of course," I said.

"Patty!" yelled Doreen. "Kat will take you."

Patty trudged over clutching her string bag that was now jammed full of canned produce, boxes of crackers, and a foil container.

"Now, just pop the oven on at four hundred degrees and give that pie about twenty-five minutes," said Doreen to Patty. "Tell Joyce I'm sorry she wasn't feeling very well. I'll call you tomorrow if Stan isn't able to come and pick you up. You really need to get your phone fixed, luv."

Patty simply scowled, grunted something inaudible, and barged her way out of the front door.

"Remember to hand out my Ravishing Romantics Book Club flyer," said Angela. "Please Doreen, *please*."

Ravishing Romantics! Seriously? Mum would get a kick out of that.

Angela's eyes glittered and she swayed slightly on her feet. I wondered how many glasses of scrumpy she had imbibed. The stuff was lethal and always seemed deceptively harmless.

"For the fiftieth time," said Doreen wearily. "I told you. I won't forget."

Outside in the car park I wasn't surprised to see that Valentine's Suzuki had gone. Judging by the amount of wine he'd been drinking earlier, I hoped that he wouldn't get stopped by the police and given the Breathalyzer test.

I helped Patty into the back of my Golf. As I expected, she didn't offer a word of gratitude.

Angela climbed into the front and grabbed Jazzbo from the dashboard. "Oh! What a cute little mouse. He's so sweet! Hello, little mousie."

She really stank of cider and chattered on in the most peculiar accent that I had ever heard.

"Do you really think we can win?" said Angela as we sped through the country lanes.

"We? We?" Patty finally spoke. "Why should you care? You're not from these parts."

"Nor am I!" I said lightly. "But I care."

"I love your auction idea, Kat," said Angela. "Is it true you used to do car boot sales, Patty?"

"What's it to you?"

"I'm just saying, maybe you can sell some of your junk for the campaign."

"Bloody cheek!" Patty exclaimed. "I've got some real quality stuff but no one is buying these days. It's programs like *Fakes & Treasures* that have ruined it for all of us. You can't get a bargain anymore."

"So sell it at Kat's auction," said Angela.

"If I'm selling anything, the money goes straight into my pocket," Patty declared. "Charity begins at home."

"Not always," said Angela. "I believe in what goes around comes around."

"You said it." Patty leaned forward and whispered into Angela's ear. "You sat in Sir Maurice's chair. He doesn't take kindly to that. Something horrible is going to happen to you. Just you see."

"What do you mean?" Angela exclaimed. "Why would you say such a thing?"

"Don't take any notice of Patty," I said. "It's just superstitious nonsense."

"You can think what you like," said Patty. "But don't say I didn't warn you."

No one said another word until we turned into the narrow lane and descended the steep hill to Bridge Cottage. I noticed that the stream that ran alongside the road was running high from all the rain.

Suddenly, Angela shouted. "An animal! Don't hit it!"

I slammed my foot on the brakes. "What on earth—?"

"It's not an animal!" Angela cried. "No, wait . . . what's on the side of the road?"

"There's something in the water." My stomach lurched. "Oh God."

Illuminated in my headlights was a mobility scooter. It had flipped over and was laying half in and half out of the stream.

Patty gave a shriek. "Mother! She's fallen! Oh!"

"Wait right here," I said quickly and cut the engine. "Angela, call for an ambulance. Stay with Patty."

But Patty was already scrambling out of the car, too. She was hysterical. "Mummy, oh Mummy!"

I grabbed Patty's arm, pulled her into my shoulder, and held onto her tightly. "Don't look. Just don't look."

But I did.

Joyce lay facedown in the water in her purple-knitted coat. Her hat had fallen off revealing a halo of gray hair that skittered in the current.

Gently, I steered Patty away and back toward my car.

Chapter Nine

Fortunately, help was close at hand. Along with Roxy and the paramedics, Tony and John Cruickshank—identical twins sporting ruddy faces and curly brown hair—had been at the protest meeting. They speculated that given the slippery conditions coupled with the age of the scooter, Joyce had just lost control and veered off the road. Even so, there would have to be an inquest.

Doreen dropped everything and bore an almost catatonic Patty back to the Hare & Hounds. It was Roxy who insisted that the mobility scooter shouldn't be touched until Shawn could take a look at it.

"Why?" Angela asked for the third time. "Do you think something weird happened?"

"No," said Roxy curtly. "I told you, this is just procedure." But Roxy seemed distracted as she trained her flashlight back and forth over the slick road surface that was covered in mud and leaves. I, too, could see what looked like skid marks. "Looks like her brakes failed."

"I mean, why was Joyce out at all?" Angela went on. "Doreen said that she wasn't feeling well."

"She must have changed her mind," I said.

"But why—?"

"I hope you're not driving, Angela," said Roxy coldly. "You've had a bit too much to drink."

"Don't worry. I'm taking her home," I said. "We're leaving. We just... I wish..."

"Are you okay?" Roxy asked.

"Not really." And I wasn't. I was feeling nauseous. I still had bad dreams about finding Vera's body in the grotto and now, here was another one! Maybe there was some truth to Sir Maurice's curses.

Angela and I got back into the car and headed up the hill for home.

"Maybe Joyce saw something," Angela banged on. "Mrs. Cropper told me about a phantom horse and rider who lured a platoon of Roundheads to Coffin Mire—Oh. My. God! It's Sir Maurice, isn't it? He did it. Oh. My. God. It could have been me."

"I didn't know you had a mobility scooter," I said.

"No. But... Joyce didn't even sit in Sir Maurice's chair and I did. If that happened to *her*—"

"Oh for heaven's sake, Angela," I said crossly. "Pull yourself together."

"Muriel from the post office told me that Eric's wife, Vera, saw a ghost in the grotto and died of fright. I didn't believe her... but now I do."

"I don't take any notice of local gossip—and you shouldn't, either."

Angela slumped back in her seat. "I've never seen a dead body before. Have you?"

"No," I lied and just wished she'd stop talking. The drive to

Honeychurch Cottages was only minutes but it seemed to take hours.

"Muriel said that William the stable manager wasn't really called William but I forget what his real name was. He's gone off on a sabbatical. Something about the Himalayas." Angela gave a really unattractive belch and I caught a waft of rancid cider breath. "I feel a bit funny in the head."

"Scrumpy will do that to you," I said. "Just drink lots of water before you go to bed."

I could feel Angela's eyes on me. "You've got really nice teeth and you're a really nice person." She gave a heavy sigh and leaned her head against the car window. "You're really nice. Really. Really. Nice. Not like a stuck-up celebrity at all. No wonder David wants you back."

I let her ramble on knowing that she'd regret it all in the morning when she woke up with a vicious scrumpy hangover.

"Still, you've met someone else now, haven't you?" Angela said wistfully. "I don't blame him for leaving the meeting. Was it true that Patty tried to shoot him?" Angela gave another belch. "Sorry."

"It was Joyce, actually," I said.

"Oh! And now look at her," said Angela. "Dead as a doornail."

I changed the subject. "What about you? Anyone special? How about Eric?"

"Eric!" Angela was so startled she had a coughing fit. "Blimey. Are you kidding? With those eyebrows? It's like they're alive!"

Despite myself, I couldn't help but laugh.

Moments later we stopped outside the Honeychurch Cottages that stood next to the Victorian walled garden. The terrace of three had been built toward the end of the nineteenth century for the gardeners when the Hall was in its heyday.

Tonight, a light burned in the upstairs middle window of number two where Mr. and Mrs. Cropper had lived for all of their married life.

"Will you come inside with me?" said Angela. "Just until I turn on the lights?"

We stepped out into the darkness. It was so quiet that when I first came to stay with Mum, I couldn't sleep. The silence made my ears hum. A fox uttered a murderous scream. Angela grabbed my arm. "Did you hear that noise? Is that a ghost?"

"You're a bit pathetic for a country girl," I joked although I, too, had had the same reaction when I'd first heard a fox's distinctive mating call.

I helped Angela indoors and she groped for the light switch. Like the other two cottages, it was a "two-up, two-down" with a kitchen and downstairs bathroom tacked on under a catslide roof. I'd heard that Angela's cottage had stood empty for a very long time. It was sparsely furnished but clean and warm, thanks to a small wood-burner stove in the corner.

Angela, still wearing her coat and clutching her handbag, flung herself onto the sofa. "Have you ever seen a ghost?"

"Not really," I said, although, in truth, I had felt a presence on more than one occasion and in more than one location at Honeychurch Hall.

"Wait! I know!" Angela rummaged in her handbag and produced a large bulb of garlic. "At least I've got this."

"I think that's for vampires."

"Oh." She laughed and delved back into her bag again. This time she withdrew a pink flyer. "I'm sorry Iris couldn't come tonight. Will you give her this?"

RAVISHING ROMANTICS BOOK CLUB
READ AND DISCUSS *GYPSY TEMPTRESS* BY KRYSTALLE STORM
OCTOBER 22ND AT 7:00 P.M.
PLACE: BUZZ CAFÉ!
CALL 07781 80529 FOR QUESTIONS

I was startled by Angela's choice and hoped my face didn't betray my surprise.

"Did you know that the author is rumored to live in Devon?" she said. "I heard it could even be somewhere around here."

"Really? How interesting." I waved the flyer. "Yes, I'll give this to my mother. Good night. Sleep well—and remember what I said about drinking lots of water."

I turned the car around and headed back to the Carriage House, passing through Eric's scrapyard and entering Mum's courtyard through the rear entrance. I thought of Angela's book club and remembered that Mum's website had mentioned she not only had an Italian villa on the Amalfi Coast but also a manor house in Devon. It was probably a coincidence that Angela had chosen *Gypsy Temptress*—although I never really believed in coincidences.

It had been a strange day that started with the revelation that Mum's stepbrother was coming to live with her, followed by discovering that Harry had run away from school again, this whole thing with Operation Bullet and all the ridiculous white lies that it had spawned within the Honeychurch clan, and finally, Joyce's horrible accident.

Fortunately, I was relieved that Mum must already be in bed. I was exhausted and just couldn't face telling her about the protest meeting and Joyce's death right now.

I headed up to bed only to find another bouquet of flowers had arrived from David to add to the half-dozen arrangements, orchids, and plants I already had in my bedroom. Mum was right—it did resemble a funeral parlor.

I put David's note into the top drawer of my bedside table to join all the others. I had to give him marks for persistence but it made no difference to me. Quite simply, it was too late.

I thought about calling Valentine to see if he had made it back to the pub safely, but decided to do it in the morning.

My mobile rang and I knew it was David who was probably checking to see if I'd gotten his latest flowers so I ignored it.

It was only when I got back from the bathroom having cleaned my teeth and changed into my pajamas that it occurred to me that I'd arrived home close to midnight and that David never rang anyone after ten. He claimed it was bad manners.

To my surprise, it was Valentine who had left a message. His voice was slurred and he sounded out of breath. "*Call me back. It's urgent. I must—*"

The end of the message was cut off. Puzzled, I hit redial but it went straight to voice mail. I tried twice more but had the same problem. I knew he'd been drinking. I felt irritated. I hardly knew the man. It would have to wait until tomorrow.

Decision made, I got into bed and fell straight to sleep.

Chapter Ten

"How was your Valentine?" said Mum eagerly. "No pun intended."

We were sitting at breakfast devouring the last of Mrs. Cropper's homemade bread toasted with lashings of butter and marmalade.

"You're quite the comedienne this morning and to answer your question, Valentine was fine."

"And?"

"And nothing."

"You're hiding something."

"No, I'm not." Not about Valentine, anyway. I knew I was putting off telling my mother about the events of last night. Knowing that she'd be furious about missing the meeting, I just needed to pick the right moment.

"I thought you liked him," Mum persisted.

"He's pleasant but I'm not looking for romance at the moment. You know that." I had tried once more before breakfast to reach Valentine but got no response and decided to let it go. I'd most likely run into him at the auction tomorrow anyway.

"So you didn't get any information about the railway line," Mum said. "Didn't you use my Dictaphone?"

"No. I did not use your Dictaphone." The truth was, I'd forgotten to turn it on. "I have a very good memory. Can't I just finish my breakfast first?"

"On one condition." Mum leaned in to whisper, "Didn't he at least try to kiss you?"

"No." I looked her full in the eye. "But we did have tiffin in the Snug."

"Good." Mum grabbed a pencil and the block of her ever-handy Post-it Notes from the counter. "Where exactly in the Snug? There's not much room—although there is that window seat—oh!" She put down her pencil. "You're joking, aren't you?"

"Mum!" I was stunned. "Seriously? You thought I would do that?"

Mum gave a heavy sigh.

"What's the matter now?" I demanded.

"Ever since *Fifty Shades of Grey*, it would seem women want more—" She shuddered. "I can't think of the word—"

"Tiffin."

"Exactly."

"Good grief. When I was typing up your manuscript I had to keep taking cold showers."

"What was it like with Dylan—"

"Mother! I am not going to discuss my sex life with you for it to appear in a novel."

There was a hammering on the front door. "Saved, thank God!" I said. "I'll get it."

I bumped into Angela in the hall. "The door wasn't locked," she said.

"I know. The lock is broken again."

Angela looked rather the worse for wear with a pale, sickly complexion and huge black circles under her eyes. She was carrying a wicker basket that was covered with a white-and-red-checked cloth emitting the most wonderful smell of freshly baked bread.

I immediately guessed what would happen. Angela would let the cat out of the bag before I had a chance to explain everything to my mother.

"Look," I said in a low voice. "Will you do me a favor?"

"For you? Yes. *Anything,*" she whispered back.

"Let's not mention Joyce's accident or the protest meeting to my mother."

"Why?"

"She gets easily upset and I need to pick the right time to tell her," I said, knowing it sounded lame. "Mum has a very sensitive disposition."

Angela's eyes widened. "You mean you want me to keep a secret?"

"Just for today."

"Yes. I'm your friend." Angela nodded. "Of course I'll keep your secret."

"Thanks. Follow me." I led the way into the kitchen.

"What a lovely smell," said Mum as we walked in.

"Mrs. Cropper said she made a fresh batch this morning," said Angela.

"Good. We've just finished eating the last loaf. I'll take that basket," said Mum greedily.

"She wanted to thank you for picking the sloes," Angela declared.

Mum set the basket on the counter but accidentally clipped the metal biscuit tin with her elbow. It clattered to the floor.

Angela clutched her head with an anguished groan.

"How's your headache?" I asked.

"Cripes. How did you know?" said Angela. "It's something awful."

"Welcome to Devon," I said. "You should ask Mrs. Cropper for one of her hangover remedies. She's into all the old wives' stuff."

"I know," said Angela. "She has this book and she told me to find some moss that grows on a human skull that I was to scrape off and then crumble into powder and take as snuff."

Mum gave a mischievous grin. "Oh yes. I know that one. It works every time!"

"For God's truth?" Angela looked doubtful. "Where would I get a human skull from?"

"You could try the graveyard."

"Oh!" Angela reddened. "You're joking, aren't you? Anyway, what's snuff?"

"It was popular in the eighteenth century," I said. "The aristocracy used to grind tobacco into powder and snort it up their nose. The Hare & Hounds keep snuff in little tins on the bar. Haven't you seen Lady Edith's snuffbox collection? Little silver boxes with enamel-painted lids?"

"Her ladyship does snuff?" Angela pulled a face. "I think I'll stick to aspirin."

Mum removed the bread from the basket. "Did Mrs. Cropper notice that I'd pricked the sloes for her?"

"Pricked what?" said Angela.

"To make the sloe gin," Mum said. "You stick each berry with a needle, then you add sugar and gin. You must know how to make sloe gin."

"Oh look!" Angela made a beeline for the huge oak dresser upon which sat Mum's extensive collection of coronation china.

Pride of place was a photograph of the Duke and Duchess of Cambridge on their wedding day.

"Isn't Kate beautiful?" said Angela wistfully. "She has the prettiest teeth I've ever seen—oh! I've been meaning to ask you something."

"What's that?" said Mum.

"Have you been in the downstairs toilet?"

"What?" Mum looked confused. "Where? Here?"

"The one at the Hall next to the library?" said Angela.

"Why?"

"There are loads of photographs of the servants who worked at the Hall in that downstairs toilet."

"They worked in the toilet itself?" said Mum.

"Oh! I didn't mean that." Angela laughed. "I meant that there's a photo gallery of all the servants through the years."

"Why? Are you hoping to have your picture taken?" I caught the gibe in Mum's voice but Angela seemed oblivious.

"And as well as the servants," Angela went on, "there are lots of pictures of a traveling boxing emporium that camped here every summer back in the old days."

Instinctively, I realized where this line of questioning was going and tried—and failed—to catch Mum's eye.

Angela regarded Mum keenly. "Don't you think that's weird?"

"I have a toilet of my own here, dear," Mum said coldly. "I don't need to go to the Hall to use theirs. And anyway, why would I think it weird?"

"Because…the boxing emporium is called Bushman's and Mrs. Cropper told that me one of your relatives is coming here to work and his name is Bushman, too."

"It's a common name," said Mum quickly.

"Is it? I don't believe in coincidences." Maybe Angela wasn't as stupid as she seemed. "Sorry, I almost forgot." Angela turned to me. "Will you come with me to pick more sloes? Mrs. Cropper told me the only place is down in Cavalier Copse and I know it's haunted. *And* you have to cut through a field of cows. I don't like cows."

I really didn't want to. "Perhaps we can go after the auction."

"I'm sure you're too busy to stay for a cup of tea," said Mum, pointing to the clock. "It's quite a walk back to the Hall."

"Cripes! Mrs. Cropper will wonder where I've gotten to," Angela said. "But I drove here. All that talk of ghosts and then when Joyce fell—I mean. Nothing." Angela shot me a look and mouthed the word *"Sorry."*

"Joyce?" Mum said sharply. "What about Joyce—?"

"Oh, Iris! Did Kat tell you?" Angela said desperately. "We've picked our book for the Ravishing Romantics."

"Ravishing Romantics?" said Mum. "What on earth is that?"

"The name of my book club. At Lindridge we had one. It was very popular."

"I'm rather busy for book clubs," said Mum.

"Mum's supervising the renovations here at the Carriage House," I said quickly. "We've just put in new plumbing."

"Surely you can squeeze in the odd hour once a month?" said Angela. "Our first book is *Gypsy Temptress* by Krsytalle Storm. Have you heard of her?"

Mum gasped. "Krsytalle Storm?"

"We are going to discuss racism among the ethnic minorities," said Angela.

Mum looked confused. "Whatever for?"

"Discrimination," said Angela. "With all the controversy with the Roma in France, we thought it very topical. You *have* heard of Krystalle Storm, haven't you?"

"My mother doesn't get time to read much, do you, Mum?"

Angela seemed smarter than she had let on. Ethnic minorities? The Roma in *France*?

"It's such a romantic story," gushed Angela. "It's all about a gypsy girl who falls in love with the son of a really uptight vicar. She betrays her family and they elope. She gives up everything for him."

"How utterly fascinating," said Mum.

"It's the first in the Star-Crossed Lovers Series. The next one's called *Forbidden* but it's not out yet."

I detected a smirk of vanity on Mum's face. "Maybe I should give it a try."

"I'm surprised you haven't heard of Krystalle Storm," Angela persisted. "Did you know that Eric Pugsley's wife—the one who died of fright in the grotto—won a contest to meet the author and spend a weekend in Italy at her villa? Can you imagine it?"

"I can't," I muttered.

"Well I'll be blowed," said Mum. "No, I never knew that, did you, Kat?"

"Amazing."

"Eric told me he's still going though," Angela went on, adding slyly, "I'd love to meet Krystalle Storm. Maybe I can persuade him to take me!" She picked up the empty wicker basket. "Pity about Eric's wife, Vera, though. She couldn't have been very old."

"Well, dear," said Mum. "If Vera hadn't died, you wouldn't be here, would you?"

"Oh. I suppose that's true." Angela smiled. "Did you know there's a rumor going around that Krystalle Storm lives in the area?"

"You don't want to believe everything you read on a website," said Mum.

Angela regarded Mum with suspicion. "I thought you didn't know who Krystalle Storm was."

"I don't."

"She doesn't," I said.

Mum grabbed a banana from the fruit bowl. She hurried over to the back door and said, "Excuse me. I must feed the cows," and slammed it behind her.

Angela turned to me with a frown. "I never knew cows ate bananas."

Angela seemed no more a country girl than I. I was beginning to wonder about her. Something didn't ring true.

Five minutes later, Angela had gone. I found Mum hiding around the back of the Carriage House shivering with cold. "Has she left? I'm freezing out here."

"Yes, she has."

"What nerve! Did *you* know about this so-called rumor? What utter lies!" Mum exclaimed. "And I bet I know who told her."

"As you said, it's on the website."

Mum shook her head. "No. Eric must have told her despite his promise to keep it secret."

"If Eric had told Angela, she would have asked you," I pointed out. "Although she's not the smartest tool in the shed."

"I don't know about that," said Mum slowly. "What was all that talk about the discrimination among ethnic minorities and the Roma in France?"

"I caught that, too."

"And why mention Bushman's boxing emporium in the photo gallery?" Mum frowned.

"I have no idea."

"Well. There's something odd about her," said Mum. "Maybe it's that snaggletooth."

"You and Angela seem to share an obsession with teeth."

We stepped back into the kitchen and were both startled to find

Lavinia and Benedict—holding a large, black, leather portfolio—hovering by the Rayburn. Both were dressed in outdoor coats and Wellington boots.

My heart sank. This time the cat would definitely be let out of the bag and there was nothing I could do to stop it.

Mum seemed flustered. "Your ladyship!" she cried. "I am so sorry. Oh, dear. Have you been waiting long?"

"Frightfully sorry for barging in," said Lavinia. "We did knock but the door just popped open, didn't it, Benedict?"

"It seems the lock is broken."

"I must get that fixed," said Mum.

"Lovely and warm in here," said Lavinia. "Frightfully cold at the Hall. Edith only keeps the heating on in three rooms."

"Your coats! Katherine! Take their coats!" Mum exclaimed. "You must think we've got no manners."

Lavinia and Benedict handed their coats to me and of course, I realized I had nowhere to hang them up so I just piled both on top of the fridge.

For once, although Lavinia was dressed in jodhpurs, she was not wearing her blond hair clamped under a hairnet. Instead it was held back in a tortoiseshell clip and I could have sworn she was wearing a smudge of lip gloss.

"Delighted to see you again, Kat, and to meet the lovely Mrs. Stanford." Benedict offered Mum his free hand to shake.

"Do call me Iris, please," said Mum, shooting me a curious look. She mouthed, "*Again?*" Before adding, "Shall we go through to the drawing room?"

I winced. The term "drawing room" was reserved for grand houses like the Hall. Most people said "sitting room" or "lounge."

"We're frightfully happy in the kitchen," said Lavinia. "Aren't we, Benedict?"

"Katherine," said Mum. "Fetch the tea tray, please."

"The tea tray? It's only half past nine in the morning."

"It's in the *pantry*!" Mum nodded to the closed pantry door.

The pantry had floor-to-ceiling shelves and a square butcher table set against a tall, narrow window that looked directly into a hedge that had been recently cut right down to practically ground level. The small room was crammed with dry goods and emergency supplies—a habit of my father's that Mum seemed to have continued in case of a nuclear attack.

On top of the butcher table was a set of Mum's coronation bone china cups and saucers, milk jug, and sugar bowl on a vintage metal tray with Queen Elizabeth II's portrait and the date June 2, 1953. There was also a china plate of McVitie's chocolate digestives carefully laid out on a paper doily.

This was going to be embarrassing.

I poked my head back into the kitchen. "Anyone prefer coffee?"

Luckily, Lavinia and Benedict agreed they did and that we were not to go to any fuss.

"Perhaps we can use some of your lovely coronation mugs," said Benedict with a smirk I saw and didn't like. Mum needed no encouragement and brought down four from the dresser. Each mug depicted a portrait of a monarch and was framed with tiny Union Jack flags. They were horribly cheesy.

"Benedict takes his coffee black with no sugar." Lavinia turned pink. "I think. Not that I would know about these things."

I brewed a fresh pot from a fancy machine I'd purchased in Dartmouth and finally we were all settled.

"We were disappointed you couldn't make the protest meeting last night, Iris," said Benedict.

"Protest meeting?" Mum turned to me. "*Protest* meeting?"

"There was a huge hullabaloo," said Lavinia. "And apparently, that frightful Prince-Avery stormed off in a huff."

"I tried to call you several times, Mum," I said desperately.

I felt my mother's fury coming off her in waves but I knew she wouldn't want to make a scene. I made all kinds of silent gestures implying that I'd explain everything later but she pointedly ignored me.

"It was supposed to be on Thursday!" Mum said.

"Eric changed it," said Lavinia. "I have no idea why."

"Oh really?" said Mum. "I think I do."

"Of course, having Kat as the face of our campaign is fantastic." Benedict beamed with pleasure. "The auction idea is excellent."

"How fantastic to have Kat's face," Mum said sweetly. "What a *treat*."

A loud *rat-a-tat-tat* sounded at the front door. "I'll go."

"It'll be for you anyway," said Mum, adding, "It's her daily delivery of flowers."

"That's an exaggeration," I said as I left the kitchen.

I opened the front door to a young woman with a pierced nose holding a large white orchid. "It's another orchid," she said. "Sorry. I try to ring out the changes but it's October and there's not much around."

"Thanks, Bethany." David had sent me so many flowers that I was on first-name terms with the delivery girl.

"How did the protest meeting go last night?" said Bethany. "I couldn't make it but Aunt Muriel told me they raised five hundred pounds at the pub."

"Would you know if Muriel met with one of the compensation consultants by any chance?" I said.

"Yes. Yesterday morning." Bethany's expression hardened. "Some twit with a fancy name."

"Valentine Prince-Avery?"

"That's right. He really upset her. I heard he was practically booed out of the pub last night. Good riddance to bad rubbish."

"He has a thankless job," I said, feeling more than a little sorry for Valentine. Needless to say I hadn't heard a squeak from him this morning.

"Well, that's his choice," said Bethany.

I agreed and, joking that I'd see her tomorrow, closed the door, popped the orchid into the sitting room, and returned to the kitchen. Benedict's map from the night before was spread over the table.

"What do all these different colors mean?" I heard Mum say. "What's a SAFETY ZONE?"

Once again I listened to Benedict's spiel and watched my poor mother's face grow longer and longer. It was only when Benedict discussed his idea of suggesting an alternate route that I noticed a glimmer of hope.

"You're hired, as far as I'm concerned," said Mum grimly.

"Good," said Benedict. "I'll contact my people and we'll get to work."

"Wonderful!" Lavinia beamed. "And I do think that since Iris and I are in a better financial position than most of my people, we should carry the brunt of the cost—at least at the very beginning, don't you, Iris?"

I looked at Mum who was nodding her head in agreement. "Whatever it takes."

"So how much are we talking here?" I demanded.

"I'd say, five thousand pounds each to begin with," said Benedict.

"Five thousand pounds!" I exclaimed.

"Take no notice of her," said Mum. "Will you take cash?"

"Cash, checks, jewelry." Benedict laughed. "Whatever you've got."

"How are you going to pull that off without telling his lordship?" Mum asked suddenly.

Lavinia looked startled. "I do have a trust fund, you know—but since you mention Rupert—" Her face turned pink. "We're all agreed that my part in this goes no further than these four walls."

"Of course, m'lady," said Mum.

"And do call me Lavinia," said Lavinia. "Now we're in cahoots I think we can drop the formality, don't you?"

Lavinia rose from her chair so we all got up.

"Where are you staying in Devon, Benedict?" Mum asked. "Presumably, not at the Hall."

"Nor at my old family home, unfortunately," said Benedict with a trace of bitterness.

"Benedict's family used to own Thornton Park on the River Tamar," said Lavinia. "Frightful shame. Place is a retirement village now. *Ab-so-lute-ly* ghastly."

"Thornton Park was listed in the *Domesday Book*," said Benedict. "So you see, I know how important it is to keep our heritage."

"So you *do* understand," Mum said gratefully.

"Iris, I'll be in touch tomorrow about the moolah so Benedict can get cracking," said Lavinia.

"Shall I see you at the yard at eleven?" I asked.

Lavinia's pink flush returned. "Actually, not this morning. I'm going to show Benedict the estate whilst you and Edith ride out."

"And those awful HS3 placards," Mum reminded her. "Don't forget to show him those."

"I've already told Eric to remove them," said Lavinia.

"Didn't you want to photograph them?" I said, surprised.

"I completely agree with Lavinia that we should protect the dowager countess as much as possible," said Benedict. "There is no need to alarm her at this point. We'll find some other backdrop to take your photograph for our campaign."

Benedict slipped the map back into his portfolio whilst I returned their coats.

"Frightful business about Joyce Gully," said Lavinia.

"What about Joyce Gully?" Mum asked.

"Didn't Katherine tell you?" Lavinia seemed astonished.

"Katherine doesn't tell her mother anything," said Mum coldly.

"I was going to," I said. "Unfortunately, Joyce was on her way to the meeting—"

"So Joyce knew about the meeting, despite the fact that she doesn't even have a phone—"

"Mum," I said horrified. "Joyce had a tragic accident. She died."

"Oh! Forgive me. I'm so sorry," Mum mumbled. "I didn't know."

"Mrs. Cropper told me that the police think it was either a heart attack or brake failure," said Lavinia. "Those scooters are death traps."

"It just goes to show we never know when our number is up," said Benedict, fixing Lavinia with a look of such admiration that she blushed. "Life is just too short, Vinnie, isn't it?"

Vinnie?

I saw them out and returned to the kitchen, preparing myself for Mum's wrath. Instead, I found her busy scribbling on her yellow Post-it Notes.

"I suppose Lavinia and Benedict are your next victims for one of your torrid love stories."

"Ah! You detected it, too," said Mum gleefully. "Poor girl. She really is so unattractive when she blushes."

"At least he calls her Vinnie," I said. "Rupert calls her Lav."

"But he is strange," said Mum. "Perhaps it's those heavy glasses? I never trust a man with a small head and he's got such a peculiar complexion. It's almost orange."

"Bad luck," I said. "They're just friends. They've known each other for years. Lavinia is besotted with Rupert, you know that."

"That may be so but when there is trouble in paradise, a woman like Lavinia is easy prey."

"So says the expert who was married for forty-nine years to the same man." I scoffed and then, "Mum, I'm sorry but I did try to phone you."

"I know," said Mum. "Tell me, was there really a riot?"

So I did but I left out Valentine's late-night phone call to me.

"I know it's none of my business but five thousand pounds is a lot of money," I said. "Do you have that amount of cash laying around?"

"Don't we all have a trust fund?"

"I've seen this sort of thing happen before," I said. "The surveyors draw up more plans, which need even more money, and before you know it, you've spent a fortune and you've gone too far to wriggle out."

"I'm not daft," said Mum.

"I just hope you know what you're doing."

Chapter Eleven

At exactly eleven o'clock Edith and I, mounted on Tinkerbell and Duchess, clattered out of the yard with Mr. Chips bearing an unwieldy stick and bounding along beside us. Just watching him making forays into the undergrowth or tearing along ahead, then racing back at great speed, made me feel exhausted.

I had been riding sidesaddle for the last three weeks and was still adjusting to feeling lopsided on what had to be the most awkward riding position ever invented.

Edith had praised my "light hands" and "excellent balance" and insisted I give it a try since she believed riding sidesaddle was the "only way a lady should ride." A part of me was vain enough to want to learn and I found I was hooked! There was something elegant and romantic about wearing a riding habit although I wore a sidesaddle apron over jodhpurs for regular hacking. Edith, however, always rode in a full habit complete with hat and veil.

I'd actually splashed out on some riding togs despite Mum's comments that it was a waste of money because "where will you ride sidesaddle in London?"

With Lavinia showing Benedict around, I found myself alone with Edith for a change. This morning she seemed very subdued and rode on ahead. I was glad. Edith wasn't stupid and I found it hard to believe that she wouldn't know what was going on literally in her own backyard.

It had rained heavily in the night with gale-force winds that had brought down dozens of boughs and the roads were scattered with broken branches. Water pooled in huge puddles along the country lanes and the bridleways were thick with mud. The wind blew in gusts and sent the falling leaves swirling around the horses' legs. Mr. Chips plunged into the hedges, snatching at sticks that he then bore away to bury.

Duchess hated the wind and I nearly came off when a squall threw open a five-bar gate with a deafening crash and she leapt sideways.

It was only when we reached Hopton's Crest that Edith finally reined Tinkerbell in and waited for me to catch up. She was gazing over the tops of the hedgerows. I braced myself for Edith's inevitable questions regarding the HS3 placards but when I joined her was relieved to see that they had all been removed. All that was left were a few telltale mounds of earth. Eric had followed Lavinia's orders.

"One of my favorite views." Edith turned to me and looked directly into my eyes. "What did Harry say? Something about a runway being built—or perhaps, he meant a *railway* line?"

I really did not want to lie to Edith and was about to come clean when I felt a peculiar fluttering in my stomach. Across the valley, parked next to a five-bar gate was a metallic-blue SUV.

Edith spotted it, too. She gestured with her hunting crop. "Harry told me that a man in a metallic-blue car was digging holes and putting in posts with big red signs."

"How is Harry?" I said, desperate to steer the conversation onto safer ground. "Did he get back to school safely?"

"But it does look like we have a mole problem in that field—" Edith fixed me with a hard stare. "And rather an odd one given the size of those molehills."

"Yes. Very odd." I could feel myself reddening.

"Well?" Edith demanded. "Are you going to tell me what's going on?"

"I just don't think it's for me to—"

"Tosh! I see. If you won't tell me then let's go and ask this so-called trespasser what he's up to, shall we?" Calling Mr. Chips to heel, Edith nudged Tinkerbell into a brisk trot.

I followed on Duchess with a heavy heart.

Moments later we came upon Valentine's car. Thankfully, it was empty. There was a banner running along the rear tinted window—OGWELL CAR HIRE YOUR CHOICE FOR LUXURY.

Edith tapped her hunting crop on the roof of Valentine's car. "How frightfully inconsiderate. Completely blocked the entrance. This vehicle is rented, I see. Well, that explains it. Obviously not from around here." Edith scanned the area. "We can get into the field down by Bridge Cottage. Come along."

The Gullys' home seemed more depressing than ever in daylight. It was made of the usual cob but in dire need of a coat of paint, the thatched roof was patchy, and the front wicket gate hung off its hinges. Half-drawn curtains hung at grimy windows. Two were boarded up with planks of wood and the whitewashed rendering was cracked and gray. Wooden pallets leaned against the outside wall together with some old car tires and sheets of corrugated iron.

I thought of poor Patty living here alone and wondered what she would do now that her mother had gone. As she had so bitterly pointed out, thanks to Operation Bullet, selling the cottage would be impossible.

Behind the hedge, a tractor engine exploded into life sending

Duchess into a frenzy of fear. I held on for grim death as she backed dangerously away from the sound, her rear hooves scrabbling to find their grip on the riverbank. She plunged forward then barged into Tinkerbell who squealed and kicked out, narrowly missing my ankle. Mr. Chips darted around in circles barking, thinking it must all be a great game.

"Turn it off!" yelled Edith as she, too, struggled to keep Tinkerbell under control but her voice was drowned out by the clatter of the diesel engine.

Eric and his red Massey Ferguson tractor appeared in the gateway. The moment he saw us he cut the engine and cried out, "Sorry, m'lady. Didn't know you were there. I didn't see you!"

But our horses continued to lunge and spin in circles as Edith and I struggled to calm them down.

Eric leapt from his seat. "So sorry," he said again.

"What on earth are you doing down here?" Edith demanded. "Have you finished clearing the ditches in Cromwell Meadows already?"

Eric's eyes met my own. He gave a tiny, imperceptible nod that I took to mean that he'd moved the placards from the field per Lavinia's order.

"Well?" Edith demanded. "Cat got your tongue?"

Eric seemed nervous. He licked his lips. "Er … well … Tom told me the water trough wasn't filling up so I came to check."

"Why?" Edith barked. "That's Tom's job."

"It needed two pairs of hands," Eric mumbled. "And then I saw I couldn't use the top gate. That damn car has been parked up there since early morning. Tom saw it when he came to feed the cows at first light."

"There's no sign of the driver at all?" I said sharply. Surely Valentine's car couldn't have been there all night.

"I'm going to get that thing towed if it's not gone by the end of the day," Eric declared.

Edith didn't seem to hear. She studied the silent tractor that—to me—seemed as monstrous as Duchess believed it to be.

"You go first, Katherine," Edith commanded. "And be firm with her. She won't like it."

Edith was right. Duchess snorted and spooked at the big red monster and its trailer before finally tearing past, bucking wildly.

"Sit down in the saddle," Edith screamed. "Keep those hands low! Show her you're in command!"

It was only later as we rode across the field that I realized that Eric's flatbed trailer had been empty. Where could he have hidden the placards? Judging by Eric's horrified expression when he saw our horses careening all over the place, he'd definitely not expected us to show up.

"What do you think about Parks, the new housekeeper?" said Edith, breaking my thoughts.

"I've never known anyone to get so excited about cleaning the silver," I said. "But there is something I'd like to ask you."

"Go on."

"Did she mention anything about the book club she plans on starting in the village?"

"Good heavens. What an extraordinary question. Why would I be interested in a book club? Especially one arranged by the housekeeper."

"Oh." Edith's disdain threw me for a moment but I plunged on. "The reason I mention it is that their first selection is *Gypsy Temptress*."

"I'm sorry?" Edith said. "Should that mean something to me?"

"That's my mother's book," I reminded her. "She's the romance writer, Krystalle Storm?" I hoped I wouldn't have to explain Mum's complicated alter ego all over again to Edith.

"Of course, of course. I remember now," said Edith. "We're all sworn to secrecy."

"You don't think—" I hesitated. "I just wondered if Eric might have let Mum's real identity slip accidentally."

"It would never have come from Eric," said Edith firmly. "He wouldn't dare defy my orders to keep Iris's secret safe for as long as she wanted."

"That's what I thought," I said. "Angela has called the club the Ravishing Romantics."

"Ravishing Romantics? Good heavens. What an extraordinary name!" Edith laughed. I'd never heard her laugh so hard and I started to laugh, too.

"Pity you're going back to London," she said with a snigger. "I like you. You've got a good sense of humor. Not like poor Lavinia. I wonder—" Edith paused before regarding me shrewdly. "Have you ever thought of conducting your business affairs from here?"

"You mean, here? In Devon?" I said, surprised. "No. My life is in London."

"I must have been mistaken," said Edith dryly. "I thought you disliked all the trappings of stardom."

"I do."

"Then . . . perhaps it is the allure of the theater, museums, and art galleries that you find irresistible?"

"Not really," I said.

"The noise? Bustle? I can see how that must appeal to one when one is younger."

"And I'm definitely not in that category anymore," I said ruefully.

"Or perhaps your gentleman friend, the art investigator, has divorced his wife at last?"

Despite the fact that Edith often admitted to enjoying the gossip columns, I was embarrassed.

"No. That's over," I said quickly. "I just think that London is the best place for business."

"Nonsense!" Edith declared. "Clearly you have not spent much time at some of our country auctions. London has such inflated prices. There are lots of bargains to be found in the West Country. Take Chillingford Court, for example."

"Yes, I'm going to the auction tomorrow," I said.

"I knew Binky Chillingford, of course." Edith shook her head as if recalling a memory. "Frightful man with peculiar tastes. But perhaps you have friends you'd miss?"

"Yes, I have friends." But then wondered, did I? Edith's comments had struck a chord.

True, I did have a handful of friends but they were no longer close. I'd committed the awful faux pas of being so besotted with the man I was dating that I had slowly dropped most of them because David thought his friends and connections were more important—or rather they could advance my career in television.

As my fame grew, I became increasingly wary of people's interest in befriending me because of what they could get rather than who I was as a person. It had all happened so slowly I hadn't really noticed—until now.

"Friends come and go but in the end, it's family that counts," said Edith. "Why else do you think I agreed to this Alfred chappy, Iris's stepbrother, working here? He's family. William is still family, no matter what he did. I regard everyone who lives on the estate as part of the Honeychurch family." Edith turned and gave me another shrewd look. "Yes. Even you."

I was touched and surprised at how conflicted Edith's comments had made me feel.

"In my grandfather's day we owned the entire village of Little Dipperton," she went on. "All the cottages belonged to the estate. As a child, we used to keep the Boxing Day tradition of delivering gifts of food and clothing to our tenants in the village. In the summer, we'd hold an annual faire at the Hall—which is how I originally came to know your mother as I'm sure you know." Edith seemed to drift into a distant memory. "But now, there are only a handful of cottages left."

"Those with the blue-painted doors?" I ventured.

"I've told Rupert we need to spruce them up. Get them re-thatched. But we can hardly afford to keep the Hall up as it is. But one does what one can."

I sensed Edith's despair and began to understand why both Rupert and Lavinia had decided not to tell her about Operation Bullet.

We didn't speak again until the Honeychurch Hall gatehouses came into view.

"What about turning one of those into an office?" Edith suggested. "You could use the other as a showroom or shop?"

"Are you being serious?" I'd always liked the eighteenth-century gatehouses with the Honeychurch family crest and motto: *ad perseverate est ad triumphum*—To Endure Is to Triumph. I often thought they could be done up and put to good use.

"Naturally, you can't live with your mother permanently," Edith continued. "Jane's Cottage is on the far side of the sunken garden. It's been empty for decades and there's no heating, awful plumbing, but if you're interested, we could come to an arrangement—oh! You stupid girl!" Edith screeched. "Put that bag away!"

Duchess stopped dead, snorting furiously. I saw flashes of

fluorescent pink and heard the sound of flapping. Suddenly, she reared up. Instinctively, I leaned forward but caught my stomach on the upright pommel, pitching me sideways. The reins ripped through my fingers and the ground came toward me at lightning speed.

There was a crack as my helmet struck a large boulder and my face and shoulder hit the dirt. I was in pain. For what seemed like minutes but was probably seconds, I lay still, severely winded and disoriented, as the sound of hooves receded in the distance.

Dazed, I tried to focus.

Angela's face stared down at me. "Are you hurt?" She was practically in tears. "Oh mercy me! This is my fault. I'm so sorry."

"What happened?" I tried to sit up but my head was spinning and I felt nauseous. Then panic set in. "Where's Duchess?"

"Her ladyship has gone after it. It ran off toward the stables." Angela waved a fluorescent-pink department store bag. "I think I frightened it with my bag."

She helped me up, studying my face anxiously. "Oh. You'll have a nasty shiner in the morning. Shall I ask Mrs. Cropper for one of her remedies? Can you walk? Lean on me, please."

"No," I said. "I'm fine."

"At least let me help you back to the stable," Angela said desperately. "Mrs. Cropper wanted more sloes and I thought there were some around here." She showed me her iPhone. "I even took a photo of the ones you picked so I could tell what they looked like."

I let Angela ramble on but wished she'd stop talking. My head was pounding and I felt shaken up. Most of all I was worried about Duchess and only hoped she'd galloped back to the yard.

Angela and I parted at the fork in the drive. "Please let me ask Mrs. Cropper for a remedy," she said for the umpteenth time. "I'm sorry. Really, I am."

"It's okay, Angela," I said wearily as I left her there and walked away with her plaintive apologies continuing to ring in my ears.

I found Edith inside Duchess's stable removing her tack.

"How embarrassing," I said. "Is she alright?"

"What a silly fool!" Edith exclaimed. "What on earth was Parks thinking, flapping that bag at poor Duchess."

"I didn't see what happened," I said. "It was so fast."

"Now run along home," said Edith. "You'd better put something on that eye. I'll take care of the horses. Off you go."

Back at the Carriage House I made a beeline for my bedroom. The last thing I wanted was for Mum to see me and start fussing.

The house seemed unusually quiet but when I stepped onto the landing, I was surprised to find a wooden ladder propped against an open trapdoor that presumably led to a loft overhead. A loft hatch pole was laying on the floor.

"Mum?" I called out. "Are you up there?"

"Go away," came the muffled response.

There was a sound of an object being dragged overhead, a thud followed by a yelp of pain.

"Do you want any help?" I started to climb the ladder.

"I said go away!" Mum shouted again.

I peered over the lip of the trapdoor. It was hard to see much in the gloom under the low eaves, mainly because Mum was kneeling down with her back to me and was blocking out the light.

As she began to shuffle backward, I got a mouthful of dust.

"Watch out for rats," I teased.

Mum reared up and hit her head with a smack. "Damn and blast!"

"Sorry. I was joking." I felt guilty. "That sounded like it hurt."

She eased around to look at me. Mum's hair was covered in cobwebs and her face was smudged with dirt. As she crawled toward the exit I caught a flash of blue plastic wedged inside the top of her Marks & Spencer V-neck jumper.

"What are you up to?"

"Never you mind," said Mum. "Get out of my way. I need the ladder."

But I didn't budge. "What's that tucked into your jumper? Are you taking drugs?"

"Good heavens," Mum cried. "What's wrong with your face? Did someone punch you in the eye?"

"You don't exactly look fit to receive royalty yourself."

As Mum leaned in for a closer look, the blue object fell out and tumbled onto the landing.

"Don't touch it!" Mum shrieked.

I scrambled down the ladder and inspected the book-size packet wrapped in blue transparent plastic. I couldn't believe my eyes. It looked like bundles of hundred-pound notes.

I looked up as Mum cautiously descended the ladder.

"Don't tell me. Let me guess," I said. "You and Alfred robbed a bank."

Chapter Twelve

"It's my money and I earned it," said Mum.

"How much money is in there?" I demanded. "No, what I really should be asking is how much money is up *there*?" I pointed to the loft above.

"You really are impossible, Katherine," said Mum. "You're worse than your father with all these questions and all your prying."

Mum looked defiant, an expression I'd occasionally witnessed at home following an argument with Dad over how she spent her housekeeping allowance.

"Haven't you heard of a bank?" I said.

"I can hardly pop to the Channel Islands when I want to withdraw some cash," Mum retorted.

I gasped. "You have an offshore account?"

"My publisher pays my royalty checks into an account in Jersey—"

"The Channel Islands!"

"Yes. That's where Jersey is," said Mum. "I don't see why the government should tax my hard-earned money. It's perfectly legal."

I took in this new information with dismay. "I thought you had to be a multimillionaire to open an offshore account."

"Don't be ridiculous. You just have to know the right people."

"And clearly, you do." I didn't want to ask, but I had to. "Who are these right people?"

"I have no idea." Mum shrugged. "Alfred organized it."

"What!" I said. "I thought he'd only just made parole."

"He set it up ages ago," said Mum airily. "I couldn't risk your father finding out. I had no choice. It was Alfred's idea."

"But—how did he do it?"

"Well, he is very well connected, dear, both on the inside, and out."

"But—how do you access the money?"

"By boat."

"How? When?"

"Not when your father was alive, obviously," said Mum. "I was quite surprised to find I had a lot more money than I realized. I just take the ferry from Weymouth. It only takes four hours both ways so I am back in time for tea. It's very civilized."

I tried to take in yet another detail of my mother's secret life. "And you bring the money back—how?"

"In my suitcase."

I looked at Mum in horror. "You're smuggling!"

"Rubbish," she cried. "I can bring in ten thousand pounds every time and not declare it. I know my rights! It's all aboveboard."

"But it's not aboveboard," I protested. "Otherwise you would have the money in a bank account here. You know as well as I do that there are strict tax laws about keeping money in the Channel Islands. It was one of Dad's pet projects."

Mum didn't answer.

"And where do the bank statements get sent?"

"I don't get them sent. I signed up for online banking."

"You don't have a computer, let alone the Internet."

"Why would I need either?"

"Because that's what online banking is," I said, exasperated.

Mum shrugged again. "I keep my own records. I have a little cashbook. What does it matter to you anyway? It's my life."

And the truth was, it shouldn't matter but it did. I wasn't clear how Mum's arrangement worked but it sounded very dodgy.

"You're right. It is your life," I said wearily.

"Good. Now that we're clear, shall we go downstairs and have a spot of lunch?"

Mum breezed on by and I followed her down the stairs and headed for the kitchen.

"Just help me understand," I said. "You bought this place for cash."

"Correct."

"And I know you spent a lot of money putting in a new bathroom."

"Correct."

"So you had to have smuggled in more than ten thousand pounds. Something doesn't add up here—" I pushed open the kitchen door. "Oh! Hello, boy." Mr. Chips was dancing around the kitchen table and seemed more excited than usual. "What are you—?"

"Angela!" Mum shot me a horrified look that had "*did she hear us*" written all over her face.

"Hello. What's happened?" she said. "You both look as if you've been in the wars."

"You could say that." We must have looked a sight. I was sure my cheek was swelling nicely and Mum's foray into the filthy loft had coated her clothes with cobwebs.

"Oh! Is that a spider?" Angela pointed to Mum's hair.

"It's only a money spider," I said and gently removed it.

"How apt," Mum said dryly.

"You've got to kill it!" Angela exclaimed.

"It's bad luck to kill a money spider," said Mum.

"Bad luck?" Angela shrieked. "But…there were hundreds of them when I cleared out the larders. I…I swept them away with my broom."

"I heard you sat in Sir Maurice's chair, too, so you'd better watch out then, hadn't you?" said Mum rather unkindly.

"What's wrong with Mr. Chips?" I asked.

The Jack Russell was frothing at the mouth and scrabbling the table leg. Loops of drool dripped onto the floor.

"He can smell the meat." Angela pointed to the brown paper bag on the kitchen table. "Mrs. Cropper gave me a raw steak for your eye."

"A packet of peas will do just as well," I said. "But thanks."

"Is that what you've got there?" Angela stared intensely at the blue packet in Mum's hand. Even I could see the imprint of a banknote through the transparent plastic.

Angela stepped closer. "Is that money? Did you rob a bank?"

"Money? Money! What a silly thing to say. These are peas," said Mum hastily. "Kat was just putting them back into the freezer. Here, Kat—catch!"

Mum tossed the packet. Badly. I fumbled. It fell to the floor. Angela made a lunge for it but was foiled when Mum inexplicably kicked the packet away. It skittered across the floor where—to our shock—Mr. Chips snatched it up and tore out of the kitchen at high speed.

"Oh! The dog! The dog!" shrieked Mum. "Quickly, Kat. Hurry."

"Excuse me." I raced after him leaving Angela standing with her mouth open.

To my dismay, the front door had been left ajar. I ran outside just in time to see Mr. Chips squeeze through the hedge and into Eric's scrapyard next door.

"Mr. Chips!" I yelled out. "Here, boy! Here!"

Damn and blast. I was wearing my house moccasins so I gingerly picked my way around the puddles to the makeshift corrugated iron gate. Ignoring the spray-painted crimson warning of TRESPASSERS WILL BE PROSECUTED & POACHERS WILL BE SHOT, I spent ages trying to unhook the elaborate chain contraption that Eric used to keep the gate standing upright. Dragging the wretched thing open, I peeped into the scrapyard. My worst fears had been realized.

Mr. Chips had vanished.

Damn and blast, I muttered again, looking down at my feet. My moccasins were already splattered with mud and if I ran back to the Carriage House to get my Wellies, I'd never catch up with him.

I hesitated for a moment. I hated going through Eric's yard but, given that his Land Rover wasn't outside the old caravan, he was obviously not around.

Slipping through the gate, I manhandled it back into place, hastily rehooked the chain, and squelched my way through Eric's scrapyard.

Surely, once Mr. Chips realized that there was no juicy steak in the packet he'd drop it. No, wait. He wouldn't do that. He'd most likely bury it.

Oh *God.* How infuriating! I felt a spot of rain and, looking skyward, saw a blanket of dark clouds overheard. Typical. I hadn't thought to take a coat, either.

"Mr. Chips!" I yelled as I caught a glimpse of tan and white pushing through the undergrowth on the far side of Eric's scrapyard.

Damn and blast! I muttered for the umpteenth time and set off after him at a jog, sticking to the hedge boundaries and keeping an eye open for burying locations like badger setts and rabbit burrows.

Two fields later there was no sign of Mr. Chips or the blue packet.

My feet were wet and I was cold. I was extremely hungry, having run off on this wild-goose chase before lunch. I was also irrationally angry with my mother for not just keeping the money in the house in the first place but for reacting the way she did with Angela.

When I clambered over the stile and stepped down into Cavalier Copse, I was about to give up and trek home when I saw something laying in the grass that made my blood run cold.

It was Valentine's ox bone walking cane with the distinctive French bulldog handle.

Looking up the valley, I was suddenly gripped by a terrible sense of foreboding.

Valentine's SUV was still visible, parked by the five-bar gate.

A wind picked up and a chill swept through me. Something felt horribly wrong.

Retrieving the ox bone cane I headed up the hill to his car—Mr. Chips and Mum now forgotten.

As I expected, Valentine's SUV was locked. I peered through each window but other than a pair of brown leather gloves and the sale catalog for Chillingford Court, the car was empty. I tried calling Valentine's phone again. It clicked straight into a generic greeting that announced his voice mailbox was full.

I was in a dilemma. My first reaction was to call the police.

I knew that my inquiry would sound lame and would run along these lines—"How well did you know Valentine Prince-Avery?" *Less than twenty-four hours.* "When was the last time you saw him?" *Yesterday. When he ran out of a protest meeting.* "Why do you feel he is missing?" *He left me a strange message and then didn't return my phone calls. I found his walking cane in a field and his car is still parked on the top road.* "Where is he staying and have you tried contacting him there?" *The Hare & Hounds, and no, I have not.*

Perhaps I was overreacting. Valentine had been drinking heavily the night before and he did drive off somewhere in his car. Maybe he'd decided he was over the limit and just abandoned his car and walked back to the pub. It wasn't far. But surely he wouldn't have left his great-grandfather's ox bone cane lying in a field.

Since I was already halfway to the village of Little Dipperton, I decided to walk on to the pub regardless of my moccasin-clad feet. At this point I'd given up caring.

And then, just as I was walking past Bridge Cottage, it began to rain.

Perhaps I could borrow an umbrella from Patty—she might even lend me a pair of Wellies.

I knocked on the front door but there was no reply so I went around to the rear of the cottage where a raised vegetable plot, abandoned and strewn with weeds, shared the tiny strip of land that passed for a garden. A concrete coal bunker stood next to a tiled outhouse that I suspected still incorporated an old loo. The cottage had a catslide roof built on at a later date. Underneath the broken guttering was a moldy-looking mattress and rusting coil-spring bed. It was as if someone had just opened a top window and pushed the whole thing out.

With most of the trees devoid of leaves, the view from the garden looked straight across the fields to Cavalier Copse. I still kept hoping for a glimpse of Mr. Chips but suspected he'd probably be back at the Hall by now—with, or without, Mum's money.

Fifteen minutes later I walked into the pub feeling like a drowned rat. Although Doreen and Stan were "open all hours," the bar was relatively empty. Fred the duck was in his usual spot nesting at the end of the counter next to the donation bucket.

"You're soaked!" Doreen exclaimed. "And what have you done to your face?"

I'd forgotten all about my fall. "I fell off Duchess."

"You need to put a nice steak on that eye," said Doreen. "I'll see what I can find."

"No need. Mrs. Cropper already gave me one."

"Good heavens, girl!" Doreen suddenly spied my sodden footwear. "What were you thinking?" She gave me a peculiar look. "Surely you didn't walk here in *those*?"

"Actually, yes, I did," I said brightly. "I've got this really painful ingrown toenail and these are the only shoes I can wear."

"And you've no coat!"

"It wasn't raining when I set out," I said.

"You could do with a hot toddy," said Doreen.

"I would *love* a hot toddy," but then I realized I had come out without any money, either. "Never mind. Actually, I've got to get back."

Doreen gave me another peculiar look. "So, what can we do for you? Have you come to see Patty?"

I hadn't. "Poor Patty," I said. "How is she holding up?"

"So-so," said Doreen. "She insisted on spending the night at Bridge Cottage though. Stan picked her up this morning. Did you want to speak to her?"

"No—that is to say I'm actually here about Valentine Prince-Avery," I said.

"He went back to London this morning," said Doreen.

"This *morning*?" I was taken aback. "I found his walking cane in the field and wanted to return it." I brandished the cane feeling more than a little foolish. "He told me it was of sentimental value."

"Not that sentimental if he left it laying in a field," said Doreen. "No, he just cleared off. Didn't even say good-bye. He already paid in cash up front. I reckon we frightened him off last night, don't you?"

"It certainly looks that way," I said. "Did he leave an address?"

"I'll ask Stan." Doreen disappeared into the kitchen.

I waited and scanned the room. The notice board at the end of the bar bore Angela's Ravishing Romantics Book Club and an enlarged color photocopy of the *Gypsy Temptress* book jacket. *Yet another disaster waiting to happen,* I thought.

The front door opened and Benedict and Eric strolled in, deep in conversation. Benedict was holding a high-end Nikon camera that I suspected cost thousands of pounds.

"There she is!" beamed Benedict. His face dropped when he saw mine. "What happened to you?"

"I'm sorry. As you can see, it doesn't look like I'll be able to do the photo shoot." I explained how I'd fallen off Duchess.

"We could meet in London," said Benedict. "I think that will be a better idea. I'll take you to dinner and we can discuss the auction. I'll be going back early next week and your mother mentioned you would be there, too." Benedict turned to Eric. "We're not having much luck today, are we?"

"Where did you hide the placards, Kat?" said Eric with a tinge of annoyance.

"Placards? I thought you took them."

"No. They were gone when I went up there this morning."

"Maybe it was someone else from the village?" I suggested.

"Maybe," said Eric dubiously. "Like who?"

"Never mind," said Benedict. "I've got a better idea. A friend of mine owns a chopper. We could get some aerial shots. He owes me a favor. All we pay for is fuel."

"That's a bit extravagant," I said.

Eric's eyes widened. "I've never been in a helicopter before."

"We'll need those aerial shots anyway to give to my chap who is working on the new route and possible tunnel—ah, Doreen!"

Doreen returned from the kitchen with Patty in tow wearing yellow Marigold gloves. I was surprised to find her actually working. Eric mumbled something that sounded like, "I'm sorry for your loss."

Benedict echoed the sentiment leaving an awkward silence all around.

"Gentlemen, go and take a seat and I'll be right with you in one moment," Doreen said briskly.

"We'd rather prop up the bar," said Benedict.

Doreen turned to me. "Stan says Prince-Avery didn't leave an address," she said. "And Patty was the one who cleaned out his room this morning."

"That's right," said Patty. "He told me he had to leave in a hurry and that he was catching a train back to London."

Patty fiddled with her gloves and wouldn't look me in the eye.

"What seems to be the problem?" said Benedict, sidling closer although I sensed he'd been eavesdropping.

"Mr. Prince-Avery scarpered back to London this morning," said Doreen.

"He left this." I showed Benedict Valentine's ox bone walking cane.

"That's a very fine cane." Benedict took it and stroked the shaft. "Very fine. I could take it with me if you'd like. I'll be seeing him in London at some point, especially once I've got the proposal all squared away."

"It's okay. I'll hang on to it," I said. "Since Valentine is the compensation consultant assigned to this area, I'm sure he'll be back."

"Let's hope so," said Benedict. "He's still got to meet with half the village, but if I run into him beforehand, I'll tell him you have it."

I thought for a moment. "I wonder how Valentine got to the railway station. He left his SUV along Hopton's Crest." I turned to Patty. "You've got a good view from Bridge Cottage. Where were you last night? Did you see—Oh—I mean—" Too late! What a horrible snafu.

Patty gasped. Her eyes filled with tears. She turned on her heel and fled back to the kitchen.

I was mortified.

"She'll be alright," said Doreen. "She's been doing a lot of crying."

Benedict laid a hand on my arm. "I think what Kat is trying to say is that it seemed a strange place to leave a rental car."

"Not if he was in a hurry to catch the train from Newton Abbot," said Doreen. "Ogwell is in the wrong direction. Why?"

"No reason," I said quickly.

"Your *Valentine* is just not into you," Eric joked. "Isn't that what they say these days?"

"Very funny, Eric," I said. "I only just met him yesterday."

"You're a fast worker," said Eric. "Someone saw you coming out of Prince-Avery's bedroom last night."

"Angela saw me, you mean," I said crossly. "I was just talking to him about my mother's options, if you must know."

"Whoa! Nice slippers." Eric laughed and gave Benedict a nudge.

"They're moccasins, actually."

"Very sexy," said Benedict.

"She's got an ingrown toenail," Doreen chimed in.

"Now, if you'll excuse me, I must get home."

"You can't let Kat walk back in all this rain," said Doreen, fixing Eric with a stare that dared him to do otherwise. "Call yourself a gentleman."

"I'm fine. Really."

"Of course I'll give her a lift," said Eric. "Talk to you tomorrow, Benedict."

Eric and I bid our good-byes and I followed him out of the pub with mixed feelings. I'd be lying if I weren't grateful for the ride home.

Even though the car park was practically deserted, a Prius was parked next to NO PARKING HERE—AND THAT MEANS YOU! Mud was spattered halfway up the body and the windows were smeared with dirt.

"Took a ride with Benedict in that," said Eric. "I felt like I was sitting in a tin can."

"They're supposed to be very economical," I said.

"Yeah. Well, give me a Land Rover any day. You should have seen the inside. Covered in mud."

"In that case, do you want me to remove my moccasins?"

"Don't be daft," said Eric. "I'm not averse to a bit of mud."

Eric gallantly opened my passenger door and helped me up. "You're cold, lass," he said gently. "Make sure you have a hot toddy when you get home or you'll catch your death."

"Thank you." To say I was surprised at Eric's concern was putting it mildly.

"Had you met Benedict before last night?" I asked as we set off.

"Nope. He's been out of the country for years. But I know he and her ladyship have been friends since childhood," he said. "In fact, if you ask me, there's a bit of *how's-your-father* going on between them, what with his lordship gone off and all."

I was torn between wanting to know the details and not being drawn into local gossip. "Hasn't Rupert just gone to London on business?"

"All very secretive about it, too," said Eric. "According to Mrs. Cropper, he won't say where he is or how long he's going to be gone."

"How is Angela getting on?" I said, neatly introducing her into the conversation.

"You asking me if I fancy her?"

"No."

"Not my type," said Eric. "She needs her teeth fixed."

What was this obsession with teeth that everyone—including my mother—seemed to have?

"Mum and I think she's angling to go with you to Italy since you decided to accept Vera's prize, after all."

"So that's what you think, is it?" Eric said. "I'm doing what Vera would have wanted. She won that contest fair and square."

"Wouldn't you rather have the money instead and put it toward a worthy cause—like this campaign, for example?"

"I've already had this conversation with Iris and the answer is no," said Eric. "Why should Honeychurch matter to you? You're an outsider." Eric's annoyance seemed to translate to his foot as the Land Rover surged forward in a sudden burst of speed.

"I'm no more an outsider than Benedict Scroope—and can we not drive so fast?"

"He's still a Devon man," said Eric. "We've lived here all our lives and our parents and grandparents before us," he exclaimed. "This is the only life we know. The folks in the village, Doreen, Stan, Muriel at the post office, and the sisters who run that fleapit of a cafe, that's all they know, too. Having this train run through here is—" His voice broke but he covered it with a hearty cough. "Is like a slow death."

"I know and I'm sorry."

"Benedict is the only chance we've got," he continued in earnest. "Did you know there is a kingfisher that lives along the river at the bottom of her ladyship's equine cemetery?"

"A kingfisher?" I said. "I know about the Honeychurch dormice in Cavalier Copse—"

"Them, too. But kingfishers are protected by law and you can get fined five grand for disturbing a nest."

"I didn't know that," I said.

"That's what Benedict said and I checked and he's right. So you see, he's going to do right by us. Take the environmental route. Shawn told us to do it properly and that's what we're going to do so *stop* meddling."

"I'm not meddling!"

"Goddamn it woman! Where the bloody hell did you put those placards!"

"Don't speak to me like that!" I felt a flash of anger. "I told you, I didn't touch them. Perhaps Lavinia beat you to it? Did you even think to ask her?"

"It's hardly the thing her ladyship would do," said Eric. "Benedict was really pissed off."

"Maybe that was why Valentine went back to Hopton's Crest?" I said. "Perhaps he put them back in the boot of his car? You have to admit that things got pretty ugly last night."

Eric fell quiet for a moment then said, "Yeah, maybe."

"You don't think Patty knows something, do you?" I said. "She went back home. Maybe she saw Valentine doing just that? It's easy

to see Cavalier Copse from Bridge Cottage at this time of year."
And then I had a thought. "You didn't see Mr. Chips earlier this
afternoon?"

"Yeah. He's always around," said Eric. "Especially now I've been
digging up those ditches. Why?"

"Was he carrying a blue packet?"

"A blue packet?" Eric hesitated. "Nope, can't help you. Maybe
he's buried it somewhere. Maybe in that upturned soil from my
ditches. I'd start there if I were you. Why? Is it important?"

"No. Not important, at all." *Damn again.* Eric's ditch digging
spanned practically the entire estate. "Are you saying you *did* see
him this afternoon?"

"No," said Eric. "After I saw you and her ladyship out riding, I
went to meet Benedict at his hotel in Dartmouth. We spent the last
few hours driving around the area taking photographs."

I drew a mental timeline. I'd been riding with Edith at eleven,
got back around noon, then Angela had turned up, and shortly
afterward I went after Mr. Chips. It looked like Eric was telling
the truth.

We drove on in silence.

"Eric," I began tentatively. "It means a lot that you've kept
Mum's identity secret. I know you don't always see eye to eye, but
she really appreciates it."

"Iris and I can't stand each other," Eric said bluntly. "Don't
worry. I'm not keeping quiet for her sake. Lady Edith asked me.
And besides, the campaign needs Iris's money."

"Wow. At least you're honest!" I actually laughed and for the
first time, Eric grinned.

We came to the fork in front of Bridge Cottage. Taking a left
would lead back to the tradesman's entrance and a half a mile farther on, the gatehouses that flanked the main drive to the Hall.

After a moment's hesitation, Eric turned right and we made the slow, winding climb up to Hopton's Crest.

The Land Rover rounded the top bend and drove along the ridge. Eric's headlights carved out a tunnel along the long, straight track that was flanked by hedges and scrub. The wind had picked up again and leaves skittered and swirled before us.

We passed the five-bar gate and reached the end where the track funneled into a narrow bridleway that was framed by overhanging trees.

There was no sign of Valentine's car.

It had vanished.

"Satisfied?" said Eric.

"Yes. Thank you." But of course I wasn't.

"As I said before—" Eric smirked. "Maybe it's your slippers."

"*Moccasins.*"

As I walked back to the Carriage House through Eric's scrapyard, I tried Valentine's phone twice more only to get the same automated message that his voice mailbox was full. In the end, I sent him a text telling him I had found his cane and to call me about picking it up.

Resolving not to waste another minute on Valentine Prince-Avery—a man who I was definitely not into—I marched up to the front door.

I braced myself for the inevitable hysterics.

Mum was going to freak out when I told her the money was gone.

Chapter Thirteen

To my chagrin, the front door was locked and I had to ham-mer and yell for what seemed like hours.

Finally, Mum threw it open.

"Are you okay?" I said warily. "You fixed the lock."

"Yes! It's fixed! Hooray!" Mum's face was flushed and her eyes bore the signs of the happy drinker. She engulfed me in a huge embrace. "Oh. You're wet."

"What's going on?"

"I'm celebrating," Mum said happily. "Guess who is waiting in the kitchen."

"I have no idea."

"No, go on. Guess!"

"The Queen of England."

"Not yet."

Mum turned on her heel and practically skipped down the hall and into the kitchen shouting, "Here she is!"

I put down Valentine's cane and kicked off my moccasins and trooped after her.

"She looks like a drowned rat," I heard her say. "Now, don't be alarmed about Kat's face!"

"Why?" said a gravelly voice with a thick cockney accent. "If's she got your face, she's a beauty."

Sitting at the kitchen table was a man in his mid-seventies wearing Dad's old striped dressing gown. I gave a start. For a moment, I was transported back into our kitchen in Tooting on a Saturday morning when he and Mum would do the crossword puzzle together.

But of course it wasn't Dad.

This man was wiry with a thatch of white hair and steel-rimmed glasses. He had a heavy jaw and reminded me of the bulldog on Valentine's cane.

"You must be Alfred?" I ventured.

"I told you she'd know who you were," said Mum.

"Sporting a shiner like a real Bushman," said Alfred, showing what few teeth remained. Presumably he'd lost them in the boxing ring.

"But I'm not a real Bushman, am I?" I couldn't help but say. "Isn't Mum your stepsister?"

Mum laughed. "Don't take any notice of grumpy pants."

"Pull up a chair," said Alfred. "Have a drink! Let's get acquainted. What's your poison?"

Alfred was nursing a Scotch—Dad had been a whiskey drinker and Mum must have kept a bottle in the cupboard. Alfred's knuckles were scarred and everything about him seemed dangerous. Both forearms were heavily tattooed with birds of prey.

"Kat drinks gin." Mum poured me a large one. "I've told her all about you."

"You don't want to believe everything you hear," said Alfred, winking at Mum. "I know how Iris loves to tell a good story. She was always one for spinning a yarn."

Mum came over with my drink and gave Alfred a playful cuff around the ear. "Sit down and join us."

Alfred withdrew a packet of cigarettes from his dressing gown pocket and fumbled for a lighter. "Want one?"

"No thanks. We don't smoke," I said. "Dad never liked it."

"Don't mind if I do," said Mum and took one.

"Since when did you smoke?" I demanded.

Mum gave Alfred a nod. "Told you she's a nag."

The two laughed at my expense. Alfred lit one for Mum and then passed it over. She inhaled deeply and didn't even cough. Yet another secret of my mother's! Next thing I'd discover would be a cocaine habit.

As cigarette smoke rapidly filled the kitchen, I opened a window and made a big deal of waving it out.

"Alfred decided to come a couple of days early," said Mum.

"Had to hitch a lift from London," he said. "You never know how long it's going to take but I got lucky."

"He walked all the way from Dartmouth and got caught in that downpour," Mum chimed in. "I gave him some of your father's clothes. I've had to wash everything else."

Mum gestured to a grubby duffel bag that had been dumped in the corner of the kitchen. "That's all Alfred owns in the world."

"Yep," said Alfred. "My life is in that bag."

I made a superhuman effort to be friendly. "That must have been pretty tough walking in all that rain."

"Nah. I've got no complaints." Alfred grinned again. "Not after all those years inside." He reached across the table and took Mum's hand. "And now I'm here and it's all thanks to Iris."

The two shared a moment and I saw an exchange of genuine affection. Mum's eyes teared up. "You're all the family I've got, Alfred," she whispered.

"Thanks, Mum," I said pointedly. "Believe it or not, you *do* have me."

"You won't regret it, Iris, I swear as I live and breathe. I'll not let you down."

"Let's hope not," I muttered.

Alfred looked around the kitchen with a critical air. "I've got a couple of days before I start working with the horses, official like. I thought I could do a bit of painting. Help spruce the place up a bit."

"He's already fixed the lock on the front door." Mum beamed and gave me a look that clearly implied, "*See, I told you all would be well.*"

"I thought the painters were coming next week," I said.

"Cancel them, Iris. I can do it. You concentrate on writing your books." Alfred turned to me. "Now what's this I hear about your neighbor, Eric Pugsley being difficult?"

"What's Mum told you exactly?"

"She said he broke her hand and now he's spreading rumors that Krystalle Diamond lives in the neighborhood."

"It's Storm," said Mum.

Alfred chuckled. "See! My mind always goes to diamonds!"

Diamonds?

Alfred took a long drag on his cigarette. "You leave that Pugsley fella to me. I'll make sure he'll not give you any more trouble." Alfred actually cricked his neck and cracked his knuckles.

Mum looked pleased. "You don't want to mess with my Alfred."

"I spoke to Eric, Mum," I said. "He denied spreading those rumors about you and I believe him."

"Of course he'd say that!"

"That Eric had better watch out!" Alfred threw a few fake punches. "I've still got it." He jumped up and began shadow boxing around the kitchen. His efforts quickly dissolved into a coughing fit.

Alfred slumped back into his chair wheezing heavily. Mum hooted with laughter and moved to thump him heartily on the back.

"Blimey. I'm a bit out of practice. I'm just so bloody happy to be here." Now *his* eyes teared up and looking at Mum, I saw hers had done so again!

"Bloody hell, Iris," he whispered. "Where do the years go to?"

"How long were you inside?" I asked politely.

"Did a ten stretch," said Alfred. "This time."

"That's ten years, dear," said Mum. "He's on a jam-roll."

"A what?"

"Parole," Mum said. "I'm learning the prison lingo. I thought I could weave it into the third installment of the Star-Crossed Lovers trilogy."

"Have you read any of Mum's books?" I asked Alfred.

"Not yet. Going to start right now. I knew she'd be a famous writer."

"And as you know, we're trying to keep that a secret here," I reminded him. "For lots of reasons, which I am sure you know about. Mum's earnings being just one."

"I know, I know." Alfred nodded in my direction. "Is she always so serious?"

"Yes," said Mum.

"Takes after your Frank, doesn't she. No sense of humor."

"I have got a sense of humor," I said hotly. "I just don't think it's very funny."

"Stay right there for a minute," said Mum and exited the kitchen.

Alfred regarded me with amusement. "Don't you worry, luv," he said. "I'm taking care of your mum. That's what a business manager does."

"Business manager!"

"Someone's got to look after her career." Alfred grinned again. "Money's my specialty."

"I'm sure it is," I said darkly. "I thought you came here to look after the horses."

"I'm a jack-of-all-trades," said Alfred. "I told her, you've got to live your life, Iris. And Kat has got to live hers. Course, she'll miss you when you go back to the smoke, but you'll come and visit, won't you?"

"Here. Remember Jazzbo?" Mum returned bearing Jazzbo Jenkins. She propped him up against the gin bottle on the table.

"Well, I'll be buggered!" Alfred exclaimed. "I remember this little fella." He picked up Jazzbo Jenkins. "What was Billy's mouse called—the one with all those badges of seaside piers?"

"Ella Fitzgerald," said Mum. "She's still wearing all those badges, too. Those were the days, weren't they?"

"Did Mum tell you how she came to have your brother Billy's mouse?" I couldn't help but say.

"No need to go into that now, Katherine," said Mum sharply.

Alfred's eyes teared up yet again! I was getting exhausted from all the emotional turmoil in the room.

"I'm glad you kept the mice," he said. "Course, I called Billy a sissy for having a toy like this but … remember the Honeychurch dormice, eh?" He wiped away a tear and shook his head. "When we were kids, Billy and I would spend hours down at Cavalier Copse hoping to see those little buggers. Poor Billy."

Mum reached across and squeezed Alfred's hand. "Alfred was there when Billy had that aneurism on Blackpool Pier, Kat."

"Dropped dead right in front of me," said Alfred.

"I know," I said. "I'm sorry. It must have been horrible."

Alfred seemed lost in thought for a moment but suddenly snapped out of it. "The old countess never liked me."

"Let's hope you'll make her change her mind," I said. "You *do* know that she has no idea that you have a prison record? Mum told the dowager countess that you have spent the last few decades working with retired circus horses in Spain."

"See, I told you Iris can spin a good yarn."

"He's good with all animals. Not just horses," Mum declared. "I told you, we used to call him Dr. Doolittle."

"So, you've never worked in a circus?"

"Course I have." Alfred's expression changed instantly. "That's where I met that *bastard* Ralph Jackson."

"You mean William," I pointed out. "Here at Honeychurch, he's known as William."

"Katherine!" Mum shot me a warning look. "Well, that's all water under the bridge—"

"I beg to differ." Alfred scowled. "I know all about bloody Ralph Jackson impersonating my poor, dead brother. *Bastard.* Called himself the strongest man in the world, did Ralph. How about the biggest *liar* in the world! He was no friend to Billy, no friend at all. All brawn and biceps—wait a minute—" He rounded on Mum, "Is that how you came to get Ella Fitzgerald?"

"Not exactly," said Mum hastily.

Alfred's scowl deepened. "So he not only stole Billy's name... he stole his mouse? He stole Ella Fitzgerald?"

I let out a snort of derision. I couldn't help it. "The strongest man in the world and his little toy mouse."

"Katherine!" Mum said again. "And don't snort. It's so unattractive—"

Alfred slammed both fists down on the table. "If I ever get my hands on that *bastard* I'll—"

"You won't," Mum exclaimed.

"Why?"

"He's in prison," I said.

Alfred looked up sharply. "Where?"

"Don't tell him," Mum said quickly. "Don't be silly, Alfred."

Alfred cricked his neck again. "I'll find out. I've got friends that would make his visit more comfortable—shall we say."

"That's a bad idea," I said. "Edith is fond of William—Ralph ... oh for heaven's sake, he's *William* to us."

"Not to me, he isn't," Mum declared. "To me he'll always be Ralph, I swear."

"Now who's lying?" I exclaimed. "Anyway Alfred, if you want to make a good impression, you'd better keep those opinions to yourself."

"Oooh! Will you listen to her!" jeered Alfred.

"I'm afraid Kat's right," said Mum. "You should."

"Alright. I'll try," said Alfred. "But I can't promise anything."

The whole thing was turning into a farce. Here was my mother, inviting her stepbrother Alfred Bushman, to work for Edith who said she'd never liked Alfred anyway. Not only that, Alfred's position as stable manager was to "temporarily" replace Ralph Jackson—aka William aka Billy—the very man who had had the gall to impersonate his dead brother, Billy. *Downton Abbey* could never have come up with a better storyline.

I had to laugh. And did.

They looked surprised. "You see!" I said. "I do have a sense of humor!" I got to my feet. "Now, if you'll excuse me, I will leave you to your reminiscing. I have phone calls to make."

"Help yourself to another drink, Alfred dear," said Mum. "Kat and I will make you up a bed on the sofa in the sitting room."

"What's wrong with William's flat in the stable yard?"

"I'm not sleeping in that ruddy flat," said Alfred firmly. "Be a blight on our Billy's memory. Your mum said I could have your room once you've gone. The couch is good enough for me tonight."

Mum followed me out of the kitchen and closed the door behind her. "Where is it?" she whispered.

"What?"

"The five thousand pounds!"

"Five thousand pounds!" I shrieked. "I thought it was a couple hundred."

"Be quiet!" Mum pointed in the direction of the kitchen. "Don't let Alfred know."

"Why shouldn't Alfred know?"

"He's got ears like a bat." Mum steered me over to the bottom of the stairs and lowered her voice. "He'll have a heart attack if he finds out I've got some of that money here."

"I thought you said it was yours and you could do what you like," I said. "And besides, isn't he your business manager?"

"Yes, yes, but the thing is—" Mum paused. "Alfred told me that he would take care of any withdrawals through his um . . . *contact* . . . and that I was not to go to the bank myself."

"Not to go to Jersey?"

"Yes. No."

I rolled my eyes. "But of course you ignored his instructions."

"Katherine! Please!" Mum grabbed my arm tightly. It hurt. "Don't say anything. Promise."

"Why? What could he do?"

"You just don't know Alfred."

"You can let go of my arm." I removed her fingers. "Look, I'm worried about this arrangement. There was a reason why Dad didn't welcome Alfred into our home. Are you sure you can trust him? He's a criminal who has been inside more than once."

"He's turned over a new leaf—now quickly, where is my money?"

"Somewhere on the Honeychurch estate," I said wearily.

Mum gasped. "You *lost* it!"

"Not lost. Mislaid. I'm sure it'll turn up somewhere," I said, although in truth, I wasn't sure at all.

"This is your fault."

"You kicked it."

"You should have caught it." Mum glowered. "What am I supposed to do now?"

"Go and enjoy the evening with your brother," I said. "I promise I will have another look tomorrow."

Mum bit her lip. "Alfred can't know about this," she said again. "It would be disastrous."

"I know."

As I picked up my handbag, Valentine's cane clattered to the floor.

"Isn't that Valentine's walking stick?" Mum asked.

"Yes."

She gave a shiver. "Hmm. Someone walked over my grave."

"Don't say that."

"Why? What's happened?"

"I know you don't like Valentine much, Mum, but I've just got this weird feeling that something is wrong."

"In what way?"

"I found his cane lying in the field and his car parked up by the gate on Hopton's Crest. And then tonight, I went back up there and the car had gone."

"Did you try calling his mobile?" said Mum.

"Of course I did," I said. "His voice mailbox is full so it's not just me that's looking for him. I went to the Hare & Hounds and they said Valentine caught a taxi to the station."

"And?"

"Why would Valentine drive to Hopton's Crest and then call and take a taxi from there? Why not leave the car at the Hare & Hounds and call from there? He had luggage. And, according to Eric, the car was seen early in the morning."

"If you ask me, it's got all the signs of being a coward," said Mum. "You said yourself he ran out of the protest meeting."

"I know but—"

"Let's ask Alfred," said Mum, snatching up the cane. "He's good at channeling."

"Mum!" I protested but she was already on her way back to the kitchen and thrust it into Alfred's hands.

"Who is Valentine?" said Alfred.

"Kat's new man," said Mum.

"He's not my new man."

"She gave David Wynne the boot."

"Who is David Wynne?"

"The art investigator. Remember? I told you?" said Mum.

"Quiet now. Let me think." Alfred closed his eyes and slowly ran his fingers up and down the shaft.

I looked at Mum and mouthed, "*What's he doing?*"

She mouthed back, "*Wait. And. See.*"

Alfred snapped his eyes open. "Did he drive a blue Suzuki SUV?"

"How do you know that?" I said sharply.

"I saw it," said Alfred. "A bloody big tow truck drove past me pulling a blue car. Didn't bother to slow down and went right through a puddle. That's why I'm wearing your dad's pajamas."

"What time was that?" I asked.

Alfred shrugged. "About four."

It must have been when I was in the pub but at least it explained why the car had vanished. But who had called for the tow truck? Edith had mentioned it this morning to Eric but Eric would hardly have driven me up to Hopton's Crest if he had arranged for the car to be towed. Surely he would have mentioned it.

Alfred suddenly flung the cane away from him.

Mum gave a cry of alarm. "What's the matter? What's wrong?"

"Can't breathe!" Alfred leapt to his feet, eyes bulging. He grabbed his throat. "Can't breathe!"

Mum grabbed me. "Do something, Kat!" she shrieked. "Help!"

I tried to restrain him but Alfred pushed me aside and fell to the floor, gasping for air. Then, just as quickly, it was over.

"Oh my God!" Mum exclaimed. "What happened?"

"I think he had a seizure," I said anxiously. "Has this happened before?"

Alfred gave us a weak smile. "Where am I?"

"You're in the kitchen with your sister," said Mum firmly. "You had a bit of a funny turn."

We helped Alfred back to his feet and sat him in the chair. Mum thrust a glass of Scotch under his nose.

"You had a vision, didn't you?" she said.

Alfred nodded. "Water. Mud—"

"Where?" I demanded. "Here?"

"What did you see, Alfred?"

"Death," Alfred whispered.

"Who? A man? A woman?" Mum said urgently. "A platoon of Roundheads?"

"Stop talking, Iris." Alfred touched the cane again. "I'm not feeling too good."

His complexion had a grayish sheen to it.

"Of course you're not." Mum turned to me and whispered, "He gets these moments after having one of his visions."

"Should we call the police?" I whispered back.

"And say what?" said Mum.

Two beeps sounded from my handbag. Someone was sending me a text message.

"That'll be Dylan," Mum said, rolling her eyes.

"Who is Dylan?"

"Mum calls my ex-boyfriend David, Dylan," I said, delving into my bag.

"Why?"

"I have no idea. Probably because she knows it annoys me."

There was a third beep. I pulled out my iPhone and stared at it in astonishment.

There were three text messages.

The first text was just the letter "*k*." The second was the letter "*j*" and the third said, "*Hello all ok*." That was it.

"It's a text from Valentine. He's fine," I said tightly. "Sorry for all the fuss."

"Oh, Katherine!" said Mum with scorn. "You and your imagination." She gave Alfred another affectionate cuff around the ear. "You and your visions."

I felt inexplicably upset. "Sorry. Excuse me," and darted out of the kitchen.

Mum caught me going halfway up the stairs. "Kat my love, wait! Are you alright?"

"I'm fine," I said quickly. "Leave me alone, please."

Mum was by my side in seconds. "I'm your mother. I know when something is wrong."

Tears stung my eyes. "So stupid. It was all so long ago. It's not even about Valentine!" I exclaimed. "I'm not even attracted to him!"

Mum gently pulled me down beside her and we sat together on the stairs. She put her arm around my shoulders and I felt a tear trickle down my cheek. *What was wrong with everyone tonight? All these tears!*

"It's bringing it all back for you, isn't it?" said Mum gently.

"So stupid," I said again.

Jem was my very first boyfriend and someone who, at age seventeen, was the love of my life. He had been on his way to pick me up on his motorbike but never arrived. He and I had had a childish argument earlier on the phone because Dad had forbidden me to ride pillion and Jem told me to choose between him and my family. I chose Jem of course because I was young and in love and couldn't imagine life without him. I wrote my parents a note, packed a tiny bag, and sneaked out of the house planning to run away. For two hours I waited for Jem at the bottom of the road but he never came. I thought he must have changed his mind and slunk back home to face the music. Dad was furious and forbade me ever to see him again. The first I knew of Jem's fatal accident was two days later when his mother called mine.

"I have the same feeling of foreboding, Mum," I whispered.

"Then we'll go to the police first thing in the morning," she said briskly. "Come on. Let's have a laugh. *Walk of Shame: Celebrity Family Secrets Revealed* is on in ten minutes."

"You certainly know how to snap me out of my misery," I said dryly. "I hate that program."

Walk of Shame: Celebrity Family Secrets Revealed was a reality TV show hosted by none other than my nemesis, David's estranged wife Trudy Wynne. The goal was to deliberately humiliate celebrities by exposing the skeletons in the family closet. It was mean-spirited and I flatly refused to watch it.

"How would you like it if your past was broadcast to gazillions of viewers for everyone to laugh at?"

"Don't be dramatic," Mum said. "It's all scripted."

"I've told you it's not. Trudy would have a field day with me and all *your* dark little secrets—haven't you ever thought of that?"

"So that's why you don't want Alfred here," said Mum. "You're afraid that it'll come out that you're related to a criminal."

"But I'm *not* related," I said, exasperated.

"So what's the problem?"

"Well...maybe Trudy will expose the boxing emporium," I said. "Oh! And find out that you're really Krystalle Storm who is fond of taking little trips to the Channel Islands to smuggle money into the country."

Mum's jaw dropped. "Well. Put like that, I suppose I wouldn't like it. But darling, seriously, the celebrities she has on there are really awful. They're just asking to be humiliated."

I got up. "Let's agree to differ. Everyone has a right to their privacy."

"If you say so." Mum paused. "But at least you are sounding a little brighter."

"I'm okay, honestly."

"Dinner is at eight. Alfred wants to cook."

"What are we having? Porridge?"

Back in the sanctuary of my bedroom I sank onto the bed and wondered whether I should respond to Valentine's brief text since he didn't mention his walking cane. I decided it was better to let the whole thing go. Maybe he'd still come to the auction and I'd be able to return it there. I didn't want to hang on to it. Maybe

Alfred was right. Perhaps there was a weird energy about the wretched thing.

My mind turned to Mum and her five thousand pounds. I'd have to resume my search tomorrow. Surely Mr. Chips had favorite places where he liked to bury his treasures. Perhaps Edith would know where they might be. But there was something I had to do first.

I returned to the landing and listened. Cries of "Snap!" and shrieks of laughter were coming from the kitchen. *Who on earth still plays Snap?* But it was good to hear Mum so happy.

I found the loft hatch pole behind Mum's bedroom door and the wooden ladder laying flat underneath her bed.

Quickly, I opened the hatch in the ceiling, primed the ladder, and heaved myself up. Mum had left a flashlight tucked in a cleft between the eaves. Plywood boards had been laid over the joists. It was horribly dangerous. Just one slip and Mum could easily fall straight through the ceiling.

The eaves sloped right to the floor. Right at the back was a leather suitcase with presto combination locks. I carefully crawled toward it. Making sure to keep my head low and my knees on the boards, I dragged the suitcase out into the middle.

I knew it was wrong but I just had to know what was in there.

A sudden burst of laughter reached my ears followed by a Native American war-whoop from Alfred. Mind made up, I keyed in the date of Mum and Dad's wedding day. The locks popped right open—Mum was so predictable.

I opened up the lid and played the flashlight over the contents inside.

"Oh. My. God!"

The suitcase was packed with bundles and bundles of twenty,

fifty, and hundred-pound bills. Tucked in a pocket at the side was a roll of empty blue self-sealing plastic bags secured with a rubber band.

Mum had definitely made more than one or two trips to the Channel Islands. I couldn't even begin to guess how much money was in there.

Her writing endeavors were seriously lucrative and I felt proud of her.

But, as I closed the suitcase, secured the locks, and pushed it back under the eaves, I began to realize just why Mum had been so freaked out about my going to the police. It was just as well that Dad never found out. No wonder he'd banned Alfred from Mum's life—and now Alfred was back.

I felt perplexed. How could I ever leave her and go back to London now?

Chapter Fourteen

The next morning my bruised face had turned an ugly yellow but the swelling had gone down. Under great sufferance, I had allowed Alfred to administer a gypsy remedy the night before. This consisted of Mrs. Cropper's raw steak slathered in a disgusting smelling herbal paste. I had to lie on the floor for an hour.

Alfred was making a supreme effort to ingratiate himself. The night before he had cooked a rather delicious dinner, washed up, and then proceeded to massage Mum's feet.

I'd never seen my mother so cheerful and realized she probably had been lonely. In fact, I wondered if she'd been lonely for most of her married life.

Mum claimed that Dad's job as a tax inspector had prevented her from forging strong friendships that now, I didn't believe for a minute. True, they weren't the most social people. Dad had his allotment and the Rotary Club and Mum had her headaches that I now knew, of course, was her cover for writing her books.

As I popped my laptop, mobile phone, and my lucky Jazzbo mascot into my tote bag, I decided I would stop in at the police station this morning—just for my own peace of mind. Someone might have turned in the money.

My good humor dissolved the moment I got downstairs. Wedged in the narrow hallway with only a foot to spare, sat the sofa with what remained of Alfred's makeshift bed.

Alfred, dressed in a pair of Dad's old work overalls with the sleeves and legs rolled up, emerged from the sitting room carrying a box of books. He dumped it on top of the duvet where it promptly slid off. All the books fell out onto the floor.

"Morning! Glad to see your face is much better," Alfred said cheerfully as he kicked the books under the sofa. "Look at her face, Iris."

Mum appeared holding a standard lamp and set it down at the bottom of the stairs.

"What are you doing?" I asked.

"Come and see," said Mum.

I followed her into the sitting room and stifled my dismay. Furniture had been moved into the center of the room and covered with old sheets. Boxes that Mum and I had unpacked just weeks ago were repacked with knickknacks. Two black dustbin liners bulged with the curtains Mum had removed from the windows.

"We're clearing out as much as we can," said Mum happily. "Alfred's going to decorate."

"I thought he was going to work for Edith at the stables," I said. "That's a full-time job in itself."

"That's not until Saturday," said Mum. "Today is Wednesday. Anyway, he thinks he can do it in a day."

"A day!" I said. "I doubt it."

"There she goes again," said Alfred, winking at Mum. "Always thinking the worst."

"But what about preparing the walls?" I exclaimed. "The wallpaper needs to come off for a start and that's a big job. Who knows what their condition is like! They're probably rotten and will need Polyfilla."

"Oh ye of little faith," Alfred joked.

"And look at windows." I pointed to the paint-peeled frames. "They'll need stripping and sanding right down. The skirting boards, too."

"Rubbish," said Alfred. "They look alright to me."

"I'll dig out Frank's paint tray and brushes," said Mum. "I knew they'd come in useful."

"Dad would take weeks to decorate a room even this small," I protested.

"Katherine! For goodness' sake! Stop whining." Mum glowered. "Can I talk to you in the kitchen for a minute?"

"If we can get past the obstacle course, yes."

The Carriage House had an L-shaped floor plan with the front door opening into a narrow hallway and flight of stairs. The sitting room was on the right. At the far end stood the kitchen and a small dining room that was still full of unpacked boxes from Mum's old house. Entrance to the carriageway itself was through a door situated in the elbow of the L. As well as room for four carriages, the stalls could house twenty-four horses. There was also a downstairs loo and a grooms' sitting room with a winding staircase leading to sleeping quarters above.

Mum and I squeezed past the sofa, past an empty bookcase and upended coffee table, and went into the kitchen.

"Do you want to live in this mess?" I asked.

"I'm used to it," said Mum. "Don't you remember how your father was always decorating?"

I remembered alright. Our house always smelled of fresh paint and turpentine. The moment Dad finished decorating one room in his favorite shade of magnolia he'd start on the next. Our home was immaculate and I knew Mum liked it that way.

"What happened to the painters, Messrs. Baxter and Sons?" I said. "Didn't you pay them a deposit?"

"Alfred insists," said Mum. "It's his way of saying thank you. Katherine are you—"

"Yes. I *am* going to look for your money."

"Maybe Eric picked it up—or Patty?" said Mum. "Mr. Chips is always hanging around that end of the estate."

"It's more likely to be down a rabbit hole."

"Can't you ask Patty?"

I gave a heavy sigh. "Fine. Yes. Okay."

"I'm supposed to give Benedict the retainer today—"

"Don't you think you should wait for him to give you an estimate of how much this is all going to cost first anyway?"

"I trust him."

"He's talking about hiring a helicopter," I said.

"I know. It's an excellent idea. I've never been in a helicopter before."

"Have you consulted your business manager about this?"

Mum hesitated. "I wasn't planning on it."

"Alfred is bound to find out about your ... *donation* ... especially when he gets involved in the campaign."

"Oh." Mum's face fell.

"And you'll obviously need to get more money from Jersey," I said slyly. Judging from what I'd seen in Mum's suitcase she wouldn't need to go there for a very long time.

"What do you think I should do?" Mum said.

"Why don't you stall until you've talked to Alfred?" I said. "Tell Benedict you can't get the money quite yet. Lavinia said she had a trust fund. Let her part with her money, first."

Mum gave a heavy sigh. "Alright. I'll phone her ladyship and tell her I've hit a snag."

"Good. I'll see you later."

"Oh—wait." Mum picked up a letter from the dresser. "This came for you this morning."

I looked at the handwriting and postmark on the envelope. "It's from Harry," I said. "He must have written it the moment he got back to school."

Harry's letter was very short and to the point.

Stanford, send help quickly. The guards are cruel.
My fellow prisoners are spies. My bed is hard and
my pillow is lumpy. I hate it here. Biggles. P.S.
Please look after Thunder and the mice.

"Poor kid," I said, handing Mum the letter. "I wish—"

"Don't get involved, Katherine," said Mum. "He's not your child. Just write a bright and breezy letter back."

I knew Mum was right but it still bothered me.

We clambered over the furniture and boxes and made our way to the front door.

"Where are you off to now?" Mum demanded.

"I told you. I'm going to find your money."

"Shh!" Mum exclaimed, gesturing to the sitting room. "Keep your voice down."

"And I'm also going to Dartmouth," I said. "I didn't get there yesterday as you know. The estate agent e-mailed me about that property in Shoreditch."

"Did you hear that, Alfred? Shoreditch!" Mum shouted. "Can you imagine anyone wanting to live in Shoreditch?"

Alfred peered out of the sitting room. "Stone the crows!

People would give their right arm to move *out* of the East End, not in."

"I think you'll find things have changed in the past ten years," I said. "The shop is close to Spitalfields Market."

"Spitalfields Market!" Alfred shook his head in presumed disbelief. "Bloody hell. Jack the Ripper's old stomping ground! What is the world coming to?"

Telling Mum I'd pick her up at noon for the auction, I made my escape.

It was another blustery day with clouds scudding across a watery blue sky. On the horizon was a rainbow.

I remembered persuading Dad to chase a rainbow once. I was eight. We were on holiday in the Lake District. Mum had one of her "headaches" so it was just the two of us that afternoon. Even at eight I knew there couldn't be a pot of gold at the end of the rainbow but Dad humored me and off we went. At every hill we crested, there it was before us, a spectrum of colors of visible light—an illusion, always tantalizingly out of reach. Yet even still, I hoped we could catch it and I would be the first person alive to prove the legend was true.

I made a wish. *Please let me find Mum's money.*

As I drew closer to Bridge Cottage, I recognized Benedict's Prius parked a little farther up the hill next to the gate Edith and I had ridden through yesterday.

I parked my own car outside Patty's cottage. Heaving the wicket gate aside, I noticed a black dustbin liner had been dumped in the corner and there, carelessly balled up on the top was a flash of blue plastic.

My stomach turned right over. I snatched it up, dismayed to discover the bag was empty. It was definitely my mother's.

I knew that Patty had been hiding something although it

occurred to me that she wouldn't have known that the money belonged to my mother. And given that she'd just lost her own, it was horribly awkward.

I rapped smartly on the door half-hoping she wouldn't be at home. In less than a minute, the door flew open.

For the very first time ever, Patty smiled.

Chapter Fifteen

"Come in," she said and stood back to let me pass.

"I just stopped by to see how you are."

Attired in another hand-knitted outfit—this time a garish turquoise, I stepped into what I could only describe as a hoarder's paradise. My senses were immediately assaulted by the smell of cabbage, cooked bacon, and damp.

"Is that the wonderful Katherine?" came a familiar voice from behind the door.

"Oh! Hello." I was startled. Although I'd seen Benedict's Prius, I hadn't expected to find him visiting Patty.

"Your face looks so much better this morning," said Benedict. "It looks like we'll be able to forge ahead with our little photo shoot on Friday, after all. Shall we go through to the kitchen, Patty?"

"Yes. Yes, of course," said Patty. "This way."

Patty had lived with her mother in a dingy two-up, two-down cottage not helped by the fact that the curtains were partially drawn at the front window, preventing what little light managed to find its way through to this depressing location.

Now I realized why Harry had called them "bag ladies." Furniture, clothing in black plastic dustbin liners, boxes, suitcases, and just an array of useless objects were piled high around the room and covered every available surface. Set against the wall was a rather nice Victorian credenza that was virtually swallowed by stacks of newspapers including the *Daily Post* and the *Dipperton Deal.* I caught a glimpse of a dusky pink velveteen sofa underneath bolts of curtain material and yarns of wool. A narrow pathway had been created that passed by an open latch door—leading to upstairs—and ended in the kitchen.

"Lead the way, Patty," said Benedict, shooting me a look that clearly implied he, too, was as horrified as I was at Patty's living conditions.

The kitchen was marginally better. Along the back wall was an ancient coal-fueled Rayburn that couldn't have been working because the cottage was freezing cold.

Next to the Rayburn were two tattered armchairs—one held a bag of knitting—and a small table holding the TV remote and a pile of catalogs. On the kitchen counter sat an ancient television set broadcasting QVC, the home shopping channel. Judging by the numerous boxes stacked haphazardly in the corner, someone had been a keen shopper. Under the counter stood a fridge and a washing machine that was speckled with mildew. On top was an electric kettle next to a tray with two chipped mugs, a box of PG Tips, and an open bottle of milk.

"I'm sure Patty would make you a cup of tea if you'd like one?" said Benedict.

"No, thank you. I'm fine." At any moment, I expected to see an army of cockroaches scuttle across the floor.

Benedict caught my eye and in his, I saw a degree of compassion.

"I've been telling Patty that she's not to worry about anything," he said. "Of course, Bridge Cottage is not entitled to any compensation but I shall personally negotiate—should we ever reach that stage—with the board to make her an exception."

Benedict went up several notches in my estimation.

"That's wonderful, isn't it, Patty?" I said.

"Again, I'm truly sorry for your loss," said Benedict.

Patty didn't comment.

"I was telling Patty that she wasn't to contribute a penny to the campaign," Benedict went on. "There are others in a much better financial position to support the cause—like Lavinia and of course, Iris." He laughed. "Even you!"

I smiled but inwardly felt very uncomfortable. I searched Patty's face, looking for any sign that she might have found Mum's five thousand pounds, but she just looked steadily at the television.

"So what brings you here this morning, Kat?" Benedict asked.

"I wanted to see if there was anything I could do for you, Patty," I said. "Perhaps I could help with the shopping since you don't have a car."

"Well . . . I can't afford to pay for the petrol."

"I wouldn't expect you to," I said. "I also wondered if you would be interested in helping me organize the auction."

I caught a flicker of interest. "How much would you pay me?"

I was taken aback. "I hadn't—"

"I think it's more a case of donating your time to the cause," said Benedict smoothly.

"Time is money," said Patty. "That's what Mother always told me. And now, I don't know how I'm going to make ends meet without her pension."

"I heard you used to do the car boot sale circuit," I said. "Maybe there are some things you'd like me to take a look at and see if I can sell for you?"

"Alright," said Patty. "Let's do it now."

"*Now?*" I exchanged looks with Benedict and could have sworn I saw a flicker of annoyance cross his features.

"In that case, I'll leave you both to it," he said. "Patty, will you see me out?"

"You know where the door is."

"Just want a quick word—" Benedict put his arm around Patty's shoulders. "In private."

I watched them pick their way through the obstacle course to the front door and was instantly reminded of Mum's own hallway. At the front door Benedict leaned down and whispered something in Patty's ear. I saw her stiffen and noticed his fingers tightening on her arm.

"I told you," I heard Patty say. "I don't know what you're talking about. I'm not hiding anything."

When Patty returned I asked, "Is everything okay?"

"What's it to you?" she snapped. "And what do you really want?"

It would appear that Patty was back to her usual sullen self.

"Are you sure you're okay?" I said suspiciously.

"Why should you want to help me? I don't know you."

"Because…" I wracked my brains. "I'm very close to my mother so I can't begin to imagine what it feels like to have lost yours. You've lived together for most of your life, haven't you?"

"What's it to you?" Patty said again.

"We must be around the same age," I went on, trying to find common ground. "I know what it's like to be an only child. After my dad died, he told me to take care of my mother. That's why I'm here in Devon."

I studied Patty's features. She had dark brown eyes and flawless skin. Even with her odd choice of dress, she would be attractive if she could do something with her hair. Maybe now she was free from her mother's overbearing clutches, she could start to have a life. But of course, I would never tell her that.

"Much as we love them—mothers aren't easy," I said. "I know how you feel."

"Do you?" Patty said with a sneer. "Unlike you, I don't have a fancy job or a wealthy mother. My dad left us in debt when he died. Mother had a hard life trying to keep food on the table and now—what's going to happen to me?"

"Perhaps you can help me uncover a mystery," I said. "There's a reward if you can solve it."

"How much?"

"One hundred pounds," I said.

Patty gave a curt nod that I assumed meant yes.

I pulled the blue plastic bag out of my pocket and showed it to her. "Do you recognize this?"

Patty stepped closer. "What is it?"

"It's a bag that banks use for money," I said, watching her expression carefully.

"But there's no money in there."

"I know," I said. "But there was. Did you see Mr. Chips yesterday?"

"Who?"

"The dowager countess's Jack Russell."

"Maybe. He's always running about down here."

"So you *did* see him?"

"I didn't say I saw him yesterday. Why?"

"Mr. Chips ran off with something that belonged to my mother in this blue bag."

"You mean there was *money* in that bag?"

"Yes," I said.

"How much money?"

"It doesn't matter how much." I could feel myself getting irritated. "I found this blue bag in the black plastic bin liner by your front gate."

Patty's eyes flashed with fury. "Are you calling me a thief?"

"No. I'm not calling you anything," I said. "I'm just asking if you saw Mr. Chips—or anyone else for that matter."

"My mother's not even cold and you come round here pretending to be a Good Samaritan and then accuse me of being a thief?"

"I didn't say anything of the sort!" I exclaimed.

"Why accuse me?" Patty shouted. "We're always getting ramblers walking by. Anyone could have taken your money—"

"From the *dog?*"

"Yes. From the dog." Patty thrust out her jaw. "And then thrown the bag away to frame me."

"Why would a complete stranger want to frame you?" I exclaimed.

"Eric was out working in the fields with his tractor yesterday," said Patty. "You should ask him."

"I have asked Eric," I said.

"Did you ask your railway man? Did you think of that," said Patty spitefully, "or were you too loved up?"

"Valentine Prince-Avery?" I said. "I hardly know him to be—as you say, loved up—"

"He's been prowling around here, why couldn't he have taken it from that dog? Stan said he paid for his room in cash," Patty went on. "Maybe that's where he got the cash from? Did you think about *that* before accusing me?"

Our conversation was going nowhere. Taking in the squalor

of the cottage, lack of heating or phone, and Patty's new circumstances, I tried a different tack.

"Look, I know you found the money, Patty," I said gently. "And
that's okay. Why don't you give it back to me and we'll say nothing
more about it."

"My word's not good enough, is it?" she spat.

"Of course it is—"

"You think you are so special, don't you? The famous Katherine Stanford! What's it like to be you?" Patty's outburst took me
off guard. "You think throwing all your money around will buy you
friends but it won't. You'll never belong here. Never! Get out! Get
out of my house and leave me to grieve."

"I'm sorry, Patty," I said quietly. "Just think about what I said.
I'm serious about the reward and we'll say no more about it."

"No! You think about what *I've* said!" Patty stabbed a finger at
my chest. "I'm going to report you for harassment. And what's more,
I'm going to the papers and I'm going to tell them everything about
you and your *Valentine*."

My stomach flipped over. It was exactly what I'd hoped to avoid.
Sympathy for Patty had rapidly changed to anger. I just knew she
was a thief! Without another word, I turned on my heel and tripped
my way to the front door.

Outside, I gave into my anger. I was going to go straight to the
police, which was exactly what I should have done right from the
start.

It was on the outskirts of Dartmouth that all thoughts of Patty
and the police vanished. Sitting on the forecourt of Ogwell Car
Hire and decorated with ribbons and silver balloons was Valentine's metallic-blue Suzuki, license plate LUXRY1.

On impulse, I pulled off the road and parked my Golf in one
of the three slots designated for customer parking.

Of course, it explained who had towed Valentine's car the afternoon before, but again, I wondered who had made the phone call. I still couldn't shake off the feeling of foreboding—not helped by Alfred's dramatic "channeling" performance from the night before.

It was no good. I just wanted to know that there was nothing sinister about Valentine's disappearance. I just had to be sure.

Chapter Sixteen

Ogwell Car Hire used to be a filling station. Three rusting Shell petrol pumps stood outside a brick building that was now boarded up although the sign—GARAGE—was still visible in stained-glass lettering above the double doors.

As car rental companies go, this establishment was definitely on the low end of the scale, which didn't tally with the sophisticated Valentine I had met—albeit it briefly. It was also such an odd location to choose. It was miles from the main line station to London Paddington and made me wonder how Valentine had gotten here to pick up his car in the first place.

I heard my phone vibrate in my tote bag and grabbed it. Unfortunately, it was from David. Again. Today's text differed from his usual "*Thinking of you*" to "*Must talk to you. Urgent.*" Obviously he was trying a new tactic.

I headed for the Portakabin that served as the office.

Inside the cramped space, two women in their late forties were standing engaged in an animated conversation next to a bank of filing cabinets. A kettle was on the boil. On top of the mini fridge sat a tower of Styrofoam cups, a jar of instant coffee, and a bowl of sugar sachets and powdered Coffee-mate. In the background I could hear the Judi Spiers Show playing on BBC Radio Devon. It was one of my mother's favorite radio programs—and mine, too.

The waiting area consisted of a small vinyl bench and a table strewn with a stack of maps of the area. The pale green walls were plastered with posters advertising local tourist attractions—most notably Greenway, Agatha Christie's summer home. On the ceiling I noticed a whisper of last year's Christmas tinsel.

On one of the two workstations along with the usual office clutter, sat a copy of the *Daily Post*.

I called out a greeting and they both turned around and seemed surprised to have a customer.

The pair reminded me of Laurel and Hardy, the comedy double act from the 1930s. One was thin and nervous-looking with short lank hair whilst the other was overweight with hard, piggy eyes. They were dressed in matching black trousers with white shirts and black ties.

"I was looking for Mr. Ogwell?"

"He's dead," said Hardy bluntly. She pointed to a name badge on her shirt pocket. "I'm his daughter, Susan."

"I'm sorry." I just couldn't seem to say the right thing today.

"Oh. My God!" tittered Laurel, who was, to my amusement, actually called Laurel. "You're Rapunzel from *Fakes & Treasures*."

Here we go.

"We love that show, don't we, Susan?" she gushed.

"I prefer the soaps."

"What have you done to your face?" Laurel asked. "Walked into a door?"

"I fell off a horse," I said.

"It's funny seeing people in the papers and then in the flesh," Laurel went on. "Like I'm in a dream. I was just reading about you this morning in the *Post*."

"Oh, is that what you were gawking at," said Susan. "She loves celebrity stories. Now we'll never hear the end of it."

Laurel reddened. "And if you don't mind me saying so, I'm glad you gave David the boot. I never thought he was good enough for you. I think his wife, Trudy, looks like Cruella de Vil from *101 Dalmations*, don't you?"

With Trudy's sharp angular bob I'd always thought the same but just gave a polite smile. This was exactly why I had turned my back on being a C-list celebrity. I loathed being public property where complete strangers felt they knew me well enough to comment on my personal life.

"And we've already met your new man." Laurel giggled. "Haven't we, Susan?"

"I told her I'd fire her if she called the papers," said Susan.

A familiar sinking feeling began in my stomach. Laurel was already reaching for the *Daily Post*. She handed it to me. "Look."

Trudy Wynne's infamous *Star Stalkers* column was on the front page. In the bottom right corner was a photo that Trudy constantly recycled showing me, wiping away my tears. It had been taken a year ago when I'd attended a "Wish-Upon-A-Star" charity event for terminally ill children. One brave little girl had fulfilled her dream of swimming with dolphins and it just made me cry. Today, however, the caption said BROKENHEARTED RAPUNZEL FINDS LOVE AGAIN. TURN TO PAGE 3 AND MEET HER NEW MAN.

"Good for you, I say," said Laurel. "He was ever so charming. A real *prince*!"

Even though I knew it was a mistake, I couldn't help myself and took up the newspaper.

I turned to page 3 to find an old photograph of David and me pictured at a London restaurant. Photoshop had put in a jagged black line between us—RAPUNZEL! DUMPED! Alongside were two

more images. One showed the Hare & Hounds pub sign—SECRET
RENDEZVOUS—and the other, a photo of me emerging from Valentine's bedroom—LOVERS' TRYST. It had been heavily Photoshopped so that Valentine's hand that had been innocently hanging
by his side was now firmly placed around my waist.

I was furious. No wonder David had been calling me. He must
have seen it.

There was no prize for guessing the culprit. It was either Patty
or Angela—both had seen me on the landing and yet could they
have gotten the photographs out so quickly? The meeting had been
held on Monday night so the images would have to have been
e-mailed immediately to make the Wednesday edition. Patty had
made it clear that she disliked me and was definitely hard up for
money but, as she kept on saying, she did not have a landline let
alone a mobile phone—and definitely not the Internet. Angela,
however, did—unless someone from the village was the culprit.

Yet over the past few weeks, I'd found the locals very protective of my celebrity status. Mum liked to compare my presence to
that of "Kate and William" when they lived in Anglesey. I just
couldn't think who else would have done it unless it was one of
Trudy's professional photographers.

I wouldn't put it past her. Her wretched column wasn't called
Star Stalkers just for fun. I recalled seeing three little alcoves dotted along the landing that could easily hide a photographer. The
pub had been full of people—many of whom I didn't recognize—
and even though I'd used the back staircase through the Snug, I
knew from experience that the paparazzi just seemed to have an
instinctive homing device for their prey.

"Do you know who took it?" Susan said, breaking into my
thoughts.

"No. There were a lot of people in the pub that night."

"Can't you sue them for libel or something?" said Laurel in a complete turn about face. "I think it's awful that people can pry into your private life like that. It's bad enough when the next-door neighbor overhears me and my husband having a row."

"It's not pleasant," I said.

"Well, you can tell your Mr. Prince-Avery that we're very annoyed with him," said Susan. "That Suzuki is our only luxury car."

"But we're very grateful that he called to tell us where it was," Laurel said hastily.

"Valentine called you?" I said.

"Yesterday after lunch," said Susan. "But he didn't bother to leave the keys in the car and Laurel lost the spare set."

"They're here somewhere, Susan, I—"

"So we had to hire a tow truck to go and pick the car up."

"The AA came out so it was okay," said Laurel.

"It was *not* okay, Laurel," Susan exclaimed. "It cost money that we won't get back. Not only that, we had to replace one of the headlights."

"I thought it was cracked before," protested Laurel.

"I would never allow a luxury car to be rented with a cracked headlight."

"Can't you ask Mr. Prince-Avery to post the keys?" I said, hoping to save Laurel from further misery.

Susan glared at Laurel again.

"I . . . I—"

"Laurel did not get his address and he is not answering his mobile phone," said Susan. "Perhaps you could ask him?"

Of course I had had no more luck in reaching Valentine than they had. "Didn't he pay by credit card?"

"Cash," said Susan. "We're one of the few car rental companies in the area that don't use credit cards. That's why we can offer better rates. We don't have to pay a commission."

"But surely he gave you his driver's license?" I said.

"What do you think?" Susan gave Laurel another icy glare.

"I've already said I'm sorry, Susan." Laurel thrust out her jaw. "We got to talking about Africa. My husband is going to take me on safari for my fiftieth birthday. He told me I should visit some island off the coast of Zanzibar. Pemba something."

I remembered Valentine's lucky key fob. "You mean, Pemba Island?"

"That's it!" said Laurel excitedly. "You see, that kind of inside information isn't in the travel brochures, is it?"

"Good. I'm glad we've got that straight," said Susan sarcastically. "I suppose you've come to pick up the stuff he left in the car? Laurel . . . ?"

"I'll get it." Laurel went to the back of the room and returned with a plastic container marked LOST PROPERTY. She set it down on the table and took off the lid, removing a pair of brown leather gloves and the Chillingford Court auction catalog.

"Here. Take them—and you can tell him that we disposed of the placards that he left in the boot."

"The placards?" I said sharply.

"We had to jimmy the lock open," said Susan. "Another expense."

"Did the placards say *HS3 CROSSES FROM HERE*?"

"Is that something to do with the new railway line?" said Laurel. "Yes."

"We thought so. I'm against it, we're all against it, aren't we, Susan," said Laurel. "And I thought, good for him for taking them down."

I didn't want to explain that it had been Valentine who had put them up.

"The placards were broken, weren't they, Susan?" said Laurel. "All smashed—"

"We chucked them in the skip out the back. If you want, I'll show them to you."

"They were like that when we found them, honest," said Laurel.

"You're welcome to take them," said Susan.

I shook my head. "No thanks."

"Do you want to take his gloves?" said Susan.

I suppressed a sigh. "Yes. Of course."

There was an awkward pause until Laurel blurted, "Susan took the two bottles of wine. It looked really expensive."

"As far as I'm concerned, that was payment for the cracked headlight," said Susan coldly.

Now I was concerned. Valentine would definitely have been able to carry the wine on the train back to London.

I hesitated for a moment. "Just one more thing. How did Valentine get here on Monday when he came to pick up the car? Did he come in a taxi?"

Laurel shook her head. "He came in on Saturday afternoon," she said. "He was a walk-in. I can tell you where he was staying if you like." She shot Susan a smug look. "We like to get a local address when someone pays cash."

"Don't worry," I said. "I know he was staying at the Hare & Hounds in Little Dipperton."

"Oh no," Laurel exclaimed. "He definitely said the Dart Marina Hotel. He asked for the directions."

"You're sure?" I said sharply.

"Oh yes. Why? Is something wrong?" Laurel's face was creased with worry.

"No, not at all," I said.

Promising I wouldn't mention the wine but I would ask Valentine for the car keys if I did see him again, I headed back to my car. If nothing else, the mystery of the missing placards had been solved.

As I opened my car door, a scrap of paper fell from the sale catalog and fluttered to the ground.

It was a newspaper cutting of me taken on my last day at *Fakes & Treasures* dated three months ago. "*Honeychurch Hall*" had been scribbled in the margin in black marker pen.

I stared at it in confusion. Mum and I had met Valentine quite by accident on Monday afternoon down at Cavalier Copse. I thought back to Harry when he was in his tree house and claimed that Valentine had been "waiting"—that was Harry's exact word—for Mum and me to arrive. Had our meeting been intentional? But if so, how had Valentine known we would have been there picking sloes? Even more alarming, how had he known I was staying at Honeychurch Hall?

You're being ridiculous, Kat! I was becoming paranoid. I also now had his wretched gloves to add to his walking cane. Maybe I would give them to Benedict after all and be done with it. I had much bigger problems of my own—Mum's stolen money.

It was time to talk to a professional.

Chapter Seventeen

The tiny police station that "operated Monday to Friday 9 to 5" was on the outskirts of Dartmouth.

I stepped into the sparsely furnished waiting area comprised of an uncomfortable-looking bench seat and two hard chairs.

The counter that divided the room was empty but next to an old-fashioned bell was a plaque saying, YOUR DESK SERGEANT TODAY IS: MALCOLM.

I hit the bell.

There was the sound of a loo flushing but instead of Malcolm emerging from the door behind the counter, I was startled to see it was Detective Inspector Shawn Cropper. He was holding a magazine called *Railway Roundup*. Shawn looked embarrassed.

"You caught me on the hop. Malcolm's got a doctor's appointment," he said by way of explaining his presence. "We're short-staffed. As usual."

There was an awkward silence.

"How was the recital?" I said suddenly.

"Very much what you'd expect from a class of five-year-olds," said Shawn. "Off-key."

"You're a good father," I said and I meant it.

"What happened to your face?" Shawn peered closely.

"I fell off a horse."

He reached out and touched it gently. For a split second our eyes met and I found myself blushing. "If you speak to your grandmother before I do, please thank her for the steak."

Shawn sprang back. "Of course. Yes. Definitely. Good old Gran and her remedies." He flashed me a smile. "What can I help you with today?"

"I'm in a dilemma and I need your advice."

"Go on ..."

"It's about Patty," I said. "I know that she worked for your grandmother at the Hall for a while."

"I don't think Gran has quite recovered from the ordeal," said Shawn. "Let's say that Patty can be rather challenging."

"Would you know why she was let go? Was she honest?"

Shawn seemed a bit taken aback by the question. "I think it was more a clash of the titans, so to speak."

"We call it creative differences in the entertainment world," I said. "So basically, they didn't get along."

"It wasn't that. Patty's priority was taking care of Joyce," said Shawn. "And Gran got fed up with her leaving early or just not showing up at all—"

"What will Patty do for money?" I said.

"Why do you ask?"

"I know she used to do the car boot circuit with her mother," I said. "But ... have you ever been inside Bridge Cottage?"

"Not yet."

"It's more of a hovel. There's no central heating."

"According to Gran, they lived frugally," said Shawn. "Joyce didn't believe in heating or wasting money. Why?"

I began to have second thoughts but after a moment's hesitation plunged in. "I've lost some money and I have a feeling that Patty might have found it."

"Presumably, you've asked her?"

"Yes," I said. "She denied it."

"What makes you think she found it?"

"It's a bit of a long story but Mr. Chips—"

"The Jack Russell?"

"Is there another Mr. Chips?" I joked but Shawn just looked stern.

"Carry on—"

"He found a small packet of money and ran off with it."

"I see." Shawn stroked his chin thoughtfully. "Obviously you gave chase?"

"Of course, but he was too quick for me."

"Perhaps he buried it?"

"I wish he had but—" I hesitated again. "I found the packet in one of the black bin liners outside Patty's cottage. It was empty."

"And you're sure it's the same packet that Mr. Chips had taken?"

"Positive," I said. "It's very distinctive."

"So you're saying that either Patty removed the money—"

"Or Mr. Chips spent it." I laughed but he didn't.

"This is a very serious accusation," he said. "How much money are we talking about?"

I cleared my throat. "Around five thousand pounds."

Shawn's eyebrows practically disappeared under his hairline. "Around five thousand pounds or exactly five thousand pounds?"

"Around. Maybe. I'm not sure."

"I'd certainly know if I had lost five thousand pounds." Shawn regarded me with suspicion. "So it's your word against Patty's?"

"I suppose it is."

Shawn frowned. "Can you describe this small packet?"

"I can show it to you."

"You have it with you?"

"Of course I do." I pulled it out of my tote bag and was about to hand it over but Shawn raised his hand.

"Wait a moment."

He disappeared through the door behind him and returned wearing a pair of disposable gloves and carrying a box of plastic wrap.

"Really," I said. "Does it have to be this big thing? I just want you to ask her."

"It is a big thing." Shawn neatly tore off a section of plastic wrap but he couldn't get it to lay flat on the counter. He scrunched it into a ball and pulled off another piece.

"Do you want some help?" I said.

"No. I've got it." This time Shawn managed to smooth it out flat. "Give that to me."

He carefully laid the bag onto the plastic wrap and studied it. "There's some wording on the bottom. But I can't see what it says."

"Here!" I took my jeweler's loupe from my tote bag and handed it to him. We were leaning quite close together—he on one side of the counter, and me on the other. I was aware of a smell of bananas— something I always noticed when I was around Shawn.

With his head bent over the plastic bag, I saw that he had the most gorgeous, tousled hair—almost boyish in the way it fell forward. It reminded me of a passage from *Forbidden*—one I knew by heart having typed it up for my mother a gazillion times.

"Lady Amelia trembled violently as she sat on the rough-hewn chair in her gamekeeper's cottage. It was all she could do not to run her fingers through Shelby's hair as he kneeled at her feet, his hands cradling her injured foot. 'Tis but a sprain,' Lady Amelia protested but he took no notice and wouldn't let go. Shelby was so close to her that she could smell his manly scent—a mix

of musk, pine and earth that sent her senses reeling. Lady Amelia was filled with confusion. He was not of her class nor even of her kin…"

"What do you think?" said Shawn, snapping me back to reality. "Are you feeling alright?"

"Yes! Fine!" I exclaimed. "Sorry."

He handed me the loupe. "Take a look at that."

I did so and my heart sank. I hadn't even noticed the miniscule line of print running along the bottom of the bag.

"It says Jersey National Bank, St. Helier," said Shawn with a degree of satisfaction. "Yes, this is definitely a bank-issued money bag from the Channel Islands."

"Oh, really? I had no idea." I didn't know what else to say.

"Do you bank in the Channel Islands?"

"No," I said and this was true, I didn't.

"Were the notes inside this bag from the Channel Islands?"

"I honestly don't know," I said. "My mother went on a short trip to Jersey—one of those mini breaks. She probably got the bag when she was there. Like a souvenir?"

Shawn's eyes narrowed and he looked stern. "So the money that was in this blue bag does not belong to you?"

"The money belongs to my mother," I said. "You know. I think I'm wasting your time. I'm sure it will turn up."

"Tell me exactly what Patty said," Shawn demanded.

"She denied it and claimed that anyone could have found the money and discarded the bag in her rubbish."

"That area is very popular with ramblers," said Shawn. "Patty could be right."

Shawn bent down to retrieve a very heavy—judging by a pained groan—incident ledger. He opened it, flicking over to a clean, empty page and picked up his pencil.

I was dismayed. "Do we have to record this?"

"Of course we do," said Shawn. "I will go and speak to Patty but as I mentioned, it really is her word against yours."

"Thank you."

Chuffah-chuffah-chuffah-chuffah.

"I think that's your phone," I said. "The Scarborough Spa Express from Wakefield Westgate to Ardsley Tunnel?"

Shawn cracked a smile. "I'm impressed!"

Of course I'd heard the ringtone before and in this case, once heard—never forgotten.

Shawn fumbled in his pocket, as the chuffing ringtone grew louder, reaching its crescendo with a loud *whoop, whoop, whoop.* Shawn hit the answer button. I wondered if he always waited for the entire sequence to play out.

"D. I. Cropper here," he said and walked into the small room behind the counter. I couldn't catch the conversation.

Moments later Shawn returned. "That was Patty on the phone calling from the Hare & Hounds," he said. "She wants to file a complaint against you for harassment."

"What?" I gasped.

"She said you burst into her house and made all kinds of threats."

"But that's not true," I exclaimed.

Shawn moved to the ledger. He pulled out a stool and sat down.

"You're not writing *that* down, are you?"

"Police procedure." He picked up his pen. "Patty suggested you should talk to Valentine Prince-Avery. Apparently, after he bolted from the pub, he was seen hanging around Hopton's Crest."

"I did consider speaking to him," I said. "But he returned to London." I hesitated again. "I know this sounds strange but I found his ox bone cane in the field next to Cavalier Copse."

Shawn regarded me thoughtfully. "And?"

"I went to the Hare & Hounds to return it to him but he'd

already left. I thought that a bit odd especially as he didn't return his rental car, either. It was left at Hopton's Crest and had to be towed back to Ogwell."

"Of course you must be worried about him." A faint pink flush coated Shawn's cheeks.

"Not really. Just curious."

"That's not what the newspapers say."

I noticed a copy of today's *Daily Post* at the far end of the counter. Clearly, Shawn had seen the photograph, too.

I felt a flash of irritation. "It's an antique cane and Valentine had told me that it belonged to his great-grandfather. I thought he'd want it back."

"Do you want to file a missing persons report?"

"Do *you* think I should?"

Shawn looked directly into my eyes and for a moment, I was startled by the intensity of his gaze. I had to look away. A silence stretched between us as I struggled to think of something intelligent to say.

"When did you last have contact?" Shawn said, all business once more. "Let's start with that."

"I received a text on Tuesday—look, never mind," I said. "I honestly hardly know him. I'd better get back. Mum and I are going to the auction at Chillingford Court—"

"Shawn! You'll never guess what!" Roxy entered the station positively bursting with excitement. "Old Reggie from vehicular recovery has been looking at Joyce's scooter and found—oh, I didn't see you there."

"Thanks Roxy," said Shawn quickly.

That same feeling of foreboding hit me anew. "What's wrong with Joyce's mobility scooter?"

"A lot," Roxy declared. "We're talking suspicious circumstances."

"We'll discuss that in a moment," Shawn said. "Kat was just leaving."

"In what way are they suspicious?" I said sharply.

"Why?" Roxy stared at me. "What do you know?"

"Mr. Prince-Avery left his rental car at Hopton's Crest, apparently," I said. "He would have driven by Bridge Cottage."

Roxy's eyes widened. "*And* he left the meeting in a hurry. Where is he now?"

"He went back to London," I said as I realized exactly what Roxy was implying. "There is something else," I went on. "Ogwell mentioned that one of the SUV's headlights had been broken."

"We'll want to see that," Roxy said. "Bastard must have run Joyce off the road."

"Let's not jump to conclusions," said Shawn.

Much as I didn't want to agree, I had a feeling that Roxy could be right. I'd seen the skid marks on the road myself. It would certainly explain Valentine's hasty disappearance.

"Thanks," said Shawn. "You've been really helpful, Kat. Roxy—we'd better get down to Ogwell and take a look at that car."

I headed back to my Golf feeling very unsettled. If Valentine had hit Joyce's mobility scooter, why would he then go and remove the placards, leave his ox bone cane in the field, and abandon his SUV on Hopton's Crest? Wouldn't he have at least called an ambulance? Pulling out my iPhone I tried to call Valentine one more time.

To my astonishment, this time it connected.

"Hello? Valentine!" I exclaimed. "It's Kat. I've been trying to reach you."

There was a long pause. I knew someone was there. I could hear the sounds of breathing. "Hello?" I said again. But with a click, the phone went dead.

I was completely baffled. What on earth was going on? Why would Valentine answer and then promptly hang up?

Frustrated, I tossed my mobile into my tote bag, switched on the ignition, and set off for Dartmouth.

I'd just had a brilliant idea.

Chapter Eighteen

At Buzz Café in Dartmouth, I ordered my coffee and bought three baguettes for Mum, Alfred, and me for lunch.

After settling into my favorite corner, I jumped on the Internet and started to search.

Valentine Prince-Avery's name popped up in several places and, yes, it would appear he had been listed as a consultant for several projects with the Department for Transport but the last entry was dated in 2012. There was, however, an article on a horrific car accident that he had caused that led to his being banned from driving for four years.

Things started to fall into place.

On Monday night, Valentine had not only been driving illegally, he'd been driving drunk as well. Little wonder he'd not reported Joyce's accident and simply rushed back to London.

I was disgusted. What a coward. I doubted he'd show his face in Little Dipperton again.

I turned my attention to finding out all I could on HS3. A paragraph confirmed that a bid for a high-speed line from Cardiff to London had been submitted to the Department for Transport. There was no mention of an "extended line" to the West Country but that didn't mean anything. When the highly controversial HS2 was first discussed, the long-term goal to have the route continue all the way to Scotland had been a closely guarded secret.

I Googled Operation Bullet and was surprised to see that a website was already in place with StopBullet as a domain name. There was one of my many recycled headshots along with the usual publicity spiel that mentioned *Fakes & Treasures.* A donation link with a barometer showed that fifteen thousand pounds had already been raised. The fund-raiser auction announcement took up half the page. I felt really uncomfortable. As I feared, the whole thing had been positioned as if the entire campaign had been my idea!

I turned my attention to Benedict Scroope but the only reference I could find was connected to the sale of the Thornton Park estate in 1995. Benedict was mentioned as the sole heir and—just as he had told us—had been forced to sell to pay the death duties. Benedict had then "gone abroad," which was exactly what Lavinia and Eric had said.

A quick check of my e-mails confirmed that my appointment with Colleen Fraser, my estate agent, was set for Saturday afternoon at 4 P.M. She'd sent a photograph of the details of the shop close to Spitalfields Market. It was a Grade II listed property that had been built in the early 1800s with large sash windows and plenty of light. The flat above had been "tastefully" renovated with the installation of a new kitchen/dining room on the first floor and two spacious bedrooms and a bathroom on the second. The attic had been extended into an open-plan sunroom with skylights in the roof and a tiny balcony. Colleen had said there were two other interested parties and urged me not to wait too long.

Even though I suspected it was just a ploy to get me to put in a quick offer, I knew I wasn't ready to leave Mum with Alfred quite yet. I stalled and sent back an e-mail saying that I had limited access to e-mail—which was true—and that I would call to discuss the property toward the end of the week. If it was sold in the meantime, so be it.

I swiftly dealt with a dozen or so work-related e-mails including two requests for me to do valuations from collectors who would pay generously for my time and travel. Once again, I was annoyed at being put on the spot for the auction. My plan of returning to London seemed to be fading fast.

I decided against checking my fan club e-mails because there was bound to be something scathing following my appearance in the *Daily Post* with my "new man." I had thought, when I retired from television that all this hoopla would be over.

Finally, out of habit, I checked my mother's "Krystalle Storm" website. There she was, airbrushed to death with her coiffed platinum hair and a string of fake diamonds around her neck. If I didn't know better, I'd never have recognized her in a million years. On Mum's lap was a caramel-colored Pekinese she liked to call Truly Scrumptious—a dog that did not exist. Since Alfred had helped create my mother's physical alter ego and now claimed to be her business manager, I knew I was making the right decision by staying in Devon a little longer.

Mum's home page on her website announced that following Vera Pugsley's unexpected "fatal accident," her husband Eric was determined to "live his beloved Vera's lifelong dream" and visit her favorite author in "honor of Vera's memory."

The three winning short stories were listed. I printed them off for Mum. Maybe she'd get inspired to spice up her current book from other lovers' tales of lust and angst.

Fiona—the barista—brought over a brown bag containing the baguettes and a carafe of coffee. She topped up my cup. "We're so pleased that you've agreed to be the spokesperson for Stop the

Bullet," she said shyly. "Eric was in here yesterday," Fiona went on. "He said the village is really determined to fight it."

"Eric Pugsley comes in here?" I said sharply.

"He uses the Internet," said Fiona. "He's got an eBay account." She pointed to her shoes—black Chanel pumps. "I bought these from him on eBay and Eric delivered them personally. I didn't realize that Eric was selling shoes. I asked him if they fell off the back of a lorry because they're designer but he told me there was nothing wrong with them. Aren't they great?"

"They're very pretty" was all I managed to say.

I was dumbfounded. Eric's wife Vera's collection of designer shoes had rivaled those of Imelda Marcos and Vera had had at least one hundred and fifty pairs. I had seen her collection at their cottage and calculated that Vera had to have spent at least thirty thousand pounds on shoes alone.

Eric selling his dead wife's shoes was a macabre idea but although it was something I could never imagine doing, I wasn't surprised to hear he was.

The moment Fiona was back behind the counter, I signed into my own eBay account. It took me less than a minute to find Eric Pugsley.

"Oh. My. God," I whispered.

It wasn't just Vera's shoes that Eric was selling.

MEET WORLD-FAMOUS AUTHOR KRYSTALLE STORM
AT HER LUXURY HOME IN ITALY
TAKE YOUR LOVED ONE OR A COMPANION ON
AN ALL-EXPENSE-PAID TRIP TO THE AMALFI COAST
TIME TO GO: 2DS 23 HRS
STARTING BID £2000
CURRENT BID: £6,575

I was flabbergasted. Eric was auctioning off Vera's prize!

Mum was going to have a complete meltdown when I told her.

Wearily, I turned off my laptop, gathered up my belongings and the bag of baguettes, and went back to my car to head home.

Twenty minutes later I pulled into the Carriage House court-yard to find my mother waiting for me outside. She was huddled in a winter coat and perched on the top step of the stone mount-ing block.

I opened the window. "You know what they say happens if you sit on a cold surface."

But Mum didn't laugh. She got into the passenger side and slammed the door.

"Did you buy any lunch?" she demanded.

"Yes." I handed her the brown bag.

Mum peered inside. "Why did you buy three?"

"One is for Alfred."

"Sod him."

I took one look at her face and knew something had happened.

"I'll give it to him," I said. "I have to get my catalog anyway."

Inside the Carriage House the mess was indescribable. There was even a hole in the plaster where a chair leg had punctured the cob wall. It was impossible to get to the kitchen without scram-bling over the furniture that now completely blocked the hall. The other option was to walk out of the front door, around the build-ing, and in through the kitchen. Primrose-yellow paint was splat-tered everywhere.

"Here," I said, handing Alfred his baguette. "I'm afraid I can't get to the kitchen to get you a napkin."

"Iris isn't very happy with me," said Alfred. "But I swear on my mother's grave that this will all be cleared up by the time you get back."

"I hope for your sake it is."

I dashed upstairs and got my catalog and returned to the car where Mum was sitting, arms folded with a long face. We drove off, back in the direction I had just come from.

"Did you see it?" Mum said finally. "Did you see all that mess?"

"Alfred said he was going to clear it up. He said, I quote, 'I swear on my mother's grave.'"

"Of course he'd say that. Aunt June didn't have a grave. Her ashes were scattered over Lake Windermere." Mum gave a heavy sigh. "Frank was so tidy. Frank wore overalls and put down dustsheets. Frank took great care with his paintbrushes." Mum bit her lip. "Why isn't Frank here?"

I reached over and squeezed Mum's hand. "I'm sorry. I'm sure Alfred will do just as good a job."

"He's not even using a primer!" she wailed. "Are you sure you can't stay longer? I know it's your life and I don't want to be a bother, but—"

"It's okay, Mum," I said gently. "Of course I'll stay a bit longer. At least until Uncle Alfred finishes painting the sitting room."

"That means you'll move back permanently." She cracked a small smile. "But I don't want him in your bedroom."

"Nor do I!"

"You know what I mean!" Mum said. "It's all coming back to me now. Getting old is a funny thing. I'm remembering odd things about Alfred now."

"It's called selective memory," I said. "And believe me, I have that, too."

"He was always messy when he was a boy," Mum grumbled on. "He's only got a few things in that horrible old duffel bag but somehow, he's just spread himself out."

"We'll just have to force him to take William's flat," I said.

"What happens if William comes back?"

I stifled a groan. "It's highly unlikely but let's cross that bridge when we come to it. Alfred may hate it here and leave of his own accord."

"From your mouth to God's ears."

Mum stared out of the window at the countryside speeding by.

"Mum . . ." I began tentatively. "There's something else I found out today."

"Don't tell me," she muttered. "You've discovered that Alfred is a serial killer."

"Of course not," I said. "It's just . . . when I was in Dartmouth I went on the Internet—"

"If this is about me and my website, I don't want to hear it—"

"Eric is auctioning off his trip to Italy on eBay."

"What!" Mum shrieked. "He's *what*!"

"I just thought you'd like to know. Maybe you can talk to your publisher. After all, they're funding the trip. Surely they can say he can't win the holiday and then sell it."

"How much is he selling it for?" Mum said suddenly.

"The bid is at six thousand seven hundred and fifty pounds and there is still two days to go."

"You bid for it."

"Why don't you bid for it," I retorted. "No one will connect Iris Stanford with Krystalle Storm."

"Don't be ridiculous. My publisher wants photographs of the winner having dinner with me. You have to bid for it. We could build a fake terrace and have Alfred Photoshop us drinking Prosecco."

"And I'll be recognized and everyone will think I'm a Krystalle Storm fanatic."

"You are a fan, aren't you?"

"Fine. If it makes you happy, I'll do it but first, call your publisher and tell him what's happening. Maybe he can prevent it."

"Oh *God*! This is going to kill me! All this worry! I can't write when I'm worried," she wailed again. "The last thing I can think about is tiffin—did you find my money?"

"Of course I didn't," I said. "I would have told you if I had."

"That dog must have buried it somewhere," Mum said with a wail of dismay. "It could be anywhere!"

I decided against telling Mum that I'd found the empty bag in Patty's rubbish. I'd wait and see how Shawn got on with questioning Patty before sending my mother off the ledge.

"As long as we keep it quiet," Mum went on. "I had visions of someone finding all that cash and turning it in to the police."

"Oh," I said weakly. "Would that be a problem?"

"Of course it would be a problem, Katherine!" Mum exclaimed. "The plastic bag alone would prompt all sorts of questions."

"Surely not," I said with a nervous laugh. "Aren't you over-reacting?"

"No, I'm *not* overreacting," said Mum. "I mentioned to Alfred that I needed to draw some money out and he told me I had to wait until he'd talked to his contact. I may as well be back living with your father. I hate asking for permission! It's my money!"

"Yes. Of course it is."

"So. I met with her ladyship this morning and we gave Benedict some money," Mum went on.

"I thought you were going to stall?" I said.

Mum waved her hand dismissively. "He's very optimistic. And I'll tell you something else, I was right about them having a little bit of hanky-panky."

"I don't believe you."

"I was outside in the barn looking for a paint roller to give to

Alfred when they turned up together," said Mum. "They didn't know I was in there. He grabbed her and said, 'I know you still love me' and then she said something which was really infuriating because I couldn't catch it."

"Didn't you ask her to repeat it?"

"Very funny."

"I told you so," said Mum. "Why else did Rupert go to London?" Mum didn't wait for me to reply.

"I asked Lavinia what his lordship thought about our little campaign group and she said she had no idea," my mother continued. "She hasn't spoken to him since Monday. I bet they're already separated and *that's* why Harry was sent off to boarding school."

"Alfred is right when he says you have a vivid imagination."

"Speaking of lovers," said Mum. "Is your Valentine coming to the auction today?"

"I doubt it," I said. "I haven't heard from him since I got that text."

Fortunately the majestic entrance of Chillingford Court came into view and Mum dropped the subject.

"Would you look at that!" she exclaimed.

A huge banner announcing AUCTION TODAY stretched across the matching gatehouses. I felt instantly depressed. Here was the end of yet another beautiful country estate.

Viewing had taken place over the previous weekend. I'd already been twice but Mum had not and I was relieved to see her mood lift as she was taking in her surroundings.

The gravel drive wound through well-manicured borders with banks of rhododendrons, azaleas, and camellias—all dormant now because of the season, but I could imagine how magnificent they would look in bloom.

Parking had been set up in the field behind the stable block and cost ten pounds for admission that I thought was a bit steep. Attendants wearing fluorescent-orange vests and waving batons directed the steady stream of cars into a field that was already rutted with mud and puddles. The place would be a quagmire by the end of the three-day event.

"I've brought the wrong shoes," said Mum with dismay.

"Don't worry. I put our Wellies in the boot this morning."

"I'm sure when you were with *Fakes & Treasures* you had a special parking area and wouldn't be slumming with the peasants."

"Yes. In the good old days."

"Don't forget to take Jazzbo for luck." Mum picked the toy Jerry mouse off my dashboard and dropped him into my tote bag.

The main auction was set up on the front lawn but to get there, we had to cut through the former stable block. People were milling around a variety of tractors and all manner of farmyard machinery that were displayed in the courtyard. There were five cars—one being a Rolls-Royce Silver Shadow—and a stunning barouche.

The nineteenth-century four-wheel carriage was in excellent condition with brasses and lamps burnished to perfection.

"I think I'm going to buy that for Lady Edith," said Mum suddenly. "Do you think she'd like it?"

"I'm sure she would."

"She can keep it in my carriageway." Mum pulled a face. "Don't you feel like we're vultures feeding off the bones of another time? This is all so sad."

"I know."

"I don't want this to happen to Honeychurch."

"Nor do I, Mum."

The largest marquee housed the action where the main lots were going under the hammer. It was already filled to capacity with many people spilling out onto the grass. A jumbo screen ran a live video feed so those outside could watch the bidding inside.

Porters dressed in uniform bearing the name LUXTONS EST. 1850 were transporting furniture, paintings, and carpets from the house on dollies and carrying the smaller items on foot into a covered holding area.

Five smaller tents acted as a payment office, shipping station, communal meeting area, VIP bar, and general refreshments.

I greeted a lot of familiar faces and introduced Mum who soon got caught up in the excitement of it all and kept telling anyone who would listen that the barouche was hers—as was the mink that had belonged to the Countess of Athlone. My friends Leigh and Rachel Gotch, toy specialists from a rival auction house, were there. Leigh was an authority on automatons and even though I knew deep down that Valentine would not be coming in person to bid on George—he could still make a phone bid—it was a shame he wouldn't get the chance to talk to a true expert.

"I thought the auction would be in the house," Mum grumbled.

"Some of the bigger items are." I told her that the fittings and fixtures, fireplaces, doors, and kitchen appliances would stay in situ but they would appear on the viewing screen.

"The porters may bring in a few pieces of wainscot paneling from the library," I went on.

Mum was horrified. "You mean they are stripping the walls as well? That's cannibalism!"

It was true. It happened a lot. William Randolph Hearst, the newspaper magnate, was famously guilty of that crime and to this day there are still millions of pounds' worth of church roofs, exquisite paneling, and centuries-old fireplaces kept in storage in vast warehouses across the USA. Even now, despite rules and regulations having been introduced to protect much of our British heritage, those with enough money could still snap up an entire room that was built in Jacobean times for a cool twenty-five thousand pounds.

"There was a beautiful Tudor house called Agecroft Hall in Lancashire," I said. "When the city of Manchester was developed, the whole house was bought by an American, dismantled, and shipped out to be reerected in Richmond, Virginia."

"What are they going to do with this place?"

"It's going to be converted into flats. The west wing, which you can't really see from here, was partially destroyed in a fire and has already been demolished."

Mum went quiet for a moment. "We can't let this happen to Honeychurch Hall, Kat," she said again. "I can't. I won't!"

I took her hand and squeezed it but she stopped dead and gasped. "Oh! I don't believe it! Why am I not surprised?"

My heart turned right over. David was hurrying toward us with his big smile.

Mum scowled. "Look what the cat dragged in."

Chapter Nineteen

"You're looking better than when we last met, Iris," said David politely.

"Thank you." Mum's voice was cold.

My stomach was filled with butterflies. I'd forgotten how handsome David was dressed in his smart Italian shoes, blazer, and pressed trousers. His hair seemed to have more streaks of gray and it suited him. Why do men get more attractive with age and women just sag?

David gave Mum a brilliant smile. "It must be a relief to have those pins out."

"How would you know?"

"I can only guess." He smiled again. "Although I did break my little finger once. It really hurt."

"Good."

I knew David was trying to be nice but he was wasting his breath. "Well, it's nice to see you—"

"Can I have a quick word?"

Mum opened her mouth to protest but I jumped in quickly, "Of course. Just for a minute."

"Yes. Just for a *minute,*" Mum echoed. "But remember what I told you, Katherine."

Mum walked three yards away and stood watching.

"Still the same old Iris." David grinned. "I wondered if you had been getting my letters and messages?"

"Yes, thank you, and the flowers are lovely." I knew my voice sounded stilted but I was determined not to let David get under my skin.

"I see you are still punishing me." He sounded amused. "What's wrong?"

"I'm surprised to see you here, that's all."

"Why? I knew *you'd* be here. It's not often a Steiff skittle set comes up for sale." David smiled again. "I took a look. It's rare and in very good condition and they all have buttons in their ears."

"I know. I've already viewed them."

"The last set sold in 2011 and fetched eight thousand pounds," David went on. "Your new business must be doing well."

"How is your father-in-law?" I said, changing the subject. "That is *why* you are in Devon, isn't it? Visiting family?"

David's face fell. "Not exactly." He looked over at Mum who continued to stare at us.

"Mother!" I called out. "Can you go and see what the lot number is in the main marquee?"

Mum rolled her eyes and hurried off.

"Thank God." David took my arm and gently led me behind the refreshment tent. "I've missed you, Kat and I know you've missed me."

"I don't—"

"Have dinner with me," he said. "There's something I need to tell you."

"Please don't do this, David."

"Okay. I'll tell you anyway. Hugh passed away three weeks ago," he said. "I've been helping clear the house, sort out family papers, deal with solicitors, and all that kind of thing."

"I'm sorry."

"You know how fond I was of Hugh," said David. "He was more like a father to me, than my own. That's why—"

"How are the children taking it?" I said.

"Sam and Chloe seem okay but Trudy—"

"I don't want to talk about her, thank you."

David unexpectedly took my hand. It came as rather a shock. He had never been one for public displays of affection.

"Don't you see? My divorce will be final any minute. I told you to be patient. I told you it was always about protecting Hugh. I just didn't want to cause him any more suffering when I knew he was dying."

A couple walked by. David abruptly dropped my hand. I fought down a mixture of conflicting emotions. Hope. Love. Anger. Confusion.

"I don't know. I just don't know," I said. "It's been—"

"Of course. You must think about it. I understand." David reached out and stroked my face. I winced.

"You're bruised," he whispered. "What happened? Did Iris beat you?"

"No," I said, stifling a smile. "I fell off a horse."

"You must be the most accident-prone person I know." He leaned over and gently kissed my bruise—again, taking me by surprise. Was it possible to change, after all? I thought of Harry and his boarding school and how little boys are taught to toughen up.

"Did you cry when you first went to boarding school?" I asked.

"What?" David seemed thrown by the question. "Yes. Of course I did. We all did. I was only seven! Why?"

"Harry is struggling, too."

"Who on earth is Harry?"

"Harry!" I said sharply. "You know, the little boy who is obsessed with Biggles. I told you all about him."

David ran his hand through his hair. "I don't want to talk about Harry. I want to talk about you. I've done a lot of soul searching. I don't care about *Fakes & Treasures*. I'm happy about your new antiques shop. If you want to stay in Devon, we'll stay down here. If you want to go to London, we'll live there. My work takes me anywhere in the world. I'll do whatever you want, Kat. Just give me another chance."

"I told you, I don't know."

"I don't expect your mother to ever truly accept me but perhaps she'll come round eventually when she realizes I'm never going to tell a soul."

For a moment I wasn't sure what David was talking about but then I remembered.

Of course! David knew everything about Krystalle Storm and that my mother had been adopted into a traveling boxing emporium as a child. At the time, it had never occurred to me that he and I would actually break up. I'd been so sure our future would be together.

David also knew about the fake robbery, masterminded by the old earl, Edith's husband, that had taken place two decades ago at Honeychurch Hall. Even though David did not have proof about the insurance scam, it wouldn't be difficult for him to find out.

In short, David knew too much.

I felt a surge of panic. "David, you wouldn't say anything, would you?"

He looked at me. "About what?"

"About my mother? About her books? The robbery? Vera and the grotto! Everything!"

David's expression hardened. "You think that little of me after all we've been through?"

"I just want you to give me your word."

David looked around him and then, suddenly, took my arm and pulled me toward him. Before I could resist his lips were on mine and he kissed me hard. I found myself responding, stunned at David doing something so out of character.

I broke away first, slightly out of breath but incredibly confused. Good grief, had I been reading too much Krystalle Storm? Or more to the point, had he? This was the David I remembered when we first met, but not the David of these past few years.

He stood back and his eyes raked over my body. I found myself blushing.

"You see," he gloated. "You still feel the same way. I know you do. Things will be different now. I promise. Oh—!" David exclaimed. "Iris! There you are."

Mum was peering around the corner of the tent and had the grace to look sheepish. "I didn't want you to miss the Steiff skittles," she said lamely.

I wondered how long she had been listening.

"Some people never change," said David ruefully.

"If you're hoping she'll come back to you, David," Mum said as she hurried over. "It's too late."

"Let me handle this, Mother," I exclaimed.

Mum opened her bag and pulled out a copy of the *Daily Post* folded to page three. She thrust it into David's hands. "I'm not sure if you've seen today's newspaper, but this is Kat's new man. So as I said, it's too late."

A smug smile crossed David's features. "I assume you're talking about Valentine Prince-Avery."

"You know him?" I was surprised. But of course David would know him. The antiques circuit was very small and collectors always knew other collectors.

"With a name like that he could be in one of your books, Iris," said David without a trace of humor. "But he'd have to be the villain of the piece, I'm afraid. He's a fake. I know. Because I checked."

"You *checked*." I was furious. "It's none of your business."

"How did you find out?" Mum demanded.

David shrugged. "I have my ways."

"It's over, David," said Mum. "Don't you understand?"

"Mum—stop—"

"In fact, Valentine's meeting Kat here this afternoon so perhaps you can both fight a duel." My mother knew full well that Valentine wasn't coming and that there was no romance between us anyway.

"Pistols at dawn," joked David.

But Mum seemed to have the proverbial bit between her teeth. "Valentine is *besotted* with Kat," she declared. "He's not just a collector, he's some bigwig at the ministry. He's a very important man. He's very close friends with the prime minister."

"Mum, please!" This, of course, was a blatant lie.

"Is he now?" David smiled again but I knew the reference to the ministry would bother him. He was fiercely competitive and had to be the best at everything. David often acted as a consultant for various investigations and I knew he still harbored dreams of being appointed the Minister for Culture.

"It turns out that your Mr. Prince-Avery hasn't worked for the Department for Transport for quite some time," David went on.

"Don't take any notice of him," said Mum. "He's just jealous."

"He was fired in 2012."

"I know." The newspaper article hadn't stated that fact but I had assumed, following the car accident, it would have been the case.

David looked taken aback. "But do you know what *really* happened?"

"No. And I don't care."

"You're just making it up!" said Mum with scorn.

"I'm not."

"Enough!" I shouted. "I don't want to listen to the pair of you bickering anymore." I strode off toward the car park. People turned to stare and I knew David and I had been recognized but I didn't care.

"Kat!" David shouted. "Wait! I'm sorry!"

He caught up with me as I entered the stable yard.

"Really. I'm sorry," he said again. "Hear me out, please."

He took my arm and steered me into an empty stall. Even though the herringbone floor had been swept clean, I could still smell horses and for a moment wished I was twelve years old again when life seemed so simple.

"You've changed," he said. "You're different."

I didn't answer.

"I've blown it, haven't I?" said David quietly. "I'm such a fool. If only Hugh—"

"Don't start that again—"

"When I saw that photograph of you and Prince-Avery together coming out of . . . well . . . I just couldn't stand it. Kat, you didn't— you couldn't . . . ?"

David left the obvious question dangling in the air. "You seriously expect me to answer that?"

"It's true. I'm jealous. And I don't know what to do." For the first time I saw defeat in David's eyes. "I can't force you to come back but if you want me, you know where to find me."

"Just let me be, please."

"But be careful, Kat," said David. "Prince-Avery is dangerous."

With one last look, he left me alone in the stall. I felt incredibly sad. He was right. I had changed. But it had nothing to do with Valentine. I'd finally had enough.

I left the stable and set off down a path that ran around the building. Although I could still hear various announcements being read on the public address system, it was far enough away from the auction. I needed to be alone.

I came upon an enclosure fenced off with chicken wire and post and rail fencing. It was quite a large area peppered with hedgerows and ancient oaks. A wooden information board stood next to a stile stating it was a conservation area. The board had beautiful illustrations of all the wildlife that lived inside its boundaries. There was a list of endangered species that included the grey-long-eared bat and, to my surprise and delight, the *muscardinus avellanarius* ... the hazel dormouse.

In an instant, I'd completely forgotten all about David. I felt a surge of excitement. As a listed endangered species, their existence on Honeychurch land could really help our campaign.

I couldn't wait to tell my mother and hurried back to find her.

"There you are!" she exclaimed. "I feared you'd eloped."

"There's no danger of that," I said. "I have an idea."

As we walked back to the main marquee I told Mum all about the dormice.

"Benedict wanted to find an environmental angle!" she enthused. "Clever you!"

I paid far too much for the Steiff skittle set circa 1908. With a kingpin in his red felt jacket and gold crown and eight other bears standing eleven inches high on turned wooden bases holding poles, they really were adorable. I knew they'd make a great centerpiece for my new shop—wherever it would be.

Valentine's "George" did not do so well. Much to the embarrassment of the auctioneer, the automaton failed to show off his smoking skills and didn't even reach his reserve.

My mother bought a raggedy mink coat for a bargain and wore it back to the car. "It belonged to Princess Alice, Countess of Athlone," said Mum. "She was the last remaining grandchild of Queen Victoria. Did you know she was ninety-seven years, three hundred and thirteen days old when she died and had lived through six reigns?"

"As did her coat, I suspect. Why on earth would you want to buy something like that?"

"I thought I'd branch out into clothing," said Mum. "Anyway, Frank always wanted me to wear mink."

"Mind you don't get paint thrown at you," I said. "There are still a lot of anti-fur activists around here."

"I don't care," said Mum, stroking the fur. "I now know what it feels like to be a princess."

We set off for home. "Well? Do I have to be worried about you going back to Dylan?"

"No," I said. And meant it.

"All that talk about buying a house together in Devon," said Mum.

"We didn't talk about buying a house in Devon today," I exclaimed. "Wait a moment . . . I don't believe it! Did you read one of his letters to me?"

"It was completely by accident," said Mum. "I went into your bedroom to look for my favorite pen—didn't I lend you my favorite pen? Anyway a gust of wind shot through the open window and . . . one of his letters just landed in my hand."

"From inside my bedside table drawer?"

"Exactly! Isn't that odd?"

"Those are private," I cried. "You would never get me going into your personal things." And then I remembered, I had done just that up in the loft.

"I must say Dylan can be quite ardent when he puts his mind to it," said Mum. "Who would have thought he had it in him? At least he's sparked some ideas for my book. I thought I'd rewrite Lady Amelia and Shelby's first kiss and set it in the stable. Originally, they bumped into each other in the woods."

"I know, I typed it."

"But in the stable, it raises the danger. What if he's seen? What if they're caught?"

"How clichéd," I said.

Mum pulled a stack of Post-its from out of her pocket. "Listen to this. *'What are you doing, Shelby?'* " said Mum, mimicking her heroine's breathy voice. *"Lady Amelia's eyes widened with surprise as the young gamekeeper slipped into the empty stable and closed the door behind them. 'I must speak with ye, m'lady.'"* Mum affected a deep country brogue. *"Shelby's breathing was heavy and his eyes glittered with lust. 'Oh, draw no further, sire!' Lady Amelia cried as she shrank into the corner. She began to tremble and, feeling his gaze upon her, slowly raised her eyes to meet his. In an instant, he was beside her, sweeping her into his passionate embrace; his lips crushed hers as she tried to fight him. She felt his hard body pressed against her own. Her head spun as she found herself drowning in a pool of lust until she finally broke free. Shelby stood back. His eyes raked her body. 'You see,' he gloated. 'You feel the way I do. Things will be different now.'"*

I felt my own face grow hot. "You saw David and me in the stable!"

"How could I have done that?" Mum said, feigning innocence. "I can't see through walls."

"You're incorrigible!"

"I know."

Back home, Mum's good humor evaporated the moment we opened the front door and were faced with a wall of displaced furniture.

"I told you so," said Mum.

"Hello?" Alfred's head popped out of the sitting room doorway. His face was speckled in primrose-yellow paint. "Nice mink, Iris. Very posh."

"How are you getting on?" I asked.

"Just need a few more hours." Alfred beamed. "Any chance of a cup of tea? It's gone four."

"You know where the kettle is," said Mum coldly. "I'm going upstairs to work and I don't want to be interrupted."

"Sorry, we had a cup of tea at the auction," I said. "But as Mum says, you know where it is—if you can actually get into the kitchen."

"Oh, you had a visitor," said Alfred. "A Benedict Snoop."

"Scroope, you mean."

"Snoop suits him better," said Alfred. "I caught him trying to climb over the sofa."

"Did he leave a message?"

"Just said he thought he'd left his mobile in the kitchen. He hadn't. I looked."

"I thought you repaired the front door lock," I said.

"Yeah well, the doorjamb's rotten." Alfred shrugged. "Don't tell your mum, though. She'll say I botched it."

And I suspected Mum would be right.

My bedroom was just as cluttered as the hall. I was collecting a lot of stock for my new shop. I thought again about the gatehouses and my nonexistent life in London. Maybe Edith had a point. Could I do it though? Was I ready to take such a big step?

I sank onto the bed. What a tumultuous day.

"Kat!" shouted Uncle Alfred from downstairs. "Someone to see you."

Oh God, I thought. *Who now? Benedict? David? The Queen of England?*

Chapter Twenty

Angela was standing at the bottom of the stairs holding Mrs. Cropper's wicker basket.

"I've been waiting for you to come back," said Angela. "You told me we would go and pick sloes."

Angela was the last person I felt like seeing but then I remembered the mystery photographer from today's *Daily Post*. Getting her alone would give me the perfect opportunity to ask a few questions.

"It'll be dark in an hour or so," I said. "We'd better make it quick."

"I like the new color scheme in the sitting room," said Angela. "Nice and cheerful. Your eye looks much better."

Alfred emerged from the sitting room with Mr. Chips cradled in his arms. The little dog seemed fascinated by Alfred's face— which was fascinating given the amount of paint on it—and seemed unusually placid.

"I didn't even know Mr. Chips was here," I said. "Usually he arrives in a fanfare of barking."

"He says he wants to go out digging," said Alfred.

Angela's eyes widened. "How do you know?"

"Why? Because he told me so, didn't you, boy?"

I was almost tempted to ask if Alfred knew what Mr. Chips had done with Mum's money.

Mr. Chips licked Uncle Alfred's face.

"Aw. He's so cute," said Angela.

"All the ladies tell me that."

"Not you!" Angela hooted with laughter and turned to me. "Your uncle's so funny!"

I wanted to tell her that we're not really related but knew that would bring forth another rash of questions.

"Alfred says he can talk to the animals," said Angela. "He was telling me all about his days in the circus."

"Oh, yes. When he worked with retired circus horses in *Spain*," I said. "Isn't that right, Alfred?"

"That's right. That's what I told her," said Alfred and winked at me.

"So you weren't part of Bushman's boxing emporium?" said Angela.

"Boxing, circuses, fairgrounds ... I'm a wanderer, that's me," Alfred said with a chuckle. "Now ... if you're talking about boxing—"

"Angela!" I said sharply. "We'd better pick those sloes before it gets dark. Come on, Mr. Chips. Bye, Alfred." I practically pushed Angela out the front door.

"Your uncle's a right card," said Angela happily. "What an amazing life he's had."

"You can say that again," I muttered.

We set off in our Wellies and raincoats with Mr. Chips darting off into the undergrowth. We cut through Eric's scrapyard, crossed the old service road, and started down the hill for Cavalier Copse.

"I didn't think you were an animal person," I said. "You don't mind dogs?"

"We had a Jack Russell growing up," said Angela. "His name was Snappy."

"Snappy."

"I know. I chose it. I got him for my eighth birthday. The rescue place warned us that he was aggressive. My mum was always rescuing pets." Angela chattered on. "At one time we had nine cats and three dogs."

"And you were allowed to keep them all at Lindridge?"

"What?" Angela seemed thrown for a moment. "Lindridge? Oh yes. We did. Could. My parents had a cottage on the estate—just like the one I have here."

"Do they still live in North Devon?"

"Yes—do you think the countess should be driving herself?"

"Sorry?" My head was still in North Devon with nine cats and three dogs. "I'm sure she knows what she's doing."

"Only it's quite far to Exeter and it would be awful if she had an accident," said Angela. "I worry about her."

My mother and I had often thought the same thing but I was surprised that Angela seemed to be so concerned.

"Mrs. Cropper tells me that her ladyship goes *twice* a week. Don't you wonder what she must be doing?"

"No."

"Must be important for her to drive herself all that way," Angela persisted. "Maybe it's got something to do with Lord Rupert?"

"I have no idea, Angela," I said.

"I mean, his lordship's been gone for days," Angela went on. "Mrs. Cropper says he and the countess were behind closed doors for hours on Monday afternoon. Then, there was all that drama with Master Harry running away and the next thing we know, his lordship packs a suitcase and drives off. Awful, isn't it? Sending kids away to school."

Angela paused and looked at me, presumably for a comment, but when I didn't respond she plunged on. "And Lady Lavinia is acting all funny as well," she said. "*And* that Benedict Scroope is hanging around a lot. Doesn't seem right. But that's the toffs for you. They're not like us, are they? Marriage for them is a mutually beneficial arrangement. They don't do things for love."

Mutually beneficial arrangement! Another classic Angela phrase.

"I don't believe in gossiping and I do hope you keep your observations to yourself," I said primly. "Lady Edith is very private and I'm sure Lavinia would be upset if she knew you were spreading rumors about her."

"Oh." Angela reddened. "I'm only telling you because you live here. I wouldn't breathe a word to anyone else. I swear."

An uneasy silence fell between us. Angela's prying questions strengthened my suspicions that she was trying to wheedle out personal information to sell a story.

We followed the line of the ditch.

"Why is Eric making all this mess?" said Angela.

"He has to keep the ditches clear so that the land can drain properly."

Mr. Chips turned his attention to the ridge of up-cast soil and had a good roll in the mud.

"I wish we could put him on a lead," she said.

I pointed to the blackthorn hedge that ran along the bottom of the hill that bordered Cavalier Copse. "You see those blue-black berries? Those are sloes."

I turned to take the circuitous route along the boundary.

"Where are you going?"

"That's Coffin Mire and you don't want to walk across there. It's a swamp and you'll sink."

As before, the wind suddenly whipped up, sending the branches swaying and clattering in the breeze. A chill swept through me.

"Mercy me!" Angela grabbed my arm. "Did you feel it? This is where it happened, isn't it? This is where Sir Maurice sent those Roundheads to their deaths—that's what Mrs. Cropper told me—oh!" She stopped dead, her eyes wide with fear. "In the pub . . . do you think . . . I mean . . . when I sat in his chair—?"

"I told you it was just silly superstitious nonsense."

"I don't like it here. I want to go back."

Mr. Chips seemed to pick up Angela's acute anxiety. He kept dashing about in circles, barking.

"Don't be silly," I said sternly. "We're not going anywhere near Coffin Mire. We're going to pick the sloes from the same hedge but on the other side."

We climbed over the stile—with Angela repeatedly looking over her shoulder—and into the bridleway that was flanked by the avenue of ancient oaks. Harry's tree house was just three trees farther down. I made a mental note to return the next day to scout out the dormice nests and take a few photographs.

"Those thorns look sharp," said Angela doubtfully.

"Just be careful."

"So what do you think happened with Joyce?" Angela chattered on. "Mrs. Cropper says that Shawn—that's Detective Inspector Cropper—smells a rat."

"What kind of rat?"

"They think that Valentine was drunk and ran Joyce off the road," said Angela. "And now he's disappeared. That's a sure sign of guilt."

It was my theory, too, but one I wasn't going to share with Angela.

"Why do you suppose Joyce went out in the dark, anyway?" Angela went on. "I mean, Patty had told us that her mother was ill."

"I have no idea and to be honest, I'd rather not talk about it," I said. "I don't want to remember seeing her laying in a stream. It was horrible."

We started picking the berries. I dreaded having to bring up the topic of Trudy's *Star Stalkers* column but I knew I had to. I had been hoping that Angela would have given me an opening gambit, but she seemed too preoccupied with her surroundings. She jumped at every sound and when there was a sudden rush of crackling leaves, she screamed.

"Oh, for heaven's sakes, Angela!" I exclaimed. "It's only Mr. Chips." For someone who claimed to be a country girl, she really was pathetic.

I knew it was now or never. "Have you seen the *Daily Post* today?"

"I don't have time to read the newspapers," Angela said quickly.

"I am going to ask you a question and I want you to be one hundred percent honest with me," I said. "If you are, then we will forget about it, okay?"

"O-kay," she said slowly.

"Have you heard of a column called *Star Stalkers*?"

"Star-what? I told you, I don't read the newspapers," Angela said. "I'm just a housekeeper."

"That's not true, is it?" I said quietly. "You seem to know a lot about my relationship with David Wynne. If you don't read the newspapers, I'm not sure where you would get that information."

"Muriel from the post office told me," said Angela. "It's common knowledge."

"There was a photograph of me on the landing with Valentine Prince-Avery in today's issue," I said. "Did you take that photograph?"

Angela's face turned crimson. "No. I don't understand. Why would I do that? Send to who?"

"Trudy Wynne," I said. "And don't pretend you don't know who she is."

"Wait!" Angela's eyes welled up with tears. "You don't think... you don't think I took that photograph and e-mailed it to the newspaper, do you? How could I? We don't even have the Internet at the Hall."

"You have an iPhone and there are plenty of Internet cafes around. Take Buzz, for example."

"Buzz?" Angela frowned.

"In Dartmouth!" I was getting annoyed. "There are flyers about your Ravishing Romantics book club in there."

"Oh! *Buzz*. Right." Angela went back to picking sloes.

"Well?" I demanded.

"Why don't you ask Eric? He took some of my flyers. I didn't know what he was going to do with them."

I faltered for a moment and felt my own face turn pink. "It's easy for me to check."

"You've seen how hard Mrs. Cropper works me," Angela said hotly. "And besides, when could I have done it? I don't have any time off."

"You were in the pub on Monday night," I pointed out.

"Oh!" She gasped. A lone tear trickled down Angela's cheek. "I wouldn't do that Kat, I really wouldn't. I want to be your friend." She pulled a handkerchief out of her pocket and blew her nose. "I bet it was Patty. She saw you. Or maybe it was someone hiding in one of those alcoves."

"Patty doesn't have a phone let alone access to the Internet," I said. "Nor does she drive a car. You do."

"Mrs. Cropper told me that Patty is always suing people. She even sued the vicar when she tripped in the church," Angela went on. "She'd never turn down a chance to earn one hundred and fifty pounds."

"One hundred and fifty pounds," I said coldly.

Angela looked horrified. "Or whatever the reward is," she gabbled on. "I don't know. Maybe there isn't a reward. I was just guessing—"

"I thought you didn't know anything about *Star Stalkers* let alone the exact amount of the reward for tip-offs!" I was absolutely furious. "I can guarantee when Edith hears about this you will be asked to leave. She's very, *very* particular about trusting her staff. Frankly, I'm disappointed in you, Angela."

Angela didn't answer but I could see she was upset. Her chin was working as she started to viciously pull the fruit from the hedgerow and hurl the berries into the direction of the basket. Most didn't go in.

"Why did you do it?" I said more gently. "Help me understand."

Angela spun round. Her anger was so intense that I stepped back in surprise. "How dare you accuse me!" she screamed. "You just can't help yourself, can you? You're so full of your own self-importance. You're a stuck-up bitch!"

I was speechless and incredibly hurt.

Angela kicked the wicker basket over in a rage. "I don't have to endure another insult from you!" she raged on. "Accusing me of lying! Why pick me? It could have been anyone in the pub that night. What about the reporter from the *Dipperton Deal*? Ask her! Why do you hate me?"

"I don't hate you!"

Angela stormed off back along the bridleway but instead of taking the stile on the right, she climbed over the one on the left.

"You are going the wrong way!" I shouted but Angela disappeared from view followed quickly by Mr. Chips who appeared from nowhere and scampered after her.

I sank onto a log, utterly exhausted. First, I had accused Patty of stealing and she reported me for harassment, and now Angela was insisting she was innocent. What was wrong with me?

Suddenly, a series of screams and frantic barking cut through the air. They became more and more anguished, then, abruptly, stopped altogether. There was a dreadful, eerie silence.

I tore down the path and climbed over the stile into the field.

Fifty yards away, Angela was crouched against the hedge, holding Mr. Chips by his collar. She was surrounded by a semicircle of extremely curious cows who stood just feet away from them both. One cow began to snort and paw the ground.

Angela saw me. "Oh! Help! Help! They're going to kill me!"

Holy crap. Harry's comment about the holidaymaker who was trampled to death hit me afresh.

"Stay still!" I shouted. "Don't move!"

Quickly, Mr. Chips jerked from Angela's grasp and broke free.

"Leave the dog!" I yelled. "He'll be fine!"

Mr. Chips darted around the legs of the herd, nipping at their heels before racing off toward the woods. Now, all the cows were snorting and pawing the ground.

Suddenly, Angela made a wild dash for safety and started running downhill toward me.

I could only watch in horror as the cows picked up the pace and thundered after her. She started screaming again, and kept looking over her shoulder as the large animals moved with surprising speed.

And then Angela tripped. She pitched forward face-first. Time seemed to slow down as the herd, unable to stop in time, trampled over her.

I jumped into the field, dragged off my raincoat, and waved it overhead, shouting, yelling—anything to try to attract their attention.

Distracted, the cows briefly looked my way but then turned back to Angela and stood around her seemingly lifeless body.

I didn't know what to do. I was absolutely terrified. With trembling fingers I pulled out my mobile to call for an ambulance. But of course, there was no signal this far down in the valley.

And then, it was over. The herd just ambled off and started grazing again.

I waited until the cows had moved to the other side of the field and hurried over, praying she had just been knocked unconscious. Angela's right foot lay at an unnatural angle. I suspected it was broken.

I dropped to my knees and gently lifted her wrist, feeling for a pulse. It was there—faint—but there.

"Angela, Angela," I whispered. "Are you okay?"

Slowly, she turned her face toward mine. Blood ran from her mouth. Her eyes flickered and then snapped open with alarm. She uttered a weak cry but it seemed too much of an effort and she fell silent.

"You're safe," I said. "They've gone. I'm going to call for an ambulance but I have to walk to the top of the field to get a signal."

"Don't leave me," she lisped. "My teeth."

It looked like she'd fallen onto a sharp stone that had knocked out her front teeth.

I helped Angela to her feet and put my raincoat around her

shoulders. She couldn't put any weight down on one leg and started to cry again.

It was a long, slow walk up to Hopton's Crest.

Emergency services said it would take at least ten minutes to send an ambulance out. I called Mum but she wasn't picking up the phone—nor was Alfred. I left a message and told her there had been an accident and to bring a blanket.

It was more like twenty minutes before we heard the wail of a siren. Angela hadn't said a word. She just lay flat on my raincoat with her eyes closed.

Swiftly Tony and John Cruickshank set to work, checking Angela's vitals and attending to her foot. An inflatable foot brace was produced and gently wrapped around her damaged limb. She had lost both top teeth but most of the blood had resulted from her biting through her lip.

Both told me they had had some experience with stampeding cows and that Angela was extremely lucky to survive and not been crushed. Angela drifted in and out of consciousness so it was left to me to answer their questions as best I could.

At last, Mum turned up in her red MINI and handed me a hip flask. "Mrs. Cropper's cherry brandy," she said.

"She just ran." I took a sip and felt a little better. "Angela just freaked out and ran, Mum. There was nothing I could do—Oh! I don't believe it!"

A Porsche SUV came into view.

"What's David doing here?" I said.

"I'm so sorry. He turned up just as I was dashing to the car and insisted on coming."

We watched David find a dry place to park, then make a meal out of removing his shoes and donning boots. "I bet he's laying out newspaper in the back of the SUV," said Mum. "You could never rely on him to make a snap decision, could you?"

David strode toward us, his face white with concern. "Thank God it wasn't you, Kat."

"She's in shock," said Mum bluntly. "And not to be taken advantage of."

"I'll be fine," I said. "But I'm not so sure about her."

If it turned out that Angela hadn't sent the photograph to *Star Stalkers,* I would feel that her accident had been my entire fault—despite how ridiculous that sounded.

Tony and John withdrew the gurney from the rear of the ambulance and gently lifted Angela onto it.

David turned to watch and let out a cry of surprise. Pushing me aside he stepped toward the gurney. "Angela? What the hell are you doing here?"

Incredulously, Mum and I looked from one to the other.

"You know her?" I exclaimed.

Angela's eyes snapped open "David! Oh! I can exthplain. I'm tho thorry."

Chapter Twenty-one

David was storming around the kitchen. His face was so purple that I was afraid he'd have a coronary. I had never seen him so angry.

"But I don't understand." I felt incredibly upset and confused. "Why would she do such a thing?"

"I told you," David fumed. "Angela Parks is a close friend of Trudy's."

"Who is Trudy?" Alfred hovered from the doorway, no doubt intrigued by all the raised voices. He was now 75 percent covered in primrose-yellow paint and reminded me of a perky canary.

"Trudy is David's wife," Mum said.

"Ex-wife," snapped David.

"Angela is an actress," said Mum.

"I thought she was the housekeeper?" said Alfred.

"Oh for heaven's sake," said Mum. "She was pretending to be the housekeeper."

"Well. She certainly fooled me," said Alfred.

"She fooled all of us," I said, although from the beginning I had had a funny feeling about her.

"I knew her accent was fake," Mum declared. "She was so over the top as well! All those stories about being a servant. Remember what she said about 'ethnic minorities'? What a little liar."

"Lies, Mother?"

"We're not talking about *me*," said Mum hotly.

"How did Angela get the job here in the first place?" David demanded.

"Apparently, she wrote to Mrs. Cropper and asked for the position," I said. "Angela claimed that she'd grown up on the Lindridge estate in North Devon somewhere. It had burned down so she moved south."

"Lindridge?" David gave a snort of derision. "Yes, it burned down alright but it burned down in 1962."

Mum and I exchanged looks of dismay. "We weren't to know," said Mum. "Anyway, why on earth would she want to work as a housekeeper?"

"I just told you why! She's an actress." David ran his fingers through his hair. It stood up on end. It was the first time I had ever seen him lose his groomed demeanor. "This is all my fault."

"Of course it's your fault," said Mum.

"Why is it his fault?" Alfred chimed in.

"We used to joke about Angela's fascination for *Downton Abbey*," said David with disgust.

I noted the "we" as in David and Trudy.

"Where is *Downton Abbey*?" Alfred asked.

"It's a television show!" Mum cried.

"Angela was determined to get on the show," David went on. "She thought that by working as a real housekeeper, it would give her an advantage."

"Hmm. That makes sense," said Mum. "Renée Zellweger did the same thing for *Bridget Jones's Diary*. She worked for a real publishing house to prepare for the role and no one recognized her."

"No." I said. "I don't believe it was just about that. It's too much of a coincidence. Angela has been spying on me and your wife put her up to it."

"Ex-wife," David said.

"So now you're saying it's Trudy's fault," said Mum. "Typical."

"Who is Trudy, again?" Alfred asked.

"I don't care whose fault it is," I said coldly. "I think you should leave, David."

David's jaw dropped in surprise. "Don't be silly."

"No one calls my niece silly."

"Niece?" David regarded Alfred with confusion. "Who are you?"

"Please! No more," I cried. "Just go."

David stepped toward me. "Kat, please listen. I'm just—"

"You heard what she said." Alfred may be small and currently bright yellow but I could tell he was spoiling for a fight. Alfred raised his fists.

Startled, David took a step back. "Of course!" He snapped his fingers. "You worked in the fairground. No. Something to do with a traveling boxing emporium?" A strange expression crossed David's features. "I think I know what this is about."

"What. Exactly?" I demanded.

"I'll handle it," said David grimly. "I'll talk to Trudy."

"What should we do about Angela?" said Mum. "Tell the police?"

"Tell them what?" I said. "She's in hospital. Isn't that punishment enough—anyway, I don't care. All this does is validate my decision."

"Yes, yes, so you keep saying," said David, exasperated. "I've already told you that ship has sailed. They've found a new host anyway."

"I'm not talking about *Fakes & Treasures*. I'm talking about you and me." I was close to tears. "It's humiliating to say nothing of how horrible it was, just watching Angela being trampled on—"

"Let's all have a nice gin and tonic—"

"I don't want a gin and tonic, Mother!"

"Kat, my divorce—"

"Didn't you hear what she said, Dylan?" Alfred chimed in. "She doesn't want you—"

"That's right," said Mum. "She's moved on."

"Which is why I came by," said David. "My friend at the ministry called me about Prince-Avery."

"Who is Prince—?"

"Shut up, Alfred," we three chorused.

"Is he the one with the walking cane?" Alfred ventured gingerly.

"There was a scandal that was hushed up," David went on.

"I'm not interested," I said.

"Your friend is rather too fond of the bottle. He was acting as a consultant on a project—the name of which I agreed not to reveal—when he caused a fatal car accident. He went to prison for a year."

"So I heard." But I hadn't known about the prison sentence.

"A *year*?" Alfred scoffed. "That's nothing!"

"Prison?" Mum exclaimed. "Good God!"

"And there's something else," David said. "I have a contact with the UK Border Agency—"

"You're so well connected, Dylan." Mum's voice dripped with sarcasm.

"Todd Gray, I know," I said impatiently. "We've had dinner with him lots of times."

"Todd has access to a vast database of people who enter and leave the United Kingdom."

Mum gasped. "Everyone? Every time?" She looked at Alfred and I caught him giving her a reassuring nod. "Even ferry crossings to Jersey?"

"What? Why Jersey?" David seemed thrown by the question.

"No reason," said Mum quickly.

"As part of my job as an international art investigator, the information the UK Border Agency can provide is highly valuable."

David's tone had grown more self-assured and pompous—he actually reminded me of Shawn. It was a side of David I never liked.

"What kind of information?" Alfred suddenly didn't seem so confident. "Aren't they just looking for terrorists?"

"Yes. Terrorists. Thieves. Fraudulent transactions—yes, yes, yes! Let me finish!" David rolled his eyes at me and went on. "The point is, Valentine Prince-Avery has been spending the last several months in East Africa. So I don't see how he can be acting as a consultant on this new high-speed train from a different continent."

"Actually, you're wrong. He's been visiting the Zanzibar Archipelago. Pemba Island to be exact," I said. "He's entitled to a holiday, isn't he?"

To say that the wind was knocked out of David's sails was putting it mildly. "You *knew*?"

"Valentine told you?" Mum said, surprised.

He hadn't but I couldn't stand David's smugness any longer. "But thanks for clarifying things for me, David. You just can't stand to lose, can you? It is over between you and me. It has been for a long time."

Shock registered on David's face. He looked to Mum—who

stood arms akimbo and was visibly gloating—and Alfred, who brought up his fists, again.

"Mum, Alfred—please. Just leave us for a minute."

They filed out of the kitchen.

"You're serious, aren't you?" said David.

"Yes. Yes, I am." And I was.

It was finished.

David bit his lip. He stood awkwardly just staring at me. "Right. Okay." He extended his hand. "No hard feelings?"

After a moment, I took it. "None."

David thrust his shoulders back and headed for the kitchen door that opened into the field behind. I wanted to warn him that it was muddy but no words came out of my mouth.

He didn't look back.

A split second later, Mum and Alfred were back in the kitchen. I knew they had been eavesdropping but I was too tired to argue anymore. I sank into a chair and put my head in my hands.

"Alfred's worried about the bank in Jersey," said Mum. "Will David cause us any trouble now that you've really ended it, Kat?"

"I told Iris not to worry," said Alfred. "As long as she did what I told her, she'll be fine."

"Of course! I wouldn't dream of trying to touch my own money without your permission, Alfred," said Mum. "Would I, Kat?"

"Leave me out of this, please."

"If you need more money, you let me handle it. You heard what Dylan said, there's a record of people who come in and out of the country."

"But surely, if you're a British citizen you don't need a passport," said Mum. "So if you don't show a passport, then how would they know you had come in or out of the country? What do you think, Kat?"

"I have no idea," I said again.

"Oh God!" she cried. "Would David say anything about me being Krystalle Storm?"

"Let's hope not." David's reaction this evening had made me realize that despite all his faults and his messy marriage and ugly divorce, he wouldn't do anything to hurt me. Maybe he really had loved me as much as he was capable of loving anyone.

"That's all right then." Mum poured herself a gin and tonic and downed it in one go.

"I'll drink to that! And I would if I had one," said Uncle Alfred.

"You can't have one until you've finished painting that front room—wait! This isn't about you. This is about me!" Mum's eyes widened. "Of course! This is all about me!"

"It's always about you, Mother."

"If Angela was Trudy Wynne's friend, that explains why she was asking all those questions about Krystalle Storm! The little minx! All that Ravishing Romantics Book Club and the rumors that I live here."

"Which you do," I reminded her.

"Remember when Vera sent those e-mails to Trudy Wynne just before she died?"

"Claiming to know who Krystalle Storm really was," I said. "Yes."

"Um. Can I ask…?" Alfred raised his hand gingerly. "Who is Vera?"

"No!" Mum and I chorused.

"Trudy Wynne must still be pursuing that lead!"

The phone rang in the kitchen and we all looked at each other. "Alfred, you answer it," said Mum.

"The Stanford residence," said Alfred. He jumped to attention.

"Yes, m'lady, I *am* Alfred Bushman." As he listened, his face was wreathed in smiles. "Yes, very much so, m'lady. I can start tomorrow. Yes. She's right here." He offered me the phone. "For you. It's the dowager countess."

I braced myself for questions about Angela's accident with the cows but instead she got straight to the point. "Is Mr. Chips with you?"

My stomach turned right over. In all the excitement following the cow incident, I had completely forgotten about Edith's little dog. I felt paralyzed and couldn't think of a thing to say.

Alfred swiftly stepped up and whispered in my ear, "Tell her you'll bring Mr. Chips back in a couple of hours."

I repeated what Alfred had said and hung up. "Why did you say that?" I said, wondering if my day could get any worse. "How did you know what she was asking me anyway?"

He tapped his forehead. "I've got gifts, luv. He's off hunting. We'll find him—but he's in trouble."

As if on cue, there was a powerful crack of lightning that illuminated the kitchen in phosphorescent light. A deep rumble began to sound from the bowels of the earth, culminating in a deafening boom of thunder. Rain hammered down on the roof, pelting the windowpanes.

"We'd best get to it quickly," said Alfred. "Where did you see Mr. Chips last?"

"Cavalier Copse," I said.

"We'll all go," said Mum. "Three pairs of eyes are better than one."

"And bring a couple of towels," Uncle Alfred added. "We may need them."

Chapter Twenty-two

Dressed in heavy raincoats and bearing flashlights, a shovel, some rope, and an old towel in a plastic carrier bag, we set off across the fields in a ferocious downpour.

Angela's brush with death continued to play on my mind. "I had no idea that cows could move so fast," I told Alfred for what had to be the umpteenth time. "The moment Mr. Chips broke for cover, she just made a run for it."

"Cows don't like dogs nipping at their heels," said Alfred. "But it was clever of the girl to play dead."

"She fainted. I thought she *was* dead."

It was heavy going but when we reached Hopton's Crest, the rain abruptly stopped and a pale three-quarter moon emerged from behind the clouds. A peculiar mist drifted along the track, creating odd shapes among the scrub.

"Did you see that?" Mum clutched my arm. "That shape? Moving?"

"It's just a hedge," I said but the truth was, I thought I'd seen something move, too. "It's a trick of the light—a mix of moonbeams dancing with the mist that creates an illusion."

But Mum wasn't convinced. "Alfred? Did you see that?"

Alfred waved us to keep quiet. "Stop all your chattering for just one minute."

He climbed over the stile and stood at the top of the field with his arms by his side, gazing up at the sky.

"Mum—"

"Shh! He's channeling," she whispered.

After a couple of minutes, Alfred turned and beckoned for us to join him. He headed for the boundary that hugged the hedge and ran downhill all the way to the bottom of the field.

An owl hooted; foxes cried but there was no sound of an answering bark to our repeated calls to Mr. Chips.

Alfred pointed his flashlight at a series of round holes peppered in the banks underneath the hedge.

"Rabbit holes and badger setts," he said. "But he's not here."

Minutes later we drew close to Coffin Mire.

"You don't want to go anywhere near there, Alfred," said Mum. "It's a swamp."

Alfred gingerly took a few steps forward and stopped. Again, he put his hand up and we fell quiet.

"Please don't tell me Mr. Chips fell in," I whispered.

"No, he's not in there but—" Alfred gasped. "Jesus, have mercy."

"What? What is it?" Mum said sharply. "What have you seen?"

Alfred turned away. "Later. Not now. Turn off the flashlights and be quiet. I need to concentrate."

The wind rushed through the trees with the clatter and chill that I experienced every time I came this way. Mum grabbed my arm again. "Can you feel it?"

"Don't be silly," I said but the hairs stood up on the back of my neck. There was a presence, I was sure of it, too.

"What's that light over there?" Mum whispered urgently. "Do you see it?"

She pointed in the opposite direction away from Cavalier Copse toward a bank of trees where a yellow light shone through in the distance.

"That's Bridge Cottage," I whispered back.

"Yes, yes, of course," Mum muttered. "I got all discombobulated."

"Be quiet, Iris," Alfred hissed.

We did as we were told and stood waiting.

Another rush of icy cold air swirled around us.

"Aye, the soldiers are here, they're all here, wandering around, lost and confused," said Alfred. "Can you hear the chink of armor? The sound of horse hooves?"

"No," I said. And I didn't want to.

Suddenly, Alfred turned his flashlight back on. "We're coming, little fella. Mr. Chips is in the bank, yonder."

Most Devon hedges are built on top of earthen banks and like most, too, were home to many woodland creatures.

Alfred made a beeline for the third hole to the far side of the stile.

It looked too small for even a rabbit to go down, let alone a Jack Russell terrier. "Surely, he can't be in there!"

Alfred put his shovel aside and knelt down at the entrance. "Mr. Chips?" he said gently. "You in there, boy?"

Far, far belowground came a faint whimper.

"Thank God!" I exclaimed.

"He's there!" Mum said happily. "But how can we get him out?"

"All right, my boy, we're here now."

Mr. Chips's whimpers turned into anguished whining.

Alfred set to with the shovel, digging out the hole as Mum and I held our flashlights so he could see what he was doing.

"Keep the light at an angle," he said. "Don't want to frighten the little bugger any more than he already is."

"Told you he could talk to the animals," said Mum proudly.

"We're lucky there has been so much rain," said Alfred. "The earth is soft. We'll soon get him out."

Alfred suddenly tossed the shovel down, lay on his stomach, and thrust his hand far into the hole right up to his armpit.

There was a yelp of surprise.

"He's got something in his mouth," muttered Alfred.

"He's got my money!" Mum exclaimed.

"I can't pull him. Drop it, boy. Come on! Drop it."

There was a series of growls. "He wants to play," I said, relieved. "He's okay."

"Got it." Alfred withdrew his arm and tossed an object aside, reaching back in. "Bingo!" he cried as he dragged Mr. Chips out by the scruff of his neck.

"He stinks!" Mum exclaimed.

And he did. Mr. Chips was coated in slick mud and what suspiciously looked like animal poop.

"Wrap him in a towel, Kat," Alfred ordered. "Don't want him to catch his death."

But Mr. Chips slithered out of my grasp, barked a few times, and trotted back to the edge of Coffin Mire.

"What's he doing?" I exclaimed.

"He wants to show us something," said Alfred grimly.

Mum found the object that Alfred had tossed aside. "What on earth is this?" She picked it up gingerly and held up her flashlight. "Good heavens! It's a man's shoe. Look, Kat."

She handed it to Alfred who dropped it with a cry of alarm. "Jesus have mercy," he said again.

"What's wrong?" I turned to Mum. "What can he see?"

Mr. Chips tore across the grass barking, then tore back again to the edge of the mire.

"He wants us to follow him," said Alfred. "I'm coming, boy."

Mum picked up the shoe again and shone her flashlight over it. "It's looks expensive. Not your average farmer's boot."

"Oh God." I felt sick. A peculiar foreboding swept over me. I'd found Valentine's walking cane in this field. Could that shoe possibly belong to him, too?

But no, that couldn't be right. We'd been sharing text messages.

"The other shoe is over here!" Alfred called out and waved us over with his shovel.

Alfred pointed his flashlight to a matching shoe partially submerged in a black inky pool of water, yards away from firm ground.

"Do you think someone drowned in there?" said Mum.

I'd initially thought the same but it wasn't logical. "No, Mum. Of course they haven't. Look, that shoe is on top of the mire and since Mr. Chips was able to get the other one, it couldn't have been far in. If someone has drowned, those shoes would be on that person's feet. Right?"

"Yes. You're right. Of course you're right. We all know this place is haunted. I just got a bit spooked. Perhaps it's Sir Maurice playing a trick," she said more cheerfully.

Suddenly the wind blew up again and the moaning seemed even louder this time. Alfred put down his shovel, removed his cap, and raised both arms to the sky again. The three-quarter moon settled directly overhead casting down a pyramid of light. I felt a rush of gooseflesh.

"Oh aye, we hear you, my lads," said Alfred. "We hear you."

"Oh. My. God. Alfred is going to raise the dead," Mum exclaimed.

"Youngsters, that's all they were," Alfred went on. "Fooled by a Honeychurch Cavalier. But wait—Oh, Jesus."

He stepped back abruptly and snapped on his flashlight. "He's here."

"Who!"

Mum grabbed my arm and gave a cry of shock. "It's over there! Shine it over there, Alfred! Quickly, shine it over there!"

Alfred slowly panned the area and Mum and I gasped in utter horror.

"You'd best call out the police," said Alfred grimly.

There, sticking out of the bog, was a hand.

Chapter Twenty-three

I spent a terrible night dreaming of Roundheads wearing Italian shoes and David flailing around in the mire, drowning a horrible death. Alfred's reaction to the walking cane now seemed heavy with meaning.

Alfred couldn't have slept much that night, either, because when I came downstairs, the hallway was completely clear of furniture. A quick peep into the sitting room confirmed my suspicion. He had just shoved everything back in there.

Mum and Alfred were in the kitchen eating breakfast. To say you could cut the atmosphere with the proverbial knife was putting it mildly. Alfred looked nervous and kept knocking his spoon off his saucer and the way my mother was biting into her toast made it clear that the two must have had "words."

"Any news from the police?" I said.

"I left a message," said Mum. "You know the station doesn't open until nine."

"It's an emergency, Mother!"

"I told Iris to call nine-nine-nine," said Alfred. "But she wouldn't hear of it."

"And I told you, this isn't London. Let's let our local plod handle it," she went on. "The dowager countess hates any kind of scandal and we don't want the paparazzi hearing about it and the place crawling with reporters. You seem to forget that Kat is a celebrity."

"Thanks, Mum," I said. "But in this case I agree with Alfred."

Mum rolled her eyes. "What's the rush? Whoever is in there can't get any more dead, can they?"

"Then let that be on your conscience, not mine." Alfred got up from the table and strode out of the kitchen. We heard the front door slam.

"What's happened?" I demanded. "Have you two had a sibling tiff?"

"Have you seen the sitting room?" said Mum. "Alfred just threw everything back. The paint isn't even dry in places."

"He promised to put the furniture back. And he did."

"Since when did you change sides?"

"When Alfred rescued Mr. Chips." I regarded Mum with curiosity. "What's really going on?"

"Don't say I told you so but—" She took a deep breath, "I think you're right. I can't live in that mess."

"I thought you didn't mind," I said, exasperated.

"Frank's mess was neater."

The wall phone chirruped and Mum snatched it up. "Good morning. Good. Yes." She listened, nodding. "A shoe. Yes. A hand. That's right, I told you all this on the answering machine. No. Isn't that your job?"

Mum put the phone down. "That was Shawn. As if I would make it up! He's on his way over right now."

My stomach was churning. "Oh, Mum. Who do you think it can be? What if it's Valentine? Maybe he fell in when he went to pick up the placards?"

"What are you talking about?" said Mum.

I summarized the conversation I'd had at Ogwell Car Hire and told Mum the placards had been found in the back of Valentine's SUV.

"Why would Valentine pick them up when he put them there in the first place?" she pointed out.

"I have no idea," I said. "But he really seemed upset on Monday evening. He was drinking heavily, too. The next morning, when I went out riding with Edith, the placards had gone. I *knew* something was wrong when I found his walking cane in that field."

"Let me see…"

Mum grabbed a piece of paper and a pencil. She drew a line to divide the sheet in half. "This is the bridleway and the bank of oak trees where Harry has his tree house." She drew a square. "This is the five-bar gate that opens into the bridleway." Then she drew a circle below the line and to the far left. "That's Coffin Mire." She drew an oval to represent Cavalier Copse in the center of the page just under the bridleway. "And this," Mum drew elaborate curlicues all around the edge of the paper, "is the boundary hedge and ditch."

A further ten crosses marked the locations of the signs that ran below and above the horizontal bridleway. On the far right, Mum drew a square—Bridge Cottage—and scribbled a cloud of undergrowth around it.

"Where did you find Valentine's walking cane?" she asked.

I picked up the pencil and made an X. "Between the five-bar gate and Coffin Mire."

"So it wasn't next to the mire at all."

"But… there is something else." Nausea hit me again as I remembered Joyce lying facedown in the water.

"What have you done, now?" said Mum.

"Not me, Valentine." I explained that Shawn and Roxy believed that Valentine could have been involved in Joyce's death.

"You mean he mowed her down and ran off? It was a hit-and-run?"

"No one knows where he is," I said. "He's disappeared."

"You heard from Valentine on Tuesday," said Mum. "Remember?"

"Yes."

"And Joyce died on Monday night—"

"I think that's why he called me," I said, recalling his urgent message. "Perhaps he was going to tell me about Joyce."

"I wish you'd told me all this," Mum grumbled. "Why am I always the last to know?"

"Do you think that Valentine may have gone back to the field the following day and bumped into Patty? Perhaps there was a disagreement."

"That would assume that Patty knew that Valentine had been involved in her mother's accident."

"You're right," I said. "And we don't know that." I thought again. "Angela told me that Patty is famous for lawsuits and even sued the vicar. What if—?"

"No, I don't like that theory." Mum frowned then gave a yelp of excitement. "I know! What if Valentine saw Sir Maurice at Hopton's Crest! Sir Maurice was so angry about this railway line that he led Valentine to his doom in Coffin Mire."

"Now you're being silly," I said.

"Of course, it could be one of those old Roundheads lying there."

"From over three hundred and fifty years ago?" I said. "I doubt it."

"Look at Lindow Man." Mum warmed to her theme. "He fell

into a peat bog in two B.C. or something and, voilà, centuries later he's discovered! Perfectly preserved."

"But in this case, the hand was sticking out," I said. "And if it had been one of those Roundheads, the hand would have been skeletal." I shuddered with disgust. "Can we talk about something else?"

"No. Seriously. It could be a Roundhead. With all the rain we've been having, the water levels must have shifted. The hand could have just popped up yesterday."

"Well, I hope you're right—but it doesn't explain the fancy shoe. Where did you put it?"

"In that piece of newspaper." Mum gestured to a package wrapped in Wednesday's edition of the *Daily Post* on the floor next to the oak dresser. I could see the photograph of my face on the outside. "Someone has big feet. It's a size eleven."

Lavinia burst into the kitchen. "Frightfully sorry to interrupt—"

"You've heard about the hand already?" said Mum.

"Hand? What do you mean?"

"Nothing," said Mum. "Tea?"

Lavinia shook her head. Dressed in her usual riding attire with her blond hair clamped under a hairnet, she looked even plainer than usual.

"Something terrible has happened," she said.

My stomach flipped over. "Has Harry run away again?"

"What?" Lavinia looked startled. "Oh. No. Why? Of course he hasn't. No, it's—" She seemed jittery. "If it's not too much of an inconvenience—"

"Do you want to talk privately, Lavinia?" Mum said, pointedly dropping the title. "Kat was just going out, weren't you?"

"Mum, the police will be here any minute."

"The police?" Lavinia's eyes widened. "We don't need the police!"

"We do need the police," I said, gesturing to Mum to say something but she just waved me away.

"This is important, dear," said Mum. "Just give us a moment."

"More important than someone laying dead in a bog?" I exclaimed.

"What is she talking about?" Lavinia cried. "Who is dead? Where?"

"In Coffin Mire," said Mum.

"Oh. *That*. The mire is riddled with bodies. Rupert found one last year."

"See!" Mum shot me a smug look. "It *could* just be a Roundhead."

Lavinia waited for me to leave the kitchen. As I pulled the door closed I overheard her say, "Benedict has gone."

"Gone?" Mum cried. "Gone where?"

"I don't know. He just disappeared yesterday."

"Oh dear."

My stomach lurched again. Benedict had disappeared. This was a conversation I was not going to miss.

In the corridor next to the kitchen was a walk-in cupboard where I could eavesdrop through the flimsy wall. I'd discovered this quite by accident one day when the plumbers were called about a blocked pipe and I had been clearing it out.

"Have you tried to phone him?" I heard Mum say.

"Of course I have," said Lavinia. "His phone must be switched off."

"Oh dear."

"It's too maddening for words." I heard the scraping of chairs and what sounded like a peculiar mewing noise. I wondered if Lavinia was crying.

"Have a cigarette," said Mum.

"I don't smoke."

"Nor do I."

There was a pause—presumably they were both lighting up.

"I'll open a window. Kat can be such a tyrant. She hates me smoking."

"So does Rupert. Oh, Iris! I'm afraid I've done a frightful thing."

"Let's try to stay calm and not panic," said Mum. "When did you speak to Benedict last?"

"Yesterday."

"What time?"

"Just before lunch. He seemed very agitated."

"Oh dear."

"Why? Why do you keep saying, 'oh dear'?"

I pressed my ear against the wood. I hoped Mum was right about her Roundhead theory but if not, perhaps it wasn't Valentine laying there after all. Perhaps it was Benedict.

"Maybe Benedict has done a runner," said Mum.

"A runner? Why would he do that?"

"He's run off with all our money."

"Has he? Good grief! How do you know?"

"He hasn't? I thought . . . never mind."

"No. This has got nothing to do with money," Lavinia went on. "This is far more serious."

"How can it be more serious than money?"

"Benedict gave me an ultimatum otherwise he threatened to tell Rupert everything."

"An ultimatum? What kind of everything?" I could detect the change of tone in my mother's voice and suspected she was whipping out her Post-its. "What exactly did Benedict say to you?"

"I knew you would understand. You write about love and relationships in your wonderful books and . . . well."

"I *am* a bit of a connoisseur when it comes to that sort of thing," Mum said. "All I can tell you is to follow your heart."

"Don't be ridiculous!" Lavinia exclaimed. "Our sort never follows our heart. We have our duty to perform and besides, I love Rupert. I love him desperately."

There was a silence. I could almost hear Mum's brain trying to process this new piece of information. I knew I'd been right about Lavinia being devoted to Rupert.

"So...since you are *not* having an affair with Benedict," said Mum. "What hold can he possibly have over you?"

"I suppose I was angry with Rupert for going off to London without a single explanation," Lavinia said. "We had the most awful fight."

"Over Benedict?"

"No! Not over Benedict! Why would we argue over Benedict? It happened years ago."

"So you've got nothing to worry about."

"Of *course* I've got something to worry about, Iris." Lavinia was getting hysterical. "I made a terrible mistake and I apologized."

"So you *did* have a fling with Benedict?"

My head was beginning to spin trying to keep up.

"It was more than a fling."

There was a distinct pause. I suspected Mum was worried about saying the wrong thing. "Why don't you tell me what happened so you can get it off your chest?" she said finally.

"Are you sure it won't bore you?"

"Of course not. You can trust me to be discreet and not tell a soul."

"Promise?"

"Cross my heart and hope to die."

I checked my watch. It was nine-fifteen. The police would be here at any moment. Mum and I had seen a hand in the mire and here she was discussing Lavinia's love affair—or whatever they wanted to call it.

"I met Benedict again after Rupert married that frightful servant girl, Kelly," said Lavinia.

"Ah yes. They eloped during your New Year's Eve party—"

"Oh. You knew about that?"

"Not all the details," said Mum quickly. "I'm just trying to get the backstory straight."

"Benedict was a school chum of my brother Piers so I've known him since I was five," Lavinia went on. "*Hopeless* with money. When Thornton Park sold he invested what was left—which was quite substantial I must say—in all sorts of ridiculous schemes. He even bought a luxury hotel on Pemba Island."

I stifled a gasp. *Pemba Island?* There couldn't be two islands of the same name. Valentine even had this key fob stamped Pemba Island. He'd also suggested that Laurel, from Ogwell Car Hire, should stop there on her birthday trip to Africa.

This was no coincidence. Something was going on.

"Where is Pemba Island?" said Mum.

"It's part of the Zanzibar Archipelago," Lavinia said. "Piers took me there on hols. Thought it would do me good to get away from the scandal. I suppose Benedict was a rebound of sorts—"

"He was a transitory object."

"Yes! Exactly!"

"But he wanted more?" Mum ventured.

"Yes! *Exactly!*" Lavinia said. "But I *was* frightfully fond of him. If Rupert hadn't been around—"

"But Rupert *was* around," said Mum. "Did you and Benedict stay in touch after that?"

"No, of course not. I hadn't seen Benedict for yonks," said

Lavinia. "He suddenly called me out of the blue to tell me he was back in the country—"

"And wanted to see you again?"

"Things hadn't gone well abroad and he wanted to make a fresh start. He'd formed an environmental consultancy firm and heard about Operation Bullet." Lavinia blew her nose. "He wanted to help. He didn't want Honeychurch to go the same way as Thornton Park."

"Only Thornton Park became a retirement community," Mum pointed out.

"Oh. That's true." Lavinia paused—probably to take another drag on her cigarette. "Benedict asked if I was happy—and of course I *am* happy but Rupert isn't the easiest person to live with."

"Well he *has* got a bit of a wandering eye," said Mum with her usual tact.

"Oh—well, yes, there is that." Lavinia sighed. "I should never have agreed to see Benedict again."

"You started an affair."

"No!" Lavinia sounded shocked. "Nothing like that."

"Affairs don't have to be physical things, Lavinia," said Mum. "Sometimes a mental affair, a meeting of the minds, a mutual love of similar things, is far more dangerous than a quick romp in the hay."

There was another odd gulping noise. "Benedict told me that when he saw me again it felt as if someone had taken his heart and squeezed it so hard he couldn't breathe. He said—and this is frightfully embarrassing—that his head actually began to spin because he'd forgotten how beautiful I was. Or something. He said he thought he had gotten over me but realized he hadn't. He told me he couldn't live without me."

"That's lovely," said Mum. "Can you repeat all that please? But slowly, dear."

Lavinia did—several times, in fact. Clearly she didn't realize that Benedict's protestations of love would end up immortalized on paper.

"Oh, I knew you'd understand," Lavinia said.

"So what hold can he have over you now? Is Rupert a jealous, violent man?"

I had begun to wonder the same thing myself.

"What do you mean?"

"Do you think his lordship might have harmed Benedict in any way?" Mum went on. "Perhaps he found out?"

"No, he couldn't have! I'm *ab-so-lute-ly* positive he doesn't know. We've been frightfully careful. And besides, Rupert is in London. No—" She gave a heavy sigh. "I'm just worried. What if Benedict does something silly?"

"Like what?"

"Well. He did threaten to kill himself—"

"Kill himself?" said Mum sharply.

"Yes! He tried before. When I left Pemba—"

"How? Think carefully now," said Mum. "Pills? Drink? A gun to the head … throwing himself into a swamp?"

"Oh! I can't … I don't want to—"

"Because it's strange that you should mention suicide," Mum said. "There was a pair of shoes found at the scene."

"Mother!" I yelled at the top of my lungs as I tore out of the cupboard.

"Would you happen to know what size shoe your—"

"Don't! Stop!" I yelled as I burst into the kitchen to find Mum already unwrapping the package on the table.

But I was too late.

Chapter Twenty-four

"Mr. Chips found this shoe down at Coffin Mire," said Mum.

"Mum!" I protested again. "Please don't!"

Lavinia sprung to her feet, eyes wide and hands flapping in horror. "Oh! Oh!"

"We couldn't reach the other shoe and—"

Lavinia crashed to the floor in a dead faint.

"Good heavens. And she didn't even look at it." Mum looked stunned. "Were you eavesdropping?"

We helped Lavinia to her feet and sat her on the kitchen chair. Mum held Lavinia's head down between her knees until she began to struggle. She handed her the hip flask from the oak dresser. "Drink up, dear," said Mum. "Mrs. Cropper's cherry brandy will make you feel better."

Lavinia took a deep draft. "Benedict's dead, isn't he?" she whispered. "He threw himself into Coffin Mire because he loved me. He drowned...because he loved me." Lavinia thrust her hand into her mouth and suppressed a whimper.

"We don't know that for sure." I glared at Mum. "First of all, Benedict would hardly have removed his shoes—"

"Of course he would," said Mum bluntly. "He'd want Lavinia

to know that she drove him to suicide. He'd deliberately want her to find his shoes."

Lavinia gave another cry of dismay. "Oh God! Must avoid a scandal. Mustn't let Edith know. Or Rupert! Oh God, he'll find out and divorce me."

"Let's not panic quite yet," I said calmly. "You said you spoke to Benedict yesterday?"

Lavinia nodded. "We call each other all the time—first thing every morning and every night but—" She wiped a tear away from her eye. "I haven't heard from him since yesterday at a quarter to one."

"Where is Benedict staying?" I asked.

"In Dartmouth at the Dart Marina Hotel," said Lavinia.

"Did you call them?"

"Oh no. Of course not," said Lavinia. "I told you. We were frightfully discreet."

"The phone directory is in the drawer, Kat," Mum said.

I dialed the hotel and spoke to a female receptionist who introduced herself as Mary.

"Are you a family member?" she asked in answer to my question.

"A good friend," I lied. "It's really important."

"We can't give out that information on the phone, it's hotel policy."

"Perhaps you could just put me through to Benedict's room?" I bluffed. "It's Kat Stanford."

There was a pause. "Kat Stanford? Not *the* Kat Stanford from *Fakes & Treasures*?"

"Yes. That's me."

There was a little squeal of excitement on the other end of the phone. "I love *Fakes & Treasures*! It's my favorite show. I heard you were living in Devon. You're organizing that protest meeting about the train line or something. My cousin's friend's ex-boyfriend was at the pub the other night and told me all about it."

I suppressed a groan. "Yes, something like that."

Mary and I made small talk whilst Mum pulled faces at me. Finally I got the answer I needed and ended the call. "Benedict checked out yesterday afternoon."

"I knew it!" Lavinia grabbed the hip flask from Mum and took another swig. "Gone. He left and went straight down to Coffin Mire."

"Something must have spooked him," said Mum.

"Didn't Alfred say that Benedict came here yesterday afternoon?" I asked.

"That's right," Mum nodded. "He called him Benedict Snoop. He was here looking for his mobile phone whilst we were at the auction."

"Oh!" Lavinia brightened. "Perhaps that's why he didn't call! He'd lost his phone."

"Damn, I forgot to ask that receptionist something else." Susan Ogwell had mentioned that Valentine had been a guest at the same hotel. I called back but this time I spoke to a man called Lester.

"Can you tell me if Valentine Prince-Avery was staying at your hotel this past weekend?"

"I'm sorry, but I can't release that information, madam. Hotel policy."

"Is Mary there?" I asked.

"No. She's on her break."

"This is Kat Stanford from *Fakes & Treasures*," I said in the warmest tone I could muster. "It's just a teeny favor, Lester. All you have to answer is yes or no."

"I don't care if you're the Queen of England," said Lester. "I'm the manager here and it's hotel policy. We could get into trouble with—"

"Don't worry," I said hastily. "Totally understand." I put the phone down. "How annoying. Why can't they just answer a simple question?"

"Why were you asking about Valentine?" said Mum.

"Because . . . not only did he stay at Pemba Island—yes, I heard you mentioned Pemba Island, Lavinia—but he was also staying at the Dart Marina Hotel last weekend."

Mum gasped. "You think they know each other?"

Lavinia turned ashen. "What do you mean? Know each other? How?"

"I'm not sure but it's too much of a coincidence," I said. "But why pretend that they *didn't* know each other? They certainly acted as strangers at the protest meeting."

I was struck by a growing sense of unease that I just couldn't get rid of.

"If I'd been at the protest meeting, I would have spotted their relationship instantly," Mum declared.

"Did *you* suspect that Benedict and Valentine knew each other, Lavinia?" I demanded. "Did Benedict ever talk to you about him?"

"No. Never." Lavinia bit her lip. "No—quite the opposite. Benedict referred to him as an idiot and a paper-pushing buffoon."

"Did Benedict ever ask you to supply personal information of some kind?" I said suddenly.

"Well, not really. He just asked me for a list of all the names and addresses of Rupert's wealthy landowner chums—"

"What about their birthdays?" Mum said.

"Oh. Yes. Those, too. Of course, I didn't know many of them but—have I done something wrong?"

Mum and I exchanged pained looks.

"What? Why are you looking at me like that?" said Lavinia. "Benedict said that the more people who signed the petition the better chance we had of playing the environmental card."

"We've been fooled!" Mum declared.

"Oh God. No. I don't believe it," whispered Lavinia. "He wouldn't."

"You'd better believe it," Mum declared.

"Identity theft," Mum and I chorused.

"When Rupert finds out, he'll kill me."

"Or kill *him*," said Mum darkly. "Unless he already has."

"Don't say such a thing!" Lavinia sprang to her feet again. "Goodness! Is that the time? Best be off. Must feed the horses."

"If Benedict is in that swamp, the police will want to ask you questions," said Mum.

"You promised you wouldn't say anything, Iris! You promised!"

And with that, Lavinia hurried out of the kitchen.

"What are we supposed to do now?" said Mum.

"God knows but I'm not lying for her and neither are you. I don't care what promises you made. Mum—"

"Don't say a *word*. I need to think. Perhaps we can get Alfred on the case—no! I can't do that. It will all come out about the money."

"You've got yourself into a bit of a pickle."

"It's all Lavinia's fault."

"This could be just a series of misunderstandings," I said but deep down I didn't think so.

"Morning! The front door was open!" came a male voice.

"Oh no! It's the police," Mum whispered urgently. "Now don't say anything about anything…just…let them do the talking."

Shawn and Roxy strolled into the kitchen looking grim.

"Would anyone like a cup of tea?" Mum said brightly.

"We've no time for tea," said Shawn. "Let's take a look at that shoe."

Mum unwrapped the package. "The other one is laying on the surface of Coffin Mire. We couldn't reach it."

"That's not a farmer's shoe," said Roxy. "Nor a rambler's shoe, either. That's a fancy dress shoe. Italian leather I would say. Hmm. Someone's got big feet. That's a size eleven."

"That's what we thought," said Mum.

"There's a bit of déjà vu going on round here," Roxy went on. "Remember Vera's shoe collection?"

"Who can forget it," Mum said. "She had more shoes than— what was that dictator called, again?"

"Imelda Marcos," said Roxy.

"Speaking of shoe collections," I said, thinking of Eric's shoe sale on eBay. "Maybe you should talk to Eric?"

"I bet he's got something to do with this," said Mum. "You heard about the protest meeting on Monday night."

"We have already spoken to Eric. He'll be here in a minute. He's just getting a few ropes and other gear together."

"What gear?" Mum said.

"We're heading down to Coffin Mire the moment he arrives."

"You can't mean that *you're* pulling out the body?" Mum was horrified. "You don't have to file papers or whatever the police normally do? Or go through missing persons reports?"

"Nope," said Roxy. "That's the advantage of being a satellite station. Don't ask permission, beg for forgiveness—that's what your dad used to say, didn't he, Shawn?"

Mum and I exchanged looks. We both knew that Shawn's father, Detective Chief Superintendent Robert Cropper, had turned a blind eye on more than one occasion—the Honeychurch insurance scam, for a start.

There was a rap on the back kitchen door. I opened it to reveal Eric standing in the doorway dressed head to toe in oilskins and hip boots. He looked as if he was about to star in *Deadliest Catch*.

"Shawn said someone fell in Coffin Mire," he said. "I got a couple of duckboards, ropes, and shovels. The tractor is out back."

"Good," said Shawn. "I'll pop to the car and get my oilskins, too. I'll meet you outside in five minutes. We'll cut across the fields. Roxy—take the shoe. We might need that as evidence. We'll meet you down at Bridge Cottage. Clive should be making his way there with Fluffy now."

"What should we do?" said Mum. "After all, we saw the hand first. Shall I show you where?"

"I think they already know that, Mother."

"No. You both stay here and out of trouble." Shawn went over to the sink and rinsed out his coffee mug.

"Thank you," said Mum. "Someone trained you well."

"Did you recover your money, Iris?" Shawn asked.

"Money?"

"Kat said that five thousand pounds had been stolen."

Mum shot me a filthy look. "I have no idea what you're talking about."

"She didn't tell you about Mr. Chips running off with your money?"

"Mr. Chips? The dog?" Mum laughed just a little too heartily. "Fancy. What would he want that for? To buy some bones?"

"I was going to tell you—" I felt my face redden. "But I just haven't had a minute with … you know … the body …"

"Well, you'll be glad to know that we were able to confirm that the blue plastic money bag was, indeed, from the National Bank in Jersey," said Shawn.

"What!" Mum exclaimed. "Whatever has a bank in Jersey got to do with me?"

Shawn shot me a look of confusion. I felt my face grow hot.

"No money has gone missing," Mum said indignantly.

"I'm so sorry, Officer," I said. "It was my mistake."

"You reported a theft." Shawn declared. "You accused Patty Gully of theft. That seems a particularly callous thing to do in the circumstances to say nothing of wasting police time."

"Yes, and I said I'm sorry."

"No wonder poor Patty made a complaint about being harassed."

"Officer—surely there are more important things to worry about than this trivial misunderstanding," said Mum. "Or do you no longer care about the body in Coffin Mire?"

Shawn blushed with embarrassment and, with a nod, darted out of the kitchen.

Mum turned on me. She was livid. "How *could* you go to the police?"

"How was I to know?" I said defensively. "Anyway you told me that the money in the suitcase was perfectly legal."

"Money in the suitcase?" Mum gawked. "Money in the *suitcase*? How do you know about the money in the suitcase?"

"I don't," I said hastily. "It's just a wild guess."

"You went into the loft and looked into my suitcase?" Mum was so angry that I thought she'd explode.

"No, of course I didn't!" I stammered. "I worked it out because … because … well, even though you *lost* five thousand pounds—"

"*You* lost it—"

"*We* lost it," I said. "You were still able to pay Benedict another five thousand pounds so I thought, if she has another five thousand—"

"You're a terrible liar, Katherine," said Mum. "And what has Patty got to do with all this? What was this harassment that Shawn was talking about?"

"Okay, okay," I said wearily. "I found the empty blue plastic bag in a black bin liner outside Patty's front gate."

"Empty, you say?"

"Yes. The money was gone."

"And you asked her?"

"She denied everything," I said. "In fact she got very nasty about it at the end. She reported me to the police."

"So she still has my money." Mum thought for a moment. "Right then. Go and get your coat."

"Where are we going?"

"To talk to Patty."

"I told you, it's a waste of time."

"And whilst we're at it, we'll make a quick detour to Hopton's Crest," Mum said grimly.

"Whatever for?"

"Don't you want to see who drowned in Coffin Mire?" said Mum.

"No, I jolly well don't." In fact just the very thought made me feel nauseous.

"Suit yourself," said Mum. "I'm going to get my coat."

Chapter Twenty-five

Twenty minutes later we were back at the five-bar gate at Hopton's Crest where only last night Angela had been picked up by the ambulance. The last twenty-four hours seemed to have been the longest of my life and now, with this new revelation that Benedict and Valentine could well be connected, I suspected the next twenty-four would be even longer. When Dad had made me promise to look after Mum, I had never expected that "keeping her out of trouble" meant, literally, just that.

"Mum, this is macabre," I said. "Do you seriously want to watch?"

"I'm not going to watch. You are." She handed me a pair of binoculars. "You've seen a dead body before. I haven't."

"It's hardly a hobby of mine," I said.

"Please, darling. Just for me?"

"Fine."

We both got out of the MINI and leaned over the five-bar gate.

Bracing myself, I raised the binoculars. Fortunately, the view was not as good as Mum had hoped. Coffin Mire itself was partially screened by the trees from Cavalier Copse but we could hear a diesel engine running far below.

"Is that Eric's tractor?"

"I can't tell yet." I focused the binoculars and scanned through the trees. Whatever activity was going on down there was out of my line of vision.

"That's weird." I zoomed in on a section of dense undergrowth where I caught a glimpse of red-on-black. Yes, I was right. It was part of one of Valentine's signs. I could read the lettering—HS3 CROSSING FROM HERE.

"Valentine must have left one of those behind," I said. "Why would he put all the other placards in the car and leave just one in the undergrowth?"

"Placards? What are you talking about?"

"Remember I told you that Ogwell Car Hire said they'd found a stack of broken placards in his SUV?"

The tractor clattered to a stop, leaving an eerie silence.

Someone shouted, "Hold up! We got him!"

Mum grabbed my arm. "They've got him!"

My heart began to pound as Detective Constable Clive Banks walked into the frame followed by a German shepherd.

"Who is that?" said Mum.

"Clive. Fluffy has found something."

"Give me those." Mum snatched the binoculars from me and readjusted the focus. "Don't you think he looks like Captain Pugwash with that black beard?"

The tractor started up again and Eric, riding his Massey Ferguson, rumbled into view. I didn't need binoculars to see that a rope was attached to the axle on one end and, on the other, a heavy black object.

It was slowly being dragged across the grass.

"Oh God, Katherine. Is that...?"

Eric cut the engine and jumped down. He walked over to what

was almost certainly a body coated in slime. Shawn, also dressed in oilskins and hip boots, strolled over to join them.

"I feel sick," I whispered. "Let's go home. Please." The whole thing was far more horrible than I could have possibly imagined.

Mum lowered her binoculars. "I wonder who it is," she said. "Valentine or Benedict?"

"Or neither." I mustered a weak smile. "Let's pray that it's an old Roundhead soldier."

We drove back along the track in silence. At the bottom of the hill, we came across Clive putting Fluffy back into the dog van.

Mum stopped and opened the window. "You've found a body, haven't you?"

"No comment," said Clive.

"We saw you," said Mum. "And we think we know who it is."

"We already know who it is," Clive said. "He had his wallet and driver's license on him."

"That counts out the Roundhead," I said.

"Just answer a yes or a no," said Mum. "Is it Benedict Scroope?"

Clive seemed startled. "I'm afraid I am not at liberty to say until we have informed the victim's family."

"Is it Valentine Prince-Avery?"

"No comment."

"At least tell us if he was wearing shoes," said Mum.

"Shoes?" Clive frowned. "Why?"

"If he wasn't wearing shoes then it'll be Benedict Scroope," said Mum firmly.

Clive's eyes narrowed. "Why?"

"Well. Lavinia—"

"Her ladyship is involved?" Clive looked shocked. "How do you know?"

"We don't," I said. "We don't know anything, do we, Mum?"

"I'm sure you'll have time to share your theories with Detective Inspector Cropper. I believe he has quite a number of questions for *you*, Ms. Stanford."

"For me?" I exclaimed. "Why?"

"Wait—you said *victim*," said Mum. "Do you think something seems suspicious?"

Clive secured the rear van door. "We'll know more once the ME has arrived."

"The medical examiner!" Mum exclaimed. "Please tell us, Clive. We won't repeat a word of it. We won't tell Shawn."

Clive didn't answer. He got into the driver's seat, slammed the door, and drove away.

"What's going on?" Patty crept out of the bushes. For once, the usual sneer on her face was replaced by acute anxiety. "What's happened? What are the police doing here?"

"They've found a body," said Mum coldly.

Patty turned white. "What do you mean? A body? Where?"

"In Coffin Mire." Mum thought for a moment. "Your cottage has a good view. Perhaps you saw something last night?"

"No." Patty shook her head vehemently. "Why? Why would I see anything?"

"Did you hear anything?" said Mum. "Any cries for help?"

"No. Nothing. Nothing at all." Patty shook her head again and began to back away.

"As a matter of fact, we want to have a little chat with you," said Mum. "Don't we, Katherine?"

"Mum!" I said. "Maybe today is not a good day, after all."

"I don't know anything," said Patty. "I didn't see anything. My mother is lying dead in the morgue. Why are you doing this? What is wrong with you people? Haven't you got any respect?" And with that, she turned on her heel and plunged back into the undergrowth. I was mortified.

"She's got my money, I'm sure of it," said Mum. "And I bet she saw something. Voices carry on the night air."

"I think we should tell Shawn," I said. "Let the police handle it."

"Handle my money? Over my dead body," said Mum. "If anyone's going to get involved, it will be Alfred."

"But I thought you didn't want Alfred to find out?"

Mum gave an unattractive grunt of annoyance. "I don't want to talk about this anymore."

"God. You're so predictable," I muttered.

As we pulled into the Carriage House courtyard Mum gave a cry of surprise. Rupert's black Range Rover was parked on the forecourt.

"What on earth is Rupert doing here?" she exclaimed.

"You see," I said. "He hasn't run off with another woman."

"You don't think—" She gasped. "He's guilty. He did it."

We found Rupert and Lavinia waiting for us in the kitchen. Rupert was standing with his back to the Rayburn. He looked furious. Lavinia sat hunched on a kitchen chair, head bowed. She didn't even look up when we walked in.

"Your lordship, Lavinia . . . I mean m'lady," Mum said nervously. "Can I offer you something—a cup of tea or coffee?"

"No, thank you. We won't stay long," said Rupert curtly. "I just wanted to inform you that there is no extended railway line being proposed in this area."

Lavinia uttered a whimper and raised her head just enough for us to see her cheeks wet with tears. "I'm so sorry."

"What on earth is going on?" I said.

"There's no Operation Bullet," said Rupert.

Mum's face fell. "So we were right."

"That's terrible!" I exclaimed as the full implications of this ambitious scam began to sink in. "How did you find out?"

"I've been in London this week talking to English Heritage and the Battlefields Trust," said Rupert. "Lavinia? Perhaps you would like to tell them?"

Lavinia looked wretched. "Apparently the line would never be permitted to come so far south."

"What Lavinia is saying is that the surrounding fields are of vast historical importance—especially the underground tunnel that runs under Cromwell Meadows," Rupert went on. "What's more, there is evidence of a Roman fort at the end of Hopton's Crest that has been slated for excavation for next summer."

Mum just opened her mouth and shut it again.

"I do not know how much money either of you gave this *blackguard* Scroope but I will find out. Lavinia will apologize to everyone in the village and repay them—that is, if we can't get the money back. The bounder has disappeared."

"I'm so sorry," said Lavinia again.

"I left a message on Shawn's mobile. We obviously want to keep this under wraps—can't afford a scandal." Rupert regarded Lavinia with utter disgust. "I told Lavinia not to meddle in matters she did not understand. I assume it was you, Iris, who persuaded her otherwise?"

I saw Lavinia shoot Mum a look of pure agony.

"I'll tell you why we did it," Mum said defiantly. "When we heard about Operation Bullet, we—I—knew that you weren't too bothered about saving Honeychurch from demolition."

"I see." Rupert's voice was icy cold.

"We did this for the dowager countess," said Mum. "We didn't want her to spend her remaining years worrying about what would happen to her beloved home."

"My mother has known all along about the proposed railway line," said Rupert.

"Lady Edith knew?" said Mum faintly.

I-told-you-so.

"It was my mother who suggested I go to London in the first place," said Rupert. "So you see, if you had both done what I specifically asked you to do—not meddle—we wouldn't be facing such an embarrassing situation!"

"I'm frightfully sorry," said Lavinia for the umpteenth time.

"You can't blame Lavinia, m'lord," said Mum.

"I'm not. I'm blaming you."

Mum gasped. "Well! If you had thought to tell *us* what you were up to . . . if you had thought to *talk* to your wife—"

"What I am struggling to understand is how you were both so easily fooled? Did you not think to check out Scroope's credentials?"

"Benedict was very convincing." I spoke for the first time. "He was incredibly well-informed with all sorts of statistics and claims to successes in other parts of the country. He's an environmentalist and his suggestions made sense. We all believed him."

"Then you're *all* idiots!" Rupert exclaimed.

"What about Eric?" said Mum. "He was the ringleader."

"Mum, he was just as taken in as we were," I said. "There is even a website, Rupert. It all looked so professional."

"And what about those placards that said HS3 CROSSING FROM HERE?" Mum put in. "They were stuck in the field. We're not that stupid! Why wouldn't we believe they weren't the real thing?"

If I'd needed confirmation that Benedict and Valentine were

in cahoots, this was it. The two men must have been operating a scam from the very beginning. They must have been playing good cop/bad cop with Valentine frightening everyone with tales of rolling stock depots and homes that would not be entitled to any compensation, and Benedict offering the perfect solution—for a fee. The pair had been counting on the desperation of people who couldn't face losing their homes. It was a despicable thing to do.

David had been right all along. Valentine was a fraud.

"Did you ever stop to think and wonder where Scroope got all his information?" Rupert raged on.

Lavinia's eyes filled with tears again. "We trusted him."

"What on earth made Scroope want to come here in the first place?" Rupert regarded the three of us keenly. "Why us? Why *here*?"

I caught Lavinia's look of terror. "I have no idea, Rupert."

"I have no idea, either," said Mum smoothly.

"Nor me," I agreed.

Rupert's eyes narrowed. I could tell he didn't believe us. "I will get to the bottom of this. No one, absolutely *no one* makes a fool out of my wife. And when I get my hands on this *cad*, he'll be sorry he was ever born."

Lavinia began to weep again. Rupert withdrew a monogrammed linen handkerchief from his jacket pocket and gave it to her. "For heaven's sake, Lav," he said roughly and patted her shoulder. "Pull yourself together. Stop all this nonsense. It's not the end of the world."

I suspected that this was the closest Rupert would ever get to a public display of affection.

Shawn and Roxy burst into the kitchen. Despite having changed back into regular clothes the smell of bog drifted in with them.

Shawn nodded a greeting to Rupert and Lavinia. "I thought I recognized your car."

"Good. You got my message?" said Rupert.

"Yes. We contacted Scotland Yard immediately."

"We need to catch this bounder, Scroope," Rupert exclaimed. "Blasted man has humiliated my wife and ripped off the entire village."

"We've already alerted airports, railway stations, and ports," said Shawn.

"Unless it's his body in Coffin Mire," said Mum.

"What the hell is she talking about?" Rupert said.

"Oh God," Lavinia groaned.

"No. It is not Benedict Scroope," said Shawn. "I'm sorry to say that the name of the deceased is Valentine Prince-Avery."

"I thought so," I whispered.

"I'm sorry," said Shawn gently. "I know you were close."

I started to protest but Rupert jumped in shouting, "Who the hell is Valentine Prince-Avery?"

"The chap from the protest meeting on Monday night," said Roxy grimly. "I know we shouldn't speak ill of the dead but in this case, the bastard deserved it."

"What a horrible way to die," Mum gasped. "Oh! How awful. Alfred had a vision! Remember when he touched the walking cane and said he was drowning?'

I did remember. It was terrifying.

"Will someone please tell me what's going on?" Rupert demanded.

"I'll tell you what's going on," said Roxy. "Valentine Prince-Avery was murdered."

Chapter Twenty-six

"Murdered?" Rupert exclaimed. "Are you sure?"

"As far as we can tell, Mr. Prince-Avery was struck over the head," said Shawn.

"Whoever did it, put his body in the mire and probably thought he'd sink straight to the bottom," said Roxy. "Of course, we'll have forensics out—eventually. As usual, they're backed up."

"I'm feeling rather faint," said Lavinia. "Must go and lie down."

"Do we need to be here?" Rupert said. "Neither of us knows of this Prince-Avery fellow."

"In light of these new revelations about this so-called scam," said Shawn firmly, "I'd prefer you to stay, m'lord."

"Surely you don't think any of us had something to do with it?" said Rupert.

"Are you positive they were running a scam?" Lavinia sounded desperate. "It seems a frightful amount of trouble to go to for such a paltry sum of money."

"Paltry?" said Roxy. "I coughed up two hundred quid!"

"That's just the tip of the iceberg, m'lady," said Shawn. "It's not about the money. It's the fact that scam artists like this get access to personal information that can lead to all kinds of mischief—identity theft being just one."

"Scotland Yard is already looking into whether they have done this in other parts of the country," Roxy chimed in, adding a deferential, "*m'lady*."

"Let's hope they have," said Rupert. "Then you won't seem like gullible idiots."

"When Doreen finds out, she'll be devastated," Roxy went on. "Everyone will be. It's just not right! How could this have happened?"

"I'm so sorry," Lavinia whispered. "So sorry."

"The existence of a website hints at a much bigger organization involving identity theft," said Shawn. "We shall be involving Interpol."

"Valentine and Benedict were in Africa at some point together," I said.

"I told you. Never trust a man with a small head and an orange tan," said Mum.

"Third-world countries are renowned for harvesting e-mail addresses that they sell to nefarious organizations," said Shawn. "Rest assured, we know what we're doing."

I had to admit that I was impressed. I had always taken Shawn for a country bumpkin type with his tousled hair and almost Lieutenant Columbo–like demeanor.

"Yes, Ms. Stanford," Shawn said, looking directly at me. "It would seem that even Little Dipperton has fallen foul to cyber-warfare."

"But we don't even have the Internet at the Hall," Lavinia protested. "Edith refuses to even entertain the thought."

"And I agree with her," said Mum. "It causes nothing but trouble."

"People get killed for four reasons," said Shawn. "They have something that belongs to the killer, they heard something they shouldn't have, they know something, or they said something."

"Don't we want to ask who stands to gain from Valentine's death?" I said.

"Kat's right," said Mum. "Maybe Benedict Scroope wanted all the spoils for himself and did Valentine in."

"There were plenty of people in the pub on Monday night who would have liked to have done Prince-Avery in," said Roxy. "But my guess is that Scroope holds the key."

"The *shoes* hold the key," said Mum.

"Shoes?" said Rupert.

"We retrieved the other one. They are a pair." Shawn took a deep breath. "I'm afraid I have to ask you about these, m'lord." He nodded to Roxy who produced a plastic carrier bag from nowhere. Gravely, she set it down on the table.

Mum whispered into my ear. "Shawn's show-and-tell again."

"Do these shoes look familiar to you, m'lord?" said Shawn.

Rupert pulled a face. "Good heavens, man, of course not. Why?"

"They were in the field," said Roxy. "One shoe was down a badger sett—"

"Mr. Chips found it," Mum declared.

"The other shoe was close to where the victim's body was found, lying on top of the actual mire itself," said Roxy. "The killer obviously left it behind."

"What size shoe do you take, m'lord?" Shawn asked.

Rupert flushed an angry red. "That's none of your business!"

"It's just a simple question," said Roxy.

"And I don't have to answer it."

"Would you like to have a solicitor present?" said Roxy with a tinge of sarcasm.

"Good God, woman, of course not!"

I stole a look at Mum. Her mouth was wide open as she looked from one to the other in amazement.

"Please answer the question," said Shawn.

"My word should be good enough. Besides, I have not been here. I took Harry back to school on Monday evening and I went on to London where I stayed at my club. The moment I discovered the truth about the campaign, I drove straight down. I have several people who can confirm my whereabouts."

"Oh for heaven's sake. Just tell them or I will." Lavinia paused dramatically then said, "Rupert takes a size five."

"A five!" Roxy gasped. "Blimey, my little brother takes a seven and he's only twelve."

"Rupert has always had a thing about the size of his feet," said Lavinia.

"Lavinia!" Rupert hissed, clearly horrified by such a personal revelation.

I heard Mum snigger and dared not look at her.

"Well, that counts you out, m'lord," said Roxy, barely suppressing a grin.

"What about Eric?" Mum asked. "He's got big feet."

"We have already spoken to Eric. He takes a size ten."

"Can we leave now?" said Rupert. "I've got a lot of phone calls to make following this debacle."

"Very well." Shawn nodded. "If we need to ask you any questions, we know where to find you."

Rupert and Lavinia left the kitchen and the four of us sat down. The shoes made a sinister centerpiece on the kitchen table. "Do you mind if we move those?" said Shawn.

Roxy put them back in the bag.

"Scams are often personal," said Shawn. "I know that there is something you are not telling me."

"There is," I said. "My mother wants to protect Lavinia but this is what happened." I recounted the conversation I'd overheard in the cupboard but left out Lavinia's so-called mental affair. "I think Lavinia felt she owed Benedict something in a way."

"They knew each other as children," said Mum defensively. "She trusted him."

"And of course, being a family friend, no one would think to question it," said Shawn.

"Seriously? Does that woman even *have* a brain?" said Roxy. "She's so gullible. She'll believe anything."

"Scroope was obviously trying to wangle in on her wealthy friends," said Shawn.

I nodded in agreement, adding, "Valentine asked me all kinds of questions about the Honeychurch family money, too."

"Why didn't you tell me that?" said Mum crossly.

"Ms. Stanford, how well did you know the deceased?" Shawn asked. *We were back to Ms. Stanford again.* This did not bode well. "You were seen coming out of his bedroom on Monday evening."

"Who said it was his bedroom?" said Mum, springing to my defense. "It could have been an upstairs sitting room."

Shawn looked surprised but nodded to Roxy all the same. She withdrew a copy of Wednesday's *Daily Post* from her bottomless bag under the table.

"You're a bit behind the times," said Mum. "We've already seen that. Didn't you realize the shoe I gave you was wrapped up in page three?"

"KAT AND HER NEW MAN," Shawn read aloud. "It must have been embarrassing finding out that you had—in essence—endorsed this scam by agreeing to be the spokesperson. When word got out, it would have damaged your reputation."

"I didn't know about the scam until about an hour ago," I pointed out. "And if you must know, I was talking to Valentine in his . . . suite . . . about my mother's options."

"And the sale at Chillingford Court," said Mum. "He was a bit of a collector, apparently."

"When you came to the police station on Wednesday, you told me that you had fallen from a horse—"

"Seriously? You think I got into a fight with Valentine?" I exclaimed. "You can check with the dowager countess if you don't believe me. She was there when I came off."

Shawn reddened. "No need to get upset. I'm just asking routine questions."

"You should ask Patty," said Mum. "She did Valentine in. He mowed down her mother and she got her revenge."

"Ms. Gully doesn't wear a man's shoe size eleven," said Shawn. "Let's go over the timing again, shall we? When did you first suspect something was awry?"

"On Tuesday," I said wearily. "I already told you this, Shawn. After I found Valentine's walking cane in the field."

"Kat said it was nowhere near Coffin Mire," Mum chimed in.

"Thank you, Mrs. Stanford," said Shawn. "Allow the police to do their job."

"And I think the walking cane was the murder weapon!" Mum went on. "The French bulldog handle looked pretty sharp. We didn't see any blood on there but of course, it's been raining."

"I'd like to take a look at that," said Shawn.

"Can't you spray illumination on it?" Mum asked.

"You mean Luminol," said Shawn. "I can assure you that forensics will take care of that."

"Or it could have been one of those placards," I suggested. "They were heavy. Did you go and talk to Ogwell?"

"Yes. The car is being examined at our vehicular recovery center as we speak."

"I still don't understand why Valentine put the placards in the SUV," said Mum. "Or do you think he panicked after hitting poor Joyce?"

"I'm afraid we can't comment on that at this time," Shawn said pompously. "What else can you tell us about Monday?"

"We met him on Monday afternoon," said Mum.

Shawn seemed surprised. "You met him earlier in the day?"

"Down by Cavalier Copse," said Mum. "We were picking sloes."

"And Harry said he'd been waiting for us," I reminded her.

Roxy frowned. "But how would he have known that you would have been there?"

"Lavinia," Mum and I chorused. "Mrs. Cropper may have told her that we were out picking sloes; Lavinia told Benedict and Benedict told Valentine."

"You two should be detectives," said Roxy dryly.

"Valentine got very jittery when I mentioned that David had friends at the ministry," I recalled. "Perhaps that was what spooked him."

"Yes," Mum agreed. "He must have known it was only a matter of time before he got found out."

"I felt that Valentine was pushed into the protest meeting," I went on. "He had seemed unprepared and claimed that none of his presentation materials had arrived. He had also mentioned that he wanted to talk to everyone personally about their options first."

"Of course he'd want to meet with them alone!" Roxy scoffed. "Far more effective speaking in someone's home and frightening them half to death."

"In fact, when Patty and I pulled into the pub car park on Monday night, I saw Valentine on his mobile outside." I distinctly remembered Valentine pacing up and down. "He seemed very agitated."

"So let's go back to Monday night," said Shawn. "After the protest meeting, where did you go?"

"I drove Patty and Angela home..." A flash of Joyce, facedown in the water, filled my vision. "You know the rest."

"What time did you get back?" said Shawn.

"Angela and I waited until the paramedics left and Doreen took Patty back to the Hare & Hounds for a little while—"

"Are you telling us that Patty didn't spend the night at the pub?" Shawn said sharply.

"Doreen said Patty insisted on being in her own bed."

Roxy leaned into Shawn and whispered something into his ear. He gave a nod. "So what time *did* you get home, Ms. Stanford?"

I shrugged. "Eleven-thirty. Maybe midnight—you can check with Angela."

"We did," said Roxy. "Angela denied it."

I gasped. "Seriously? I walked her into her house because she was so freaked out by everything."

"Not according to Angela," said Roxy.

"Of course she'd deny it," Mum said crossly. "She blames Kat for the cow incident."

"Oh for heaven's sakes!" I said. "I was at the auction with my mother all of Wednesday afternoon and evening—apart from when Angela Parks was trampled by cows. I haven't seen Valentine since Monday!"

"Speaking of Angela Parks," said Roxy. "She is suing you for negligence claiming that she will never act again because of losing her front teeth. Apparently she was going to audition for that upstairs-downstairs drama."

"*Downton Abbey*?" said Mum with a snort. "Who are they killing off this time?"

"We're not talking about yesterday." Shawn was getting exasperated. "Valentine Prince-Avery was killed in the early hours of Tuesday morning."

"That's not possible," I said. "I've been exchanging text messages with Valentine—oh, but . . . there was a message."

"A message?" Shawn exclaimed. "We'll want to listen to that."

I grabbed my tote bag and handed Shawn my mobile. He dialed voice mail and hit speaker.

"*Kat, I will never give up. I know you don't believe me but when you kissed—*"

"Sorry, wrong one." I snatched the phone away and hit delete. My face was burning with embarrassment.

"That was David Wynne," said Mum. "In case you were wondering."

"We weren't," said Shawn gruffly.

"Here, this is it." I handed Shawn the phone again and we all listened to Valentine's last message. "*Call me back. It's urgent. I must—*"

"And did you call?" said Shawn.

"Yes. Several times but the voice mailbox was full."

"What about the text messages you got the night Alfred arrived?" said Mum.

"Here, three text messages." I showed Shawn. "The first text was just the letter '*k*.' The second was the letter '*j*,' and the third said, '*Hello all ok*.'"

"These messages were sent at ten-thirty Tuesday night," said Roxy. "Valentine was dead by then."

"How can you be so sure?" I said.

"I studied anthropology at uni," said Roxy. "These valley mires are really deep deposits of peat that originate from sphagnum moss. A body can be perfectly preserved in peat—we're talking skin, hair, and internal organs. It means we can pinpoint the exact time of death. Look at Lindow Man."

"Valentine only died on Monday," said Mum. "Not in the middle of the first century."

Shawn snapped his fingers. "When we recovered the body, there wasn't a mobile phone on him—was there?"

"The only things in Prince-Avery's pockets were house keys, car rental keys, and his wallet with a driver's license," said Roxy.

"So who made the phone call to Ogwell telling them to pick up the car?" Mum asked. "My brother Alfred saw it being towed around four o' clock."

"Probably Benedict trying to buy some time and keep up the pretense that Valentine was still alive," I suggested.

Shawn gave a heavy sigh. "I think we can safely assume that Benedict Scroope is our prime suspect."

"And I think we can safely assume that he's probably halfway back to the Zanzibar Archipelago by now." Mum scowled. "With our identities, money, and God knows what else."

"I'm afraid you are probably right." Shawn rose from the table. "We'll obviously do all we can but unfortunately, it looks like Scroope has had a head start. Come on, Roxy, we'd better get back to the station."

Mum saw them out and returned to the kitchen grim-faced.

"At least your money in Jersey is safe," I said lightly but Mum didn't laugh.

"He'll get away with it," said Mum. "It's too late and we'll never be able to prove anything. Even if they catch him, no one can confirm those shoes were his or that he was even anywhere near Coffin Mire."

"Unless Patty saw something, after all?" I suggested.

"Let's have a gin and tonic," said Mum. "Gin always gives me a clear head."

Armed with a glass each, Mum took a large gulp. "If Benedict was there that night and those were his shoes, he must have driven back to the hotel in his socks!"

"Clever you! Gin *does* make you clearheaded!" I exclaimed. "You call the hotel this time in case it's Lester and he recognizes my voice."

Mum called the Dart Marina Hotel and fortunately got Mary. She handed me the receiver. Mary was only too happy to tell me about the night porter's tale of a strange guest who had returned in the early hours of Tuesday morning wearing muddy socks. She also confirmed that Benedict checked out early. He had been booked to stay until the coming weekend.

"And speaking of socks," said Mum after I'd rejoined her at the kitchen table. "Since Valentine *also* checked out early at the Hare & Hounds, what happened to his clothes?"

"You're right," I said. "He had an overnight bag. I saw it when I went into his room. Let's call Doreen and ask if he left it behind."

Doreen was predictably outraged the moment she recognized my voice. News of the scam and the body in the mire had traveled as quickly as only news in a small village would. Instantaneously.

"We're all gutted," Doreen went on. "And of course, it's hard not to blame Eric. He was the one who brought this crook into our lives."

"You can't blame Eric completely," I protested. "He was just as taken in as the rest of us."

"No. Apparently, his lordship has insisted that Eric repay every single penny any of us invested. Personally."

It would appear that Eric had taken one for the Honeychurch team to protect Lavinia's reputation. That took a lot of guts.

"Looking on the bright side," I said. "At least Fred the duck will be safe now along with all the wildlife—one more thing, who cleaned Valentine's bedroom?"

I put the phone down. "Yes. Patty definitely cleaned Valentine's bedroom."

Mum gave a squeak of excitement. "I remember! I saw her on Tuesday after I'd met Lavinia for the money drop. Patty was carrying a leather holdall bag and walking home in the pouring rain. I offered to give her a lift but she refused."

"She stole it—just like she took your money," I said. "That's just the kind of thing Patty would do."

"What if the police are wrong and Patty had something to do with killing Valentine after all?" said Mum.

"Patty hasn't the strength to drag a man across the grass and roll him into the mire," I said. "And if he was drunk, it would be practically impossible to move him."

"Let's go back to Monday night," said Mum. "You left the pub with Patty and Angela. Was Valentine's car still in the car park?"

"No. It had gone."

"So then you drove down the lane to Bridge Cottage and see Joyce's mobility scooter laying—where exactly?"

"It had toppled over and thrown Joyce out." I shuddered at the memory. "That part of the lane is very steep and it's covered in mud and leaves."

"So *then* Patty goes to the Hare & Hounds with Doreen but changes her mind and heads back home to bed."

I nodded.

"She saw something," said Mum firmly. "I'd bet my last pound she did."

"And we know that at this time of year it is possible to see Cavalier Copse from Bridge Cottage through the trees."

"Patty looks out of her rear window and sees Valentine removing the signs and taking them to his car. How many placards were there?"

"Ten placards—excluding the one left behind in the undergrowth," I said. "Valentine would have had to have made several trips."

"Patty watches him and starts to get angry. She's already in a state of shock—"

"So she goes to confront him."

We both paused.

"And then what?" I said.

"Patty phones Benedict?" Mum ventured.

"Why would she and anyway, Patty doesn't have a phone," I reminded her. "Maybe Benedict was the man who called Valentine *before* the meeting when he was in the car park," I went on. "Maybe Benedict got worried when Valentine left in a huff. Maybe he knew where he was going. There was an argument. It turned violent..."

"And as far as Benedict was concerned, Valentine's body should never have been found. It was supposed to sink to the bottom of the mire."

"Exactly!" I said. "When I went to the pub with the walking cane Benedict was there. Patty, too. She said that Valentine had already caught the train back to London. Valentine even offered to return the walking cane for me!"

"I bet Patty still has Valentine's overnight bag," said Mum.

"There was an iPad as well in there—and maybe Valentine's mobile."

We book looked at each other and came to the same conclusion at the same time.

"We've got to talk to Patty."

Chapter Twenty-seven

It was dusk by the time we reached Bridge Cottage. The place was in darkness. As expected, no one answered the front door despite our repeated calls. We were able to get the front door open a crack but it looked as if a piece of furniture had been pushed against it.

"Let's try the back," I said.

"This place gives me the creeps," said Mum.

We headed around the side of the building, trying our best to navigate the rubbish.

"Why didn't you bring a flashlight?" I said.

"I thought you would have one."

The kitchen door stood ajar.

"I don't like this, Kat," whispered Mum.

My stomach began to churn. "Nor me."

We stepped into the kitchen and were plunged into darkness.

"What's that funny plasticky smell?" said Mum. "Can you smell it?"

"Yes. It feels warm in here, too," I said, recalling how cold the place had been just the day before.

I fumbled for the light switch and flipped it.

Mum gasped. "Patty's been robbed!"

"No, she lives like this," I said. "But wait—" The kitchen cupboards stood wide open, drawers had been upended, and all the contents dumped on the floor.

We picked our way through the chaos into the sitting room and I flipped the light there, too.

"Oh. My. God. You weren't joking when you said she was a hoarder," said Mum. "This is disgusting."

The mess that I'd seen just days ago was the same—but different. Black dustbin liners of clothes had been upended, too, furniture had been moved, and the reason we couldn't get in through the front door was because a large armchair had been wedged against it.

"Someone has been here looking for something," I said.

"Listen!" Mum hissed. We both fell quiet. "Can you hear that dragging noise?"

Up above, over our heads, was the same sound I'd heard not so long ago in the loft at the Carriage House.

"Patty's upstairs," I said. "Come on."

We carefully climbed over more rubbish and went up the narrow staircase.

"Will you look at all this stuff?" said Mum, pointing at the rows and rows of empty jam jars that lined either side of the staircase.

A loud bang followed by a rush of cold air sent scraps of paper and plastic bottles clattering down the stairs.

"What the hell was that?" Mum exclaimed.

The small window on the landing swung open and shut as the wind picked up outside. I stared out into the darkness but couldn't see a thing and pulled it closed.

"Just the wind," I said.

Mum grabbed my arm tightly as we climbed over a mound of

dolls with broken limbs and headless bodies. We stepped into a room that could only be described as a junkyard with boxes filled with old candlesticks, knickknacks, broken mirrors, tea trays, cups, and toys. There were brown carrier bags filled with wool and scraps of knitting.

"Joyce and Patty used to do car boot sales," I said. "This must be their stock."

We retraced our steps into what was probably Joyce's bedroom. The curtains were drawn. The room smelled musty and damp. Paper was peeling off the walls. A large chest of drawers blocked another door in the corner.

All around were mounds of linens, towels, and clothing. A framed photograph was just barely visible on the nightstand. It showed a severe-looking woman in 1960s dress with a young girl in pigtails holding a pet rabbit.

"That's Joyce with Patty."

"I used to braid your hair, too," said Mum.

"But I wasn't allowed to have a pet."

Next to an unmade single bed was a steel-framed camp bed with a pillow and duvet on top. "You think Patty slept on that?" I said, horrified. "She didn't even have her own room."

"At least you have yours," said Mum, attempting a joke but I didn't laugh.

Something was bothering me. "Where is the bathroom?"

Mum snapped her fingers and pointed to the chest of drawers. "Behind there."

"Patty!" We shouted again but there was no answer.

"You take one end of the chest of drawers and I'll take the other," I said.

"Someone deliberately moved this against the door," said Mum anxiously. "Why?"

We found Patty laying under a pile of clothes in the bath. Her mouth had been taped and her arms and legs bound with rope.

"Quickly, let's get out of here," I said. "I don't like it. Something is wrong."

We lifted her out and gently removed the tape bindings. Patty was in deep shock. She'd had a lot to deal with these past few days. We carried her into the bedroom and laid her down on the bed.

"We'd better call an ambulance," I said.

"I don't have my phone."

"Well, neither do I. You stay here, I'll drive home."

Mum pulled a face. "Can't I drive home and you stay here?"

"I'll be quicker."

Two seconds later, I was back, struggling to stay calm. "Mum, the house is filling up with smoke. I can't get downstairs."

"*What?*" Mum bolted out onto the landing. "The smoke is coming up the stairs!" she shrieked. "We're going to burn alive!"

The roof was made of thatch and, along with all the rubbish, the entire place would become an inferno in minutes. There was a crash and boom as the fire took hold below.

"The window," I said. "Hurry."

We grabbed Patty and frog-marched her onto the landing that was already heavy with thick black toxic smoke. Thanks to her mother's preference for nylon furnishings, if the flames didn't get us, the smoke would.

"You can slide down the roof," I told Patty. "There's an old mattress underneath. Quickly!"

But she just hung on tightly to the sides of the window frames.

Mum pushed Patty hard and she tumbled out into the darkness. "Oh. Sorry."

Mum skittered down the sliding roof with me right behind her. There was a roar and earth-shattering *whomph* as the thatch caught fire. A series of cracks and explosions suggested that the flames had found the empty glass jars.

The three of us sprawled on the old mattress in a heap, winded and breathless.

"Mum? Your bad hand?" I said. "Is it okay?"

"I'm fine," said Mum. "I landed on top of Patty. I think I crushed her."

We dragged Patty to relative safety at the edge of the garden and watched her home burn. In the flickering light, I looked over at her and saw a slow smile begin to creep across her face.

"Benedict did this," Mum said suddenly. "And now we'll never be able to prove a thing."

On the horizon, lights flared. "Look!" I exclaimed. "There's a car on Hopton's Crest."

"It's *him*." Patty spoke for the first time. "It's Benedict."

"How do you know?" I said.

"That's where he left his car," said Patty. "I saw him walking across the fields."

"So no one would see him," Mum said grimly.

I got to my feet. "I'm going to stop him."

"Are you insane?" said Mum. "He's a killer! We could all have been burned to a crisp in there if it hadn't been for your quick thinking."

"All I'm going to do is block his escape," I said. "The track dead ends at the bridleway, remember? He has to turn his car around to get out."

"At least wait until the police arrive, please, Kat," Mum cried. "Wait—"

But I was already running for my car.

I sped up the hill and the moment I turned into the track was instantly engulfed in thick mist. At first, I thought it was coming from the cottage that was burning below where, in my rearview mirror, I could make out hazy orange flames shooting high into the air.

The visibility along Hopton's Crest was practically zero. I slowed down to a crawl and edged my way forward. All I could see in the distance were two headlamps rapidly coming toward me. Fast.

I started to panic. I felt closed in.

And then I saw it and slammed on my brakes.

It was a large, black object that seemed to emerge from nowhere and almost floated just yards away in front of my car before being swallowed up into the mist. I sat there in utter shock and disbelief until a sickening crash of metal followed by a deafening car alarm snapped me back to my senses.

As suddenly as the mist had descended, it vanished to reveal a brilliant canopy of stars and a bright moon.

Benedict's Prius was slammed up against one of the ancient oak trees with the hazard lights flashing. White airbags filled the windows. The alarm stopped abruptly, leaving an eerie silence.

Trembling, I grabbed the Mace I always kept in the glove box— old London habits die hard—and hurried toward the car where Benedict was gripping the steering wheel, staring blindly ahead.

I wrenched open the driver's door. "The police are on their way," I said, hoping they were. I primed the Mace and held it close to his face.

Benedict slowly turned to look at me. His nose was bleeding profusely and a nasty gash sliced across his forehead. He looked terrified. He also couldn't move. The airbags had him fully trapped.

"You saw it, too, didn't you?" he said in a tremulous voice. "It *was* him, wasn't it—Sir Maurice, the phantom Cavalier? I thought it was just a legend."

"Yes, I saw something." And I had and it had shaken me to the core.

"My legs hurt," he whispered. "They're tingling."

In the distance I heard the comforting sounds of fire engines with their sirens blaring.

Benedict slumped back into his seat. "Is Patty—?"

"She's alive but no thanks to you," I said. "And so is my mother. Why did you do it?"

"I never meant any of this to happen," said Benedict. "If Patty had just given me back Valentine's mobile."

"Why was it so important?" I said. "It was just a phone."

Benedict gave a bitter laugh. "Oh, you know—all kinds of incriminating messages from me to Valentine. The bloody fool, the bloody, drunken fool."

"Valentine hit Joyce's scooter, didn't he?"

"He swore he never touched her," said Benedict. "He said he swerved to miss her but she just veered off the road."

"He didn't think to call an ambulance?" I exclaimed.

"And have everything come out?" said Benedict. "The driving ban—"

"Everything would have come out anyway! I already knew about the driving ban."

"Yes. This is all your fault, Katherine Stanford," Benedict said bitterly. "You've ruined everything. The moment Valentine realized that David Wynne would be asking questions, he wanted out. But there was too much to lose. I've spent years building up my company—"

"Your fake company, you mean," I said. "You might think that we're just a tiny backwater down here where no one understands the Internet but I can assure you, the police are investigating all your little scams as we speak."

"You'll never prove a thing," said Benedict.

"The police have your shoes," I said.

"What are you talking about?"

"The shoes you were wearing the night you killed your friend."

Benedict gasped. "You think I killed Valentine?" he cried. "No. Never. It was an accident. He was drunk. Angry. There was a struggle. We fought—"

"You hit him with one of those placards," I said.

"He hit me first."

"What is this? The school playground?" I said.

"No. No. It was an accident. I told you." Benedict shook his head with horror. "God. It was awful. Valentine just stumbled off. I couldn't get to him. Couldn't reach him. He told me it was a mistake coming down here. He told me that my feelings for Lavinia got in the way of our plan. He was right."

"Yes. And then there is Lavinia," I said. "You almost destroyed her marriage."

"She chose money over love," said Benedict quietly. "I suppose in some way, I wanted to get my own back. Wanted to see Rupert suffer."

"She didn't choose money over love," I said. "Lavinia has always loved Rupert. And there was no Honeychurch money. There never was. Lavinia felt guilty for leading you on all those years ago."

A panda car came screaming toward us with its blue light flashing. Shawn leapt out of the driver's seat and rushed to my side. "Kat! Are you okay? Are you hurt?"

"Yes. Fine. Just a bit shaken," I said and realized I was trembling and tears stung my eyes.

To my surprise, Shawn took me in his arms and even when Roxy turned up, he didn't let go.

Chapter Twenty-eight

"**You were gone for hours!**" **Mum exclaimed as I strode into** the kitchen having had a wonderful ride.

"Edith took me to look at Jane's Cottage," I said, removing my riding helmet. "Let's just say it's got potential."

"What on earth have you done to your hair?" Mum sounded appalled. "You're morphing into one of them!"

I touched the old-fashioned slumber-net that Lavinia had insisted I try. "I know, I know. Hat hair and all that, but it really does keep the hair in check—what's going on? You look like the cat that swallowed the canary."

"Speaking of canaries," said Mum. "Alfred is moving into William's old flat—but I don't want to talk about him—" Mum handed me a brown paper bag. "Look inside."

"It's money!" I exclaimed.

"Five thousand pounds, to be exact," said Mum. "It was Eric who found the cash in the bridleway near Bridge Cottage. He had no idea it belonged to me and said he thought he'd found the end of the rainbow."

"Wow. Eric is full of surprises."

"And he took the blame for Lavinia's mess with Scroope—

although of course, he'll be using Lavinia's money to repay the villagers."

"So I heard."

"Which just goes to show you can't judge a man by his eyebrows." Mum laughed at her own joke. "He's in an awful financial mess. Up to his ears in debt having spent all that money on that stupid Massey Ferguson tractor, which was why he's selling all Vera's shoes and—you'll never guess..."

"Don't make me."

"It was Eric who sold your photograph to the *Daily Post*. Angela took it but he sold it. He even admitted that she begged him not to."

"Oh, no." I groaned. "So not only did I accuse Patty of stealing the money, I was wrong about Angela, too. I owe them both an apology. Maybe I'll go into Totnes this afternoon and take them some flowers. Do you want to come?"

"No."

To my astonishment, Patty had booked herself into a private room at Totnes Hospital. Not only that, when she saw me, she smiled. For once she looked clean and wore a smattering of lipstick.

"You're looking better," I said. "Nice room."

It turned out that Patty's mother had not just been frugal but she'd been smart with her money. Bridge Cottage had been heavily insured meaning that Patty had inherited a large sum of money.

"Enough for me to buy a little flat down in Dartmouth by the river and not feel guilty about my mother anymore."

"You can start a new chapter," I said firmly.

"Can I show you my iPhone?"

Patty then admitted that the afternoon I'd seen Benedict at her cottage he'd been asking if she'd found Valentine's phone and had become very threatening. She was so frightened of him that she lit the Rayburn and tried to burn it. It certainly explained the odd smell of plastic that Mum and I had detected.

The irony was that even though Benedict had set the fire to destroy the cottage, only one thing had survived—the cast-iron Rayburn. And inside was Valentine's iPhone that would be totally salvageable. Benedict would get his just desserts after all.

"Where did you find Valentine's iPhone?" I asked.

"It was in the hedge," said Patty. "And it worked. I thought that if I answered your messages no one would find out that Valentine had lost it."

"I hope your texting skills improve," I said.

Patty grinned. "I'm getting the hang of it, now."

"What about Valentine's overnight bag?"

Patty's face fell. "*He* found that. He came back for it. That's why he was there the afternoon you stopped by." For a moment, she seemed small and very alone.

"It's over now, Patty," I said briskly.

"Will you come and see me again?" she asked.

"Of course."

It was a good feeling knowing that Patty faced a brighter future—although I suspected my next visit would not be so uplifting.

Angela lay in a packed geriatric ward. She had to be the youngest patient there by fifty years.

I found her sitting up in bed flicking through a copy of *The Stage*.

"What do you want?" she lisped. "You're not therpothed to be here."

"I owe you an apology," I said. "It was Eric who sold the photograph to the *Daily Post*. I'm really sorry."

"Look!" Angela opened her mouth wide and pointed to two

stumps. "I need crownth put on theeth but I can't afford them. I'm going to mith my audithion."

"Are you suing me so you can get your teeth fixed?" I said bluntly.

Angela nodded miserably. "Thrudy won't pay," she said. "Thee told me that I didn't keep up my end of the bargain."

I thought for a moment. "Tell you what, I'll pay for your orthodontist."

"Oh. My. God. Really?"

"Yes. You're a very talented actress," I said. "But just tell me one thing, why did you agree to spy on me?"

"Thpy on you?" Angela looked confused. "Thrudy thaid we could fluth out the real Krythalle Thorm. Thee got a tip-off from Vera the houthkeeper before me. Do you know who it could be?"

I felt a huge wave of relief. "No, I'm afraid I don't."

Angela sighed. "Oh well. Let Thrudy do her own dirty work. They'll thoon find out who Krythalle Thorm ith anyway."

"What do you mean?"

"Thrudy won Ericth prithe on eBay."

"She *what*?" I whispered. I'd put in my final bid with just five minutes to go. "You mean . . . Trudy's going to meet Krystalle Storm in Italy?"

I was too late. It looked like Trudy Wynne had won after all.

Half an hour later I pulled into the courtyard with a heavy heart to find Mum, perched on top of the mounting block.

She hurried over and yanked open the passenger door. "Thank heavens you're back. Awful news."

My heart sank. "You've heard about Trudy Wynne and the contest?"

"What? No. Harry's missing," said Mum. "The school called

Lavinia this morning. He ran off again in the night. What's more, Thunder is missing from his stable."

"Oh, no," I said. "Rupert had threatened to sell his pony if he ran away again."

"Where shall we start to look?"

And then I knew.

We sped back down the service drive, past the burned-out shell that—along with the Rayburn—was all that remained of Bridge Cottage.

"Where are we going?" Mum exclaimed as we passed the bridleway entrance to Cavalier Copse.

"You'll see."

Up on Hopton's Crest I stopped the car just yards away from the spot where Benedict had hit the tree. Only two deep grooves gouged into the surface marked the accident.

"What are you doing?" Mum demanded as I got out of the car.

"You'll see," I said again.

I was right. On either side of the track were two wide gaps in the hedgerows. Both bore the signs of fresh hoofprints and on one side, there was a small mound of horse manure.

"You're kidding," said Mum when I told her my theory.

"I'm sure it was Harry riding Thunder last night. He would have crossed over Hopton's Crest to get down to Cavalier Copse and with all that mist..."

"So it wasn't Sir Maurice, the phantom horseman, after all."

"You seem disappointed," I said.

"I suppose I am."

Ten minutes later we arrived on foot at the base of Harry's tree house. There, tethered to a nearby bush stood Thunder.

"Harry? Are you up there?" I shouted.

A face peered out but it wasn't Harry's. It was Rupert's dressed in an old flying helmet, goggles, and white scarf.

"Good afternoon," said Rupert. "We're manning the look-out here and I'm receiving orders from Squadron Leader Bigglesworth."

"Be quiet, Honeychurch," I heard a voice say. "You'll wake up the dormice! They're hibernating."

"We'll come down," whispered Rupert.

Moments later, father and son emerged from behind the tree. They were dressed identically. Harry was clutching Ella Fitzgerald.

Rupert pointed to his outfit. "Found these in the attic. Incredible stuff up in our attic. Had no idea. There's an old Hornby train set that belonged to my grandfather. Still in original boxes. You should look at it. I'd appreciate your opinion."

"A train set," I said slowly. "I think I've had enough of trains for the time being but maybe in a week or two."

"Flying Officer Stanford," Harry barked in his alter-ego voice. "It's official. I am not going back to the front. This war is over."

"As a matter of fact, sir," I said. "Neither am I."

"Oh Kat!" he yelled. "Wicked!"

"We should celebrate!" Mum exclaimed. "Come along, Kat. What a day!"

Back at the Carriage House, a bouquet of flowers sat on the front doorstep.

"David just won't let go, will he?" I grumbled.

"Let's look at what he has to say this time." Mum picked up a large embossed envelope. "Oh," she said. "These flowers are not for you, they're for me."

"A ha," I said. "So he's trying to win *you* over now so you will put in a good word for him."

"How very transparent." Mum turned the envelope over and frowned. "How odd. This is the Goldfinch Publishing crest."

"Go on. Open it, Mum. Maybe your books have just been sold to a big Hollywood producer!"

Mum's jaw dropped. "Well I never. Look."

Inside was a travel wallet holding two airline tickets and an itinerary with details of a luxurious long weekend in a private villa on the Amalfi Coast.

Mum handed me the cover letter. "Read it to me."

"*Your hostess Krystalle Storm sends her regrets that she can't join you but hopes you will have a pleasant stay.*"

Mum looked to me in confusion as a note card fluttered to the ground.

I picked it up. "I don't believe it." I gasped. "Listen to this. '*Thought you girls might like a holiday. Regards, David.*' Oh, Mum. That's so thoughtful. So sweet of him."

"I thought *you* bid for this on eBay," said Mum sharply. "What's it got to do with David?"

"Didn't I tell you?"

"You don't tell me anything."

"There was a last-minute snafu—but now everything is alright. But of course we can't—"

"Let's go," said Mum suddenly. "Let's go tomorrow! It will probably be the last holiday you'll get now that you're opening your new business down here."

"Yes. There's a lot of hard work ahead."

Mum gave me a hug. "I'm so happy you are staying."

"Someone has to keep you out of trouble, but promise me one thing," I said. "Let's agree never to end up like Joyce and Patty."

"I'll drink to that."